SPUN BY SORCERY

BARBARA BRETTON

THORNDIKE PRESS

A part of Gale, Cengage Learning

Detroit • New York • San Francisco • New Haven, Conn • Waterville, Maine • London

GALE
CENGAGE Learning™

LIBRARY OF CONGRESS CATALOGING-IN-PUBLICATION DATA

Bretton, Barbara.
  Spun by sorcery / by Barbara Bretton.
    p. cm. — (Thorndike Press large print romance)
    ISBN-13: 978-1-4104-3404-3
    ISBN-10: 1-4104-3404-4
    1. Women merchants—Fiction. 2. Magic—Fiction. 3. Salem (Mass.)—Fiction. 4. Domestic fiction. 5. Large type books. I. Title.
  PS3552.R435S68 2011
  813'.54—dc22
                  2010043425

Published in 2011 by arrangement with The Berkley Publishing Group, a member of Penguin Group (USA) Inc.

Printed in the United States of America
1 2 3 4 5 6 7 15 14 13 12 11

PERMISSIONS

ACKNOWLEDGMENTS

A big thanks to all of my pals at Romancing the Yarn including Fran Baker, Maura Anderson, Devon Monk, Dallas Schulze (who taught me spinnerese), Nancy Herkness, Mary Ann Mohanraj, Caroline Leavitt, Janet Spaeth, Elizabeth Delisi, Terri Du-Long, Rachael Herron, Jean Brashear, Laura Phillips, Flo Moyer, Cindi Myers, both Nicoles, Kim H, Shirley, Mandy, Penny, Adrienne, Monica, Sharon, Cathy, Jill, New Zealand Kim, Kat, Sara, Rho, Renna, Lynda, Leslie, Rusty, Tanya, Michelle, Linda, Pat, Ellen, Carol N, Holly, Anne, Mary, Grandma Moo, The Georg, Lynda, Laura, Turtle, Susan, Anonymous 1-2-and-3, and everyone else who has taken time to visit over the last few years.

Much love to Jeremy Bredeson, who gave me a refresher course in believing when I needed it most.

Thanks to Dawn Brocco for the magical

spice cookies and the friendship!

A shout-out to the knitters at Fiber Fiction on Ravelry who make it fun to check for messages every day. (Okay, twice a day.)

A knitterly welcome to our niece Tricia who has been lured over to the dark side of fiber obsession.

And, most of all, to my husband, Roy, who has shared more road trips with me than I can count. I love you, BDH.

1

CHLOE
SUGAR MAPLE, VERMONT

What would you do if the people you loved, the places you knew, disappeared without warning? Your town, your home, the knit shop you'd built from scratch, your best friends, your enemies, the familiar landmarks that had been part of your world since the day you were born, all of them suddenly wiped off the face of the earth in the time it took to take your next breath.

You would probably think you'd had too much to drink or that maybe someone had slipped a weird mushroom into your salad when you weren't looking. People disappear. Cats and dogs go missing. Car keys, stitch markers, your favorite sunglasses.

But not your hometown.

Hometowns aren't portable. You can't load them onto the back of a flatbed truck and roll them to a new location. Every now and then Mother Nature reaches into her bag of tricks and tests the mettle of a small town. She flings tornadoes and blizzards, fires and floods at them then watches in admiration as they bend, but never break.

And they definitely never disappear without a trace.

At least that's what I thought until it happened to me.

I'm Chloe Hobbs, a half-human sorceress-in-training. When I'm not studying the Book of Spells, you can find me either at Sticks & Strings, my wildly popular yarn shop, or at our town hall, where I serve as de facto mayor of Sugar Maple, a small tourist town in northern Vermont.

But there's a whole lot more to Sugar Maple than meets the eye. Our folksy, small-town façade hides truths that could endanger our existence. Sugar Maple is inhabited by the descendants of oppressed creatures who fled Salem during the Witch Trials. Desperate for sanctuary, my ancestor Aerynn led other endangered souls north to an Indian town named Sinzibukwud, where they were welcomed with open arms and generous hearts.

Our hardware store is owned by a family of werewolves. Our head librarian is a gorgeous Norwegian troll. My best friends are

12

a shapeshifter and a witch. A family of vampires runs the funeral parlor. Traveling house sprites handle most of our home repairs. And who could forget Forbes the Mountain Giant, who walks in his sleep.

And that is only a tiny portion of our current population.

Most of the time the human side of my lineage doesn't win me any points with the townspeople but it does come in handy when we have to deal with the bureaucrats down in Montpelier. For the most part, we haven't had to deal with them much over the years but lately it seems as if we've been getting more than our share of attention from the fine folks at the state capital.

The shocking death of a tourist named Suzanne Marsden at Snow Lake last December is a good example. We had flown under the radar for so long that I guess we'd grown complacent. That was what centuries of being a town without crime could do to you. You dropped your guard. You forgot that evil actually existed and that sometimes it was right there sitting next to you.

The one good thing to come from that tragedy was Luke MacKenzie. Luke is one hundred percent *Homo sapiens* and our newly minted chief of police.

More important, he is also the love of my

life, a fact which seems to have turned Sugar Maple on its collective ear.

Isadora, the powerful leader of the New England Fae, had never been one of my biggest fans but we had somehow managed to coexist until Luke came to town to investigate Suzanne's death.

From that moment on, Isadora and I were at war. The thought of a full-blood human living in Sugar Maple pushed her over the edge and she set out to find a way to pull the town beyond the mist into the realm of the Fae, where she could reign supreme.

She knew before I did that love was the key to unlocking my inner sorceress and that my emerging powers would turn our fight into a war between (almost) equals. I thought I had managed to banish her back in December but I underestimated the Fae warrior's need for revenge. She found a way to break through the banishment shield and tonight, at the once-in-a-lifetime moment when the sun and stars were in magickal alignment and I was at my most vulnerable, she struck.

I won't lie to you. It was touch and go there for a while tonight as we battled for the spirit of a little girl and the future of Sugar Maple. When the earthquakes started and that crazy light show flashed across the sky and Luke's ex-wife — well, let's say that I had to call upon every secret I could access from the Book of Spells to come out on the winning side.

Not to brag or anything, but in the space of an earth hour I fought the battle of my life, defeated my archenemy, reunited a mother and child, and saved my hometown from certain disaster. Finally I was in sync with my magick. The nonhuman part of my lineage didn't scare me any longer. (Okay, maybe it still scared me a little but I was on my way.)

And even better, it didn't scare Luke. Flying cars. Enchanted waterfalls. Demons with an ax to grind. Most other human males would have headed for the exit the first time they found themselves accidentally turned into a Ken doll, but not Luke. He hung in there through it all, and a few minutes ago he said the words I always wanted to hear.

You're not alone anymore.

Chloe Hobbs, the woman who had pretty much been alone her entire life, had finally found her soul mate. Now when I looked into the future I saw a home and a family of my own, which, for a Hobbs woman, is the ultimate pot of gold at the end of the rainbow.

Hobbs women love only once. I know that sounds crazy and kind of eighteenth century but that was how we were made. When a descendant of Aerynn falls in love, she falls in love forever and there isn't enough magick in the universe to change that simple truth. Wouldn't you think one of us would have managed to get it right in three hundred years?

But not one Hobbs woman had until now.

Luke loved me for who I was, magick and all, and he didn't want to change me. He knew that my destiny was tied up with my quirky little Vermont town and he was okay with it. To my delight he loved Sugar Maple as much as I did and was looking forward to building a future here with me.

The battle with Isadora had been decisive and brutal. She slammed Luke against the rocks repeatedly as he tried to save his daughter's soul from eternal damnation and I was terrified that his all-too-mortal body would succumb to the punishment Isadora flung his way. My sorceress genes protected me from the worst of Isadora's attacks but my human side still took a beating.

Finally I linked the power of my ancestors with the preordained future of the solar system and banished the Fae leader forever or until the sun died. Whichever came first.

No matter how you looked at it, she was history.

And now the rest of my life could begin. Luke and I were going to settle down together in the cozy cottage I had inherited from my surrogate mother, Sorcha. He would keep the town safe from harm in the form of nosy bureaucrats and rowdy tourists. I would grow my yarn business, and together we would bring another generation of Hobbs women into the world.

With a little luck (and maybe a touch of magick) we might even end up like one of those wonderful old couples who ate dinner at four o'clock and finished each other's sentences.

I looked over at the man I loved and my heart melted. So this was how it felt. Who knew? His left eye was swollen shut, his right cheekbone had a wicked gash slanting down toward the corner of his mouth, and he was covered in grime. His breathing was shallow and he walked slowly in an attempt to keep the pain of his battered ribs from knocking him down for the count.

He caught my eye. "You don't look much better," he said with a tired grin.

"You look pretty good to me," I said. He was alive. It didn't get much better than that.

"Blueberry pancakes," he said and I laughed. "A tall stack with eggs, bacon, and a gallon of that syrup you guys are always bragging about."

"No pancakes," I said. "I want a big fluffy omelet with melted cheddar and jalapeño peppers." Who knew that fighting the forces of evil could make a girl so hungry?

"Lots of coffee."

"With cream and sugar," I said. "This is no time to count calories."

"Fully Caffeinated won't be open for at least another hour," he said.

"Who needs Fully Caffeinated? I make a mean breakfast."

He looked skeptical. I didn't blame him. So far my Food Network addiction hadn't translated into more than an infatuation with butter and garlic.

"You do the pancakes," he said. "I'll make the eggs."

It just kept getting better and better. We were the ultimate dream couple. We could battle demons and make great breakfasts without missing a beat. If this was how being happy felt, I could definitely get used to it.

See where I'm going with this? I should have known it was too good to be true.

The faintest light of approaching dawn

filtered down through the towering trees as we approached the clearing less than twenty feet ahead. I heard the rustle of leaves off to my left and the faint hooting of an owl somewhere in the distance. We were almost home.

The happy ending my ancestors had been searching for was within reach. Next to me Luke reached for my hand and I felt the golden circle close around us. This was it. This was my path. This was my destiny.

The brush was badly overgrown. I followed him single file into the clearing. The set of his shoulders changed and the air around him went still in a way that almost buckled his knees.

He turned to face me. Our gazes locked. He didn't need to say the words because I felt them deep inside my bones.

Sugar Maple was gone.

2

CHLOE

I moved past Luke and stared across the wide expanse of open field toward Sugar Maple and my mind literally went blank.

No raging inferno had engulfed the town, reducing it to a mountain of ashes. A tornado hadn't shredded the buildings into toothpicks. A flash flood hadn't washed away the homes and shops and creatures big and small.

It was just . . . gone.

It was as if the town had never existed. No paths, no trails. Only mature trees and dense undergrowth in the spot Sugar Maple once occupied.

Where a town once stood there was nothing but grass and trees. And not seedlings or saplings, either. The grass was thick and summer lush even though we were barely out of winter. The treetops scraped the sky, branches budding wildly weeks before their time. In the distance I could see the mountains that surrounded Sugar Maple.

My brain shut down. White noise filled my head. Suddenly I was in motion, tearing across the open field with Luke hot on my heels as I ran toward the place where Sugar Maple used to be.

I don't know if it was adrenaline or magick or maybe some otherworldly combination of the two, but I left him in the dust. I could have qualified as an Olympic sprinter. Almost there . . . almost there . . . a couple more feet —

Splat!

I'm not even sure how the splat happened but one moment I was about to break through the dense tree line where Sugar Maple once began and the next I was lifted up by an invisible wave and sent flying backward straight into Luke.

The man I loved let out a grunt when I slammed into him and we hit the ground with a thud. I lay there on top of him, struggling to catch my breath, while his eyes rolled back into his skull.

I scrambled off him like he was on fire. "Are you okay, Luke? Say something! Are you okay?"

He groaned and rotated his eyeballs back into position. "What the hell was that all about?" he asked as he pulled himself up. "You looked like you were windsurfing."

"That's exactly what it felt like."

"Stay here," he said as he slowly got to his feet. "I'm going to check it out."

"You don't really think I'm going to stay here, do you?"

He shook his head. "I gave it my best shot."

You could almost smell the cop on him. I felt like I was in an episode of one of my favorite shows, watching him be all focused and professional.

Too bad caution wasn't catching. He approached the perimeter of what used to be Sugar Maple with detached, methodical precision. It made me totally crazy. I ran toward a small opening in the stand of trees and this time I slammed face-first into invisible memory foam with a mind of its own.

I was flung back by the rebound only to be sucked back in again by some unknown force. The more I struggled, the tighter it held me. I tried to pierce it with my nails but it was like trying to pierce Jell-O. I tried to bite it, kick it, punch it into submission but nothing worked.

I had trouble drawing in a full breath. My lungs felt depleted, turned inside out by the exertion. I tried to scream for Luke but no sound came out. *Let me go let me go let me go —*

Strong hands grabbed me by the ankles and pulled hard. I snapped backward like a rubber band and flew up and out, landing hard on my right side with my leg bent behind me.

Luke checked me for injuries but, as far as we could tell, the only damage was to what remained of my dignity.

"Thanks for the help, but you know I could have gotten out of there on my own," I said as we regrouped.

"You think?"

"Sooner or later I would have."

"We needed sooner."

No argument there.

"Why don't you try?" I suggested. "Maybe a human can get through."

Then again, maybe not.

He was played like a handball. He ricocheted between invisible walls then finally skidded to a stop about twenty feet away from me. I felt horribly guilty for even suggesting he try. He was big and strong but he was still only human. There were limits to how much punishment his mortal body could take.

We were back to square one and I was no longer convinced there was a square two.

"She won," I said as reality (never my best friend) crashed over me like a tsunami. "I don't know how she did it. I don't know when it happened. But Isadora somehow managed to win."

"We were at the waterfall," Luke reminded me. "That's the only portal referred to in Sugar Maple history. If the town was pulled beyond the mist, we would have seen it happen."

I gestured toward the dense forest where my hometown used to be. "It happened."

"Agreed," he said carefully, "but maybe not the way you think."

My pulse rate bumped up. "Go on."

He looked horribly uncomfortable as his dark green eyes met mine. "Maybe it was something you said."

Flames shot from my fingertips and he leaped back.

"Hey," he said, fanning the space between us. "It's just a theory. I'm a cop. We throw everything against the wall and see what sticks."

I blew on my fingers and shot him a sheepish smile. "Sorry. It's genetic."

"The flames or your temper?"

I opted for the high road. "Do you really think I might have said something to cause this?"

24

He shrugged and kept his distance. "You're the sorceress-in-training. You tell me."

I tried to replay the mental tape of the battle at the waterfall but it was a jumble of crazy images, wild emotions, and unintelligible words. "I remember saying *fortress against evil* and *through time and space* but nothing that could banish a town."

Or could it? A sick feeling of doubt blossomed deep inside.

"Do you remember when I said *moves to blackness?*"

"You mean while I was having my head bashed against the rocks or when my leg was being bent back like a Pepsi pop-top?"

"Excuse me for thinking you might have been paying attention," I said with more than a little edge to my voice. "I was busy too."

"Yeah, but I was busy trying to keep my brains inside my skull."

Point made.

"This isn't getting us anywhere," I said.

"No argument there."

I held out my hands to him, palms up. "I'm sorry. I get it now. Flying through the air hurts."

"Actually, the flying part isn't so bad. It's the landing that sucks." His expression softened. "I'm thinking a little magic wouldn't hurt right about now."

I made a face. "Magick might be what got us into this mess in the first place. I mean, what else could it be? Isadora was busy battling us and nobody else in town has that kind of power."

His silence told me I'd made my point. Normally I loved dazzling him with my logic but today it only made me sad. This was one time I'd rather be wrong.

"You think the Book of Spells might have some answers?"

I tried to laugh. "It's either that or a Magic 8 Ball."

The Book of Spells was like a celestial hard drive that contained over three hundred years' worth of magickal wisdom gathered by the Hobbs women who had come before me. There had to be something in there to help a struggling sorceress recover her missing hometown.

I closed my eyes and pulled in a long, shaky breath. Everything I had learned about the Book over the last few months danced just beyond reach. I couldn't even remember how to access the table of contents.

Calm down, I cautioned myself. Magick was like a six-month-old Great Dane. You had to show it who was boss or you'd be the one sleeping in the giant crate.

"Book of Spells," I intoned in my best sorceress-in-training voice. "I command you appear before me."

"Command?" Luke sounded way too amused.

"Perps and *vics?"* I shot back.

Okay, so maybe the language of magick was a tad seventeenth century. I'd worry about updating the jargon after I found our missing town.

"Book of Spells!" My voice rang out across the dawn-lightened field. "Come to me now!"

I waited for the shiver of awareness that preceded the appearance of the Book but it didn't come.

I pumped up the volume. "Now, Book! I command you appear before me!"

You would almost think I had no magick at all.

"Damn it, Book!" I shouted, dropping all pretense of wizardly mastery. "You've gotta give me something here!"

I'd take anything. A whisper. A glimmer of light. The tiniest clue that I was still connected to all those things that made me a struggling sorceress with an all-too-human heart.

27

Somehow I had made a mistake. Now all I had to do was undo that mistake and everything would be back the way it was. Maybe even better than before because the troubles with Isadora were finally over.

Denial. Where would we be without it? And the sad thing was I believed every word.

It was still early days when it came to my magick. My skills had taken a major leap forward over the last few weeks but I was still the new clerk at the local supermarket, the one with the big long line snaking all the way through frozen foods. She knows what she's doing but she's slow and deliberate and has trouble distinguishing Swiss chard from rhubarb.

The only difference between me and the clerk at Stop & Shop was that when I made a mistake I didn't screw up someone's dinner, I screwed up their life.

"Anything?" Luke asked.

I shook my head. "For all I know the Book is gone, too."

I'm not one of those women who burst into tears the second life gets a little rough around the edges. And I'm definitely not the kind of girl who would dump all of her problems in her man's lap and expect him to carry the load.

But the second Luke pulled me into his

arms and I saw those familiar silver and white sparks arcing between us, I fell apart.

"They're gone," I said between sobs. "Everyone is gone. . . ."

My cats Pyewacket, Dinah, Blot, and Lucy watch over the cottage I inherited from my surrogate mother, Sorcha. EZ came and went at will. And my favorite of all, wise old Penelope, who kept me company at the shop and provided her own brand of magick when necessary.

Gone? They couldn't be gone. They were the family I never had, true companions of the heart with a yen for Fancy Feast and catnip mice.

My mind spun down streets that were no longer there. There was the old church that served as our town hall, the one with the big stained-glass window of Saint George slaying the Dragon. The village green with the out-of-place lighthouse that stood in tribute to Salem where we all began. Our world-class flower beds, courtesy of the Sugar Maple Garden Club and Horticultural Society, and the bike path that wound through town all the way to Snow Lake.

And my yarn shop, Sticks & Strings, the place where I met Luke and we set off sparks for the first time over my self-replenishing basket of roving.

"My stash," I choked out then cried even harder.

"You're crying over your knitting?" Luke looked horrified, but he wasn't a knitter. I couldn't expect him to understand. I mean, he still hadn't mastered the difference between yarn and wool.

"I know it sounds t-terrible and I'm ashamed — well, I'm not really ashamed. I should be. I know I should be and — Luke, stop looking at me like I'm an ax murderer. I'm a knitter!"

My stash was part of my history. Losing it was like losing a piece of myself. A really *big* piece of myself. Grand Canyon big. Cashmere, mohair, angora, qiviut, sport weight, worsted, DK, lace weight fine as cobwebs. Bags of fleeces and baskets of handspun, including one very special basket handed down from Aerynn that replenished itself with the silkiest, finest roving you've ever seen. Needles made from local hardwoods, smoothed by the hands of the Hobbs women who came before me. The drop spindle that had belonged to Sorcha. My mother's spinning wheel.

Some people kept handwritten journals, secret books where they spilled their lives onto paper. My knitting was my journal. My life in fiber. Every skein of yarn came with a story: where I was when I found it, who I was with, the way it made me feel.

Every gauge swatch triggered memories of projects completed and projects frogged, of laughing with my knitting pals as one of the cats rolled around on an uncombed fleece or got all tangled up in a hank of hand-dyed merino. Teaching Janice how to cable without a needle. Helping Lynette master lace charts. All the wonderful friends and strangers who had passed through Sticks & Strings over the last ten years.

That shop, those people, my beloved cats — they were my life. They were my family.

Luke loved me but he only knew me within the context of Sugar Maple.

Without Sugar Maple, I wasn't sure I would know myself.

3

LUKE

I'd seen a lot of crap during my years as a big-city cop. Murders, kidnappings, gang fights, armed robberies, and a few grisly ritual slayings that still haunted my dreams if I let them. All cops have their demons. It comes with the territory. If it could happen, it will happen on your watch at least once.

You've watched cop shows on TV. Nobody goes into police work without at least a glimmer of what the job entails.

We keep the good guys safe and the bad guys behind bars.

Pretty straightforward.

Simplistic? I wouldn't argue the point but simplistic gets the job done.

I'm a guy. Guys solve problems. How doesn't matter. Intellectual gymnastics or brute strength, just as long as you get the job done.

But they hadn't covered How to Reclaim

a Missing Town from Fae Warriors at the academy, so all I could do was hold her until she stopped crying and hope this turned out to be a cosmic punking.

The sky had lightened a little bit more by the time she pulled herself together.

"I'd kill for those pancakes we talked about," she said as she wiped her eyes on her sleeve and looked up at me.

"And a big pot of coffee."

She forced a smile. "Now we know why the Queen keeps her purse with her. She's been carting around candy bars and Slim Jims in case of emergency." Her smile faltered and I could see reality pushing its way in. "We're in trouble, aren't we?"

MacKenzie's first rule: never lie to a woman who is smarter than you.

"Big trouble," I said.

"That's what I thought." She was quiet for a moment. "So the bad news is we don't have any food."

"And the worse news is there's no place to get any." The coffee shop, pizzeria, take-out Chinese, mini supermarket all were gone and the nearest Golden Arches was a good ten-mile walk.

She reached deep into the pockets of her jeans. "I can top that: we have no money to buy food, assuming we could find some in

33

the first place."

"I lost my wallet back at the waterfall."

"I left mine at the shop," she said.

And since we weren't feeling bad enough as it was, we decided to compile a reverse inventory.

No family.

No friends.

No food.

No cars.

No house.

No clothing.

No furniture.

No cats.

No money.

No ID.

No laptops, no cell phones, no pagers, no BlackBerrys, no iPods.

"I'd try to magick up an ATM but I'm afraid you'd arrest me," she said.

"Go for it," I said. "And while you're at it, throw in a truck with a full tank and some Egg McMuffins."

"Don't want much, do you, Chief?" She closed her eyes and started mumbling.

I waited.

She mumbled some more.

Three singles, two quarters, and half a dozen pennies appeared at our feet in a cloud of Kelly green smoke that smelled like mint juleps on Derby Day.

"Oh, crap," she said, bending down to retrieve the pocket change. "I was trying for a fistful of Franklins." She aimed an assessing look in my direction. "I think your cop vibe is screwing with my magick."

"My cop vibe?"

"You reek of cop, but I mean that in a good way."

Like hell she did, but I let it pass. "So what should I do about it?"

"Go stand over there by those white birches and I'll try again."

I'd been around long enough by now to know that when it came to magic I was so far down the food chain that roadkill ranked higher. I jogged thirty feet away from her and waited while she fired up her powers and tried again.

A spit of green smoke. A spurt of orange flame. Then a string of sailor's curses followed by a crack of thunder that reminded me that the woman I loved was anything but ordinary.

It also reminded me that the hotter her temper grew, the more trouble we might be in. I'd spent an afternoon last month as a Ken doll after a spirited exchange, so I had some personal experience.

"Chill, Tinker Bell," I said as I rejoined

her. "We don't need any more natural disasters."

Chloe grabbed my arm. "Did you hear that?"

A faint rumble sounded from the far end of the field.

"Thunder?" I asked.

"I don't think so."

"Damn," I said. "That sounds like your car."

I was right. Chloe's monster Buick leaped into the meadow in a wild yellow and red and orange hailstorm and headed straight for us.

Chloe took off at high speed toward the car but I tackled her around the waist and knocked her to the ground. "Let me go!" she screamed, but the more she struggled, the tighter I held on.

Even though I was a big Stephen King fan, I wasn't about to let either of us star in a remake of *Christine.*

The Buick swerved from one side of the field to the other like a crazed bumper car, wheels spinning, engine straining. I tossed Chloe over my shoulder in a fireman's carry and we dived into the brush. I rolled her under me, which, under different circumstances, would have been a good thing but right now it was all about survival.

In the world I grew up in, cars didn't drive themselves but here in Sugar Maple anything was possible.

So the sight of a two-ton, two-decades-old Buick appearing out of thin air didn't surprise me.

But as it skidded to a stop the familiar face behind the wheel sure as hell did.

4

CHLOE

I'd never seen anything more beautiful in my life than the sight of my friend Janice Meany behind the wheel of my beloved old Buick.

Unless it was the sight of my beloved Penny the cat in the passenger seat, perched high atop a wondrous mountain of yarn.

Janice leaned through the driver's-side window. "Where have you guys been?" she demanded. "I thought you'd —" Her voice caught and she swallowed the rest of the sentence but I knew exactly what she had been going to say.

I leaped to my feet and ran toward the car. My friend, my car, my cat *and* some of my stash!

Luke swung open the driver's-side door and Janice jumped out. I grinned as he gave her a clumsy hug that she returned with more warmth than she had ever shown him before.

"Your ribs?" she asked as he winced. She moved her hands along his sides while whispering an incantation I didn't recognize. "Give it an hour. You'll be fine."

Luke looked skeptical but I knew that sixty minutes from now he'd be a believer in my friend's healing gifts.

Janice wasn't a touchy-feely kind of woman but she grabbed me in a hug that almost cracked my perfectly healthy ribs.

Penny the cat erupted in an ear-splitting yowl and we burst into laughter.

"Come on, Pen!" I said, and she leaped into my arms with the energy of a kitten. Her familiar lawn-mower purr sounded like a symphony. Penny was my touchstone. She had been with me all my life, and with my mother and her mother before her. Legend had it that Aerynn had brought Penelope with her when she fled Salem and I believed it was true. On more than one occasion, Penny had served as a conduit between dimensions and even though it sounded crazy when the going got tough, I knew Penny had my back.

And as if that wasn't great enough, Janice had rescued my stash! Clouds of purple and green, yellow and red and orange, rich browns and saturated blacks and every variation possible on creamy white billowed out the open windows. Noro and Colinette, Rowan and Malabrigo, one-offs from local indie dyers, batts and rolags, Aerynn's wheel and everything else Janice could wedge inside or tie on the roof.

I was so excited my words tumbled out all over themselves. "I didn't — we couldn't — I mean, we thought we would never —" I stopped and pulled in a long breath. I met Janice's eyes. "So where is Sugar Maple?"

Her brown eyes widened and she looked from me to Luke then back again. "I was going to ask you two the same thing."

"But you're here. I thought —"

"You're here, too," she pointed out. "I was hoping you had some answers."

"How the hell did you manage this?" Luke asked, gesturing toward the yarn-stuffed car. Men didn't stand on ceremony. "Why didn't the spell that took Sugar Maple take you, too?"

"Hello," Janice said. "And here I thought you were happy to see me."

"You were right," I said to Luke. "It *is* my fault. When I tied Isadora's fate to the death of the sun, I must have somehow referenced Sugar Maple."

"Where did you get that idea?" Janice demanded.

I recited the chain of events as I knew them. "What other answer is there?"

"It wasn't Isadora and it wasn't you," Janice said. "That's not how it went down at all."

Luke was in full cop mode. "If it wasn't Isadora and it wasn't Chloe, what happened and why weren't you dragged away with everyone else in town?"

Janice eyed him long enough to make me swallow hard. When Janice looked like that, anything could happen. Luke was lucky he wasn't squatting on a lily pad somewhere, croaking for help.

I didn't breathe easy until Janice broke the stare and started talking.

"The town was pretty evenly divided about whether or not to let Isadora take us beyond the mist. Probably more divided than either of you realized. Anyway, the closer we moved to the zero hour, the uglier it got. The Weavers threatened Lilith's family if they didn't go along with Isadora's plan. Cyrus tried to step in and broker some kind of understanding when Renate —"

Luke broke in. "Where the hell is the town?"

"I'm getting to that." She shot me an exasperated look while I resisted the urge to turn him into the speak-no-evil monkey

41

while she finished her story. "As I was saying, the two sides were having a throw-down and Renate started screaming that they were going to miss the opportunity and Paul Griggs said over his dead body and that's when those mini earthquakes really started popping and you just knew —" She shook her head. "Lynette headed over to your cottage to get the girls. I raced to the shop for Penny and the basket and as much of your private stash as I could cram into the Buick. I planned to drive them over the township line where they'd be safe from whatever was about to happen.

"I waited as long as I could for Lynette but she didn't show. I was just about to abandon the car and jump back onto the Sugar Maple side of the line and get back to Lorcan and the kids when the town blinked out like a dying lightbulb and disappeared."

"Disappeared?" I was having trouble following the chronology. "You said disappeared, not pulled beyond the mist?"

"Disappeared," Janice repeated. "And I'll bet my last remaining Fig Newton that Isadora had nothing to do with it."

She had Fig Newtons?

"So who did?" Luke asked.

"This is just a guess but when they didn't

get a signal or whatever it was they were waiting for from Isadora, I'll bet that the Weavers and the rest of the Fae contingent tried to pull Sugar Maple beyond the mist on their own."

Luke considered Janice's words for a long moment.

"They had that kind of power?"

"Not individually but together they might."

I met Janice's eyes. "You've read about town transport. You know it's a rough business. If they'd succeeded, the process would have left the same kind of footprint behind as a Cat 5 hurricane and we would have seen it happen."

"Well, *something* happened," Janice said, her eyes filling with tears, "because my husband and kids are gone and I'm —" This time she couldn't choke back her tears and I hugged her while she cried it out against my shoulder.

Luke was like most men, human and otherwise, in that raw emotion made him uncomfortable. He turned toward the place where the town had been and pretended to study the landscape until Janice's sobs slowed down to a few random hiccups.

I was on the edge of another crying jag myself. Janice would be with her family right now if she hadn't taken time to rescue Penny and my stash and drive the jam-packed Buick over the township line to safety. For that matter, maybe none of this would have happened at all if I hadn't screwed things up in the first place.

"Maybe this is temporary," I said as she blew her nose into a Fully Caffeinated napkin I'd found on the floor of my car. "Maybe they had enough power to make Sugar Maple disappear but not enough sustained power to keep it away for long. For all we know it's going to reappear any second."

"I wouldn't bet the yarn shop on it," Janice said. "Never underestimate Renate Weaver and her clan. They're more powerful than they let on."

Not exactly what I wanted to hear. "I wish I knew why they flipped allegiance."

"You know why they flipped. You started consorting with the enemy." She looked over at Luke. "Sorry, but it's true."

If it bothered him, he didn't show it. He was still in cop mode.

"What if the town was pulled into the mist somehow and Isadora cast a spell to help cover the tracks?" Luke said.

"Come on," I snapped at Luke. "If Isadora thought there was a chance in hell that

44

they could pull Sugar Maple beyond the mist, she wouldn't have bothered to cover her tracks. She'd rent a billboard in Times Square." I took a deep breath. "I think I did it."

Janice burst into laughter. "Honey, I love you but when it comes to magick, you're still in diapers. You couldn't possibly pull off something like this, especially not by mistake."

When this was over, Janice and I were going to have to talk. A lot had changed in the hours since I last saw my friend. I wasn't the same scared-of-her-own-shadow sorceress she'd known and loved. I would never be afraid of my growing powers again.

"I mean I think I screwed up somehow and banished the town along with Isadora."

Janice made a face. "Impossible. There's no spell linkage between towns and individuals. The power you needed to destroy Isadora was nothing like the power you'd need to banish a town."

But to me the logic was unassailable. I had created a spell that linked Isadora's banishment with the death of our sun and then, not long after, we discovered our town had gone missing, too. Why was I the only one who seemed able to connect those dots?

Penny the cat meowed and began to

squirm against me. I put her down on the dewy grass and she wandered off to do what she needed to do while we leaned against the Buick and stared across the field at the large expanse of trees that used to be a town.

"What's wrong with this picture?" Janice muttered.

"You mean, besides the fact that Penny deigned to put her paws on damp ground?"

"I was thinking more like why aren't we in there instead of out here?"

"Because we can't get in," I said.

"You tried?"

Luke and I exchanged eye rolls. "Of course we tried," I said. "What do you think we were doing before you showed up?" I was having trouble keeping the *duh* out of my voice.

Luke brought her up to speed on the shield that guarded the perimeter.

"What about the field?" Janice asked.

"Neutral territory," he said.

"Well, it made for some hella bad driving," Janice said.

"That's the Buick," Luke said with a grin in my direction, "not the spell."

"How did you know we were here?" I asked, ignoring Luke's comment. "I mean, what did you do between the time Sugar Maple vanished and now?" For that matter, how did she even know we were here?

Janice's eyes widened. "I — I'm not sure."

"You must've done something," I said. "It's been a couple of hours."

She seemed lost in thought. "I can't remember anything after the town blinked out. Next thing I knew I was driving that bucket of bolts you call a car across the field."

"Do you think you fell asleep for a while?" Luke asked.

"Not exactly the time for a nap," Janice pointed out.

"In a trance of some kind?" I asked.

"I guess it's possible but until you asked I hadn't thought about the time lapse."

"We need to make a list." I rummaged through one of my knitting bags for paper and pen. And ignored the laughter behind me. "I don't hear any better ideas." I pulled out a battered Bic that was almost as old as my car and a take-out menu from Wong Foo's with the first few rows of a lace pattern scribbled across the back. "You first, Luke. What did you see when you walked the perimeter?"

"You mean, besides the missing town?"

I loved him, but he was a wisecrack away from being turned into a hood ornament.

"The town is gone," he acknowledged,

47

"and so is the bridge. There's a forest there instead."

Janice groaned but I tried to put a positive spin on things.

"That's a good thing." My Pollyanna imitation needed a little work. "No bridge means no traffic into town, which means we'll go undetected a little longer." The Toothaker Bridge was the only way in or out of town.

"What town?" Luke retorted. "Just wait until UPS comes rolling in with a delivery for Sticks & Strings. This story will explode."

"Crap!" Sometimes passion trumped eloquence. I checked the time on Luke's watch. "Joe usually hits my shop around nine fifteen."

For three hundred years Aerynn's protective charm had shielded our truth from prying eyes but now that there was no town to shield, the protective charm no longer existed and a missing town would be impossible to explain.

"Anybody have a really big tarp?" Janice asked and we laughed despite ourselves.

"Maybe one of Forbes's granny square afghans," I said. Forbes was our resident mountain giant.

"One of Midge Stallworth's bathrobes

might work."

"Or you could create another protective charm," Luke offered.

Leave it to the cop to come up with a solution. He was definitely more optimistic than I was. So far my powers seemed to have gone the way of Sugar Maple itself. Had he forgotten my pathetic attempt to call down some spending money?

"Go for it," Janice said to me. "There has to be something in the Book of Spells that will help."

I didn't have the heart to tell my friend that so far the Book of Spells was MIA and we just might be on our own.

5

LUKE

The Janice I had known up until now was a wisecracking, self-confident Julia Roberts look-alike who had the real world and every other world by the short hairs. She balanced a big family, a happy marriage, and a thriving business and made it look easy.

Sometimes I almost forgot she was a witch descended from a long line of witches who could take me out without breaking a sweat.

I'm not sure she ever forgot I was human.

The Janice next to me now was a mess. She grabbed my hand as Chloe tried to call the Book of Spells to her side and she squeezed tighter and tighter with every failed attempt.

"She's struggling," Janice whispered in my ear. "What happened at the waterfall? Is she okay?"

"She's exhausted," I said as her nails dug deeper into the palm of my hand. "She'll be fine." I was straddling the line between lie and wish.

The more Chloe tried, the more tongue-tied she grew. Her hard-won magick seemed a distant memory. Bursts of yellow flame erupted at her feet with every failed effort, then fizzled swiftly and died. Mostly it was like watching a slow-motion train wreck.

"Where's Penny?" Chloe darted over to where we stood by the car. "I need Penny!"

She swept the enormous cat into her arms then dashed back to the center of the field.

"Uh-oh," Janice said. "That doesn't sound good."

I'm not going to tell you I understand it, but that mellow old cat served as some kind of interdimensional courier between Chloe and the world the rest of us can't see. Today, however, not even Penny made a difference.

I shot a quick look at my watch. We had maybe another ninety minutes before the real world and all its problems descended on what used to be Sugar Maple.

"I'm getting nowhere," Chloe said as she rejoined us. Penny was draped across her shoulders like a knitted shawl. "I've tried every spell I know short of abracadabra."

A brisk wind blew in from the west and I realized the sky had grown noticeably grayer over the last few minutes. Early April in

Vermont is a crapshoot. The day can start cold, turn warm, and end with a blizzard, all within one twenty-four-hour period.

On cue, a few big fluffy white flakes drifted down.

"Oh, great," Chloe muttered. "Just what we need."

"I hate snow," Janice said. "Our ancestors should have settled in Boca."

A few more pieces of the puzzle shifted, collided, then dropped into place. "I'm thinking snow is exactly what we need." Lots of snow. A blizzard of it, aimed right at the heart of the place where Sugar Maple used to be.

Chloe and Janice exchanged a *what can you expect from a human* look.

I blew it off. I knew I was onto something. "This is the answer. Maybe if you combine your powers, you can create a blizzard and block out the town."

"I don't have much right now," Chloe said, clearly distressed. She turned to Janice. "How about you?"

Janice put on her game face. "We'll find out."

The plan was simple but if it worked it would buy us time to figure out what was going on and, with luck, a way to restore the town.

Janice's powers were of the earth. The natural world was her element and, under normal circumstances, this should have been child's play. Chloe's powers were less easy to characterize and more mercurial. Their potential, however, seemed unlimited.

They moved to the middle of the open field that separated us from the woods that were once Sugar Maple, then Chloe called to Penny the cat, who had wandered off while we talked. Penny glided across the field then leaped effortlessly and once again draped herself across Chloe's shoulders as the two women clasped hands. I'd been warned to keep my cop vibe at a distance so I leaned against the Buick and watched the show.

CHLOE

I went deep, deeper than ever before, and came up empty every time. Sugar Maple wasn't the only thing that was gone. The Book of Spells was gone and so was my magick.

"Come on," Janice urged. "You can do it."

"I can't. The Book isn't responding."

"What do you mean, it's not responding? It has to respond."

"It doesn't have to do anything. It's the Book of Spells."

"It's not the boss of you. Make it listen!"

Easy for her to say. She'd been magick all her life. Magick was as natural to Janice as breathing in and out. For me it was still like patting my head and rubbing my stomach while standing on one foot in a hurricane.

"I can't make it listen, Jan. I'm still learning."

"You can make it do anything you want."

"No, I can't. It does what it does and I go along for the ride."

"You sound like you're giving up."

She was right. I was giving up. In the face of trouble, I was sliding back into my nonmagick self. Except my nonmagick self didn't exist anymore. I owed it to everyone who had come before to remember that.

"Try again," Janice urged. "You're the alpha dog around here now."

I saw the fear in her eyes and tears welled up in sympathy. I had cried more in the last few hours than at any time in my life and I didn't like it.

"Don't you dare," she warned me. "If you start, I'll start again and this time I won't be able to stop."

I had no blood family of my own at stake but she had a husband and children, a mother and father and siblings and nieces and nephews, an entire web of family lost out there somewhere with Sugar Maple. If I was in any way responsible for this, I had to try to make it right.

I burrowed down and gave it my best shot. I begged, coaxed, cajoled, pleaded with, and downright ordered the Book of Spells to show itself and help us out of this jam but it remained out of reach.

"Screw it!" Luke looked over at me in surprise. "To hell with the Book of Spells," I said. "I can do this without the Book."

I would gather up what skills I'd already mastered and put it all in the hands of my ancestors. *Aerynn, if you're out there, please help us!*

Luke was watching us but there really wasn't much to see. Whatever had occurred here had changed more than the landscape. Both Janice's and my magick had been severely depleted and would take time to replenish. Time that we didn't have.

But we were relentless. The air around Janice moved in vertical waves, like heat rising off a summer pavement, but there was still no sign of magick.

Janice had laid the groundwork and it was up to me to figure out a way to build on it. Last night I had done the impossible and saved a little girl's spirit from an eternity in hell. Conjuring up a snowstorm — even with diminished powers — should be easy.

Of course there were women who said childbirth was easy, too, so I guess it was all relative. I wove my spell around Janice's energies, adding mine to the mix, commanding the clouds to open up and spill a blizzard exactly where we needed one.

But no matter how hard I tried, nothing happened. I knew what magick felt like now. I knew how it felt when magick moved through my body, the way the muscles in my arms and legs tensed, the accelerated heartbeat, the almost sexual feeling of anticipation. And, believe me, it wasn't there.

Penny had abandoned us and returned to the car and was now peering out at me through the rear window. Her golden eyes, strangely like mine, seemed to glow with an energy that warmed my skin like summer sunlight. I could feel myself growing loose and relaxed. The moment lengthened and I sensed a change. Instead of speeding up, my heartbeat slowed. A chill washed over me, raising goose bumps up and down my arms.

Next to me Janice let out a shriek. "It's snowing!"

Flurries at first, big soft white snowflakes that landed like powdered sugar, then it quickly upshifted into serious snow.

The kind that showed every intention of turning into a blizzard that closed down schools and shops and roadways and took a town off the grid.

I mean, seriously, you've got to love magick.

Luke was euphoric when we joined him by the car. "Another fifteen minutes and nobody will be able to get within a mile of home."

The heavy storm would also make aerial views impossible. There would be no planes flying overhead in the foreseeable future. No nosy news choppers looking to fill a twenty-four-hour cycle.

But still we couldn't leave anything to chance.

"I'll call the county and report the downed bridge and the whiteout conditions and tell them I'll let them know when to send in the plows and the repair crew," Luke said. As chief of police, his word would be taken at face value. Besides, if Mother Nature and our powers cooperated, they'd have more than enough snowplowing to keep them busy once the storm stopped.

With a little luck, that would give us forty-eight hours. I didn't know what we were going to do with those hours but we would figure that out as we went along.

Except for the fact that Sugar Maple was still MIA and we were tired, hungry, and broke, things were really working out.

"Did you say something before about Fig Newtons?" I asked Janice. I may have drooled a tiny bit but I wouldn't swear to it.

"You're not getting my Fig Newtons."

"Jan, we're starving. We have no food and no money to get any food. Give up those cookies or I'll hurt you."

"Check the glove box, honey," Janice said. "I promise it's better than cookies."

6

CHLOE

Not only was Janice's surprise better than cookies, it was almost better than magick.

She'd stuffed my favorite felted knit purse into the glove box, along with my wallet, my credit cards, and all of the cash we'd had on hand in the shop. Not only that, she'd taken time to pop into Luke's office next door to my shop and raid his petty cash.

"You also had an AmEx card, your cell phone, and your old Massachusetts driver's license in there," she told him, "so I grabbed them, too."

It didn't take much to make us happy. A partially charged phone, some plastic, and a handful of dead presidents and we were suddenly masters of the universe. Janice could have gone for days without eating but Luke and I shared the human need for meals at regular intervals. I couldn't speak for Luke but I knew I would think better after I got some of those hash browns under my belt.

"Have fun, guys," Janice said. "I'm staying here."

"Are you crazy?" I asked. "The snow's only going to get worse."

"I'll take my chances with the blizzard."

I started to laugh. "She's afraid I'm going to drive," I said to Luke. "That's what this is all about."

Janice didn't deny it. "Honey, the only thing worse than driving your Buick is riding around in your Buick with you behind the wheel."

Who could blame her? Everyone knew how much I hated driving. And to make matters worse everyone seemed to agree that I was horrible at it at the best of times. The only wheel they wanted to see me behind was a spinning wheel.

To Janice's relief, Luke agreed to drive. It occurred to me that might give us an advantage. If we were pulled over, having the chief of police driving should guarantee us no questions asked.

The snow was hellacious but, true to the spell we cast, it centered on Sugar Maple and the mile or so immediately surrounding it. By the time we were halfway to the Golden Arches we had outpaced the storm and were free and clear.

McDonald's anchored a huge outlet mall two towns away. We debated eating in the car but the lure of indoor plumbing was too tempting to resist. Penny opened one eye as I exited the car then promptly went back to sleep when I promised I'd bring something back for her.

Twenty minutes later, Luke, Janice, and I were eating our way through a mountain of Egg McMuffins, piles of hash browns in those nifty paper envelopes, and enough coffee to keep us awake until Thanksgiving. Conversation was limited to "Pass the ketchup" and "I need another creamer."

There was only so much chaos the mind could process without flaming out. It was good to sit there in the toasty warm restaurant, scarfing eggy-cheesy muffins, chugging coffee, and pretending our lives hadn't been turned upside down.

And then it was time to get serious. We disposed of our trash. I ordered an Egg Mc-Muffin for Penny and grabbed a few extra coffees for the road. We might be up the creek without a paddle but at least we weren't going to starve.

"It's snowing!" I said as we exited Mc-Donald's and walked across the parking lot toward the Buick.

Janice stopped in her tracks. "It's not supposed to be snowing here. We made sure of that."

"Probably a coincidence," Luke said, glancing up at the flurries swirling around our heads. "Flurries might have been part of the weather report."

I was wondering if we had done too good a job with the snow. If the roads were impassable for delivery trucks and tourists, they would be impassable for us too.

Then again, we had magick to help us, out. I refused to worry about it until I had to.

Walmart anchored the opposite end of the strip mall and, luckily for us, it opened early. We wrote up a list of emergency items on the back of a paper napkin (cat litter, bottled water, Chips Ahoy). Luke went off in search of an ATM while Janice and I did the shopping.

"Now what?" Janice asked when we met back up in the parking lot and considered our options.

"I guess we go back to Sugar Maple," I said. What else could we do? It wasn't like we had anyplace else to go.

"There is no Sugar Maple," Luke, back from the ATM, reminded me.

"I know that." I hit each word hard. "That's why we need to go back there." Wasn't that the first rule of detecting? Keep your eyes on the scene of the crime. Sooner or later the guilty party would return for a victory lap and a smart detective would be there waiting.

Unless, of course, the guilty party turned out to be one of the detectives, which called up a whole different set of complications I didn't want to consider. I know both Luke and Janice believed I had nothing to do with Sugar Maple's disappearance but it would take more than loyalty to convince me I was totally innocent.

"Did you forget about the blizzard?" Luke sounded maddeningly calm and more than a little annoying. I felt like turning him into a hot-pink stitch marker but we needed him to drive. "The roads are probably impassable by now."

"We have to go back," I said. "I need to find the Book of Spells." He knew as well as anyone how important the Book was.

"What makes you think it's there?"

"Hey," Janice said, whirling on him, "back off, MacKenzie. I don't see you coming up with any bright ideas."

"Janice is right," I said. "You're the hot-shot big-city detective." I was so ticked off even I could see the raging red aura forming all around me. "If you're so smart, what would you do?"

"Easy," he said. "I'd go to Salem."

7

LUKE

Chloe stared at me like I'd turned into a frog. "Salem's not a great idea, Luke."

"Salem!" Janice's voice shot up at least two octaves. "Are you freaking nuts?"

"What's wrong with Salem?" I demanded. "Hell, you guys have a monument to the place on your collective front lawn." The replica lighthouse that illuminated the village green. Even the street names were based on Salem references. And those were only two of many shout-outs. Once you caught on, you realized Salem was everywhere you looked.

"Think about it, Einstein." Janice was practically spitting fireballs at me. "Witch Trials sound familiar?"

"They happened over three hundred years ago."

"And nothing's changed since then."

"Come on," I said. "Get real, Janice.

When's the last time someone was burned at the stake for being a witch?"

"They were *hanged* in Salem," Janice corrected him. "Get your facts straight."

"Come on, guys." Chloe sounded a warning a wiser man would have heeded. "Let it go. It's a Sugar Maple thing, Luke. You'll never understand."

"And you do?" She might be magick but she was human, too, and that powerful connection was something we shared. She had been raised as a mortal woman. She had to see the absurdity of Janice's position.

Instead I saw only uncertainty in her wide golden eyes. "As much as I can," she said softly.

I'd taken at least two dozen sensitivity courses during my years on the force. Workshops on racial discrimination, religious intolerance, sexual harassment, hate crimes of every type. I'd role-played both sides of every issue. No matter how you parsed it, the message was simple. Diversity was good. Bigotry wasn't. I got it. I agreed with it. I always had.

However, this whole issue of humans versus the Others was above my pay grade. That alone should have stopped me but it didn't. My gut said I was onto something, and a good cop never ignored his gut even if it got him in trouble.

I grew up two towns over from Salem. I knew the area like I knew the sound of my own heartbeat. Salem was a Massachusetts seaport and fishing village and nothing more.

"Have you ever been to Salem?" I asked both Chloe and Janice. "Walked the streets, talked to the people, stood on the docks and breathed in the salt air?"

The look of pain in Janice's eyes surprised me. "Once," she said. "I lasted three minutes before I bolted. I couldn't breathe."

"I drove over there one weekend when I was at BU," Chloe said. "I couldn't get past the Entering Salem sign." She'd broken out in hives and ended up in the ER.

I regrouped.

"We're in deep shit," I said. "We have maybe forty-eight hours before somebody out here in the world notices Sugar Maple's gone. We're not going to find the answers on the Internet or in the public library and there's no point trying to collect fingerprints or DNA. Salem is our best shot."

"Are you always this cheerful?" Janice wisecracked. "No wonder you humans spend so much money on shrinks and Prozac."

Great. Another antihuman dig from Janice. I wondered how she'd ended up best friends with Chloe, whose father had been one hundred percent mortal.

"What do you think we'll find in Salem?" Chloe asked. "Another Book of Spells? A welcoming committee?"

Janice flashed me a look. "Santa Claus with a marching band and the key to the city?"

"Maybe nothing," I admitted. "Maybe everything. We won't know until we get there. That's how you find out."

"Are you sure you were a detective?" Janice asked. "That's not how it is on television."

I let it pass. Detective work was actually a hell of a lot like advertising. Maybe only ten percent of your efforts would amount to anything but nobody knew which ten percent it would be so you covered all your bases.

Chloe looked at me over Janice's head. "I think we're better off here. Our connection with Salem has no relevance to what's happening now."

"Then why all of the Salem references in town?" I challenged her. "Why keep the connection alive all these years? It has to mean something."

"Sure it does," she said. "History . . .

tradition."

"Maybe it's time to push it into the twenty-first century."

Both Chloe and Janice scowled at me.

I regrouped again. "I know we all believe that the best way to bring Sugar Maple back is to retrieve the Book of Spells, and since the Book isn't answering Chloe's call, we've got to assume it's with the town."

"Go on," Chloe said.

"The way I see it, this all comes down to figuring out where can we find another Book of Spells."

Chloe laughed out loud. "There's only one Book of Spells."

"Are you sure?" I asked.

She hesitated. "That's what I've always believed."

"Okay, let's say you're right and there's only one Book. We know the Book began in Salem and that the knowledge was acquired there. What if some of that knowledge stayed there in Salem?"

Janice surprised everyone, including herself, when she said, "Luke might be onto something."

Luke? She called me Luke. Most of the time I was either a third-person pronoun or "the human."

Chloe seemed uneasy. "It's taken me four

69

months to even master a tiny percentage of one section of the Book. The knowledge contained in it definitely predates Aerynn's arrival in Sugar Maple."

Janice nodded her head in agreement. "Most of us in town believed the knowledge was accumulated over the ages, not just a few centuries."

Chloe glanced from her friend to me. "So you're saying that maybe not all of our ancestors fled Salem with Aerynn?"

I could almost hear the click as more puzzle pieces dropped into place.

"I'm saying it's a possibility. It's also possible that some folklore still exists that could provide a clue." That was the thing about police work. You had to follow every lead because you never knew where the answers might be hiding.

"Luke's right, Chloe. Salem might be our only hope."

I met Chloe's eyes. "Salem is the only other place on earth with a connection to Sugar Maple. It's a four-hour drive. If we come up empty we can be back here and up shit creek again by nightfall."

We had nothing to lose.

CHLOE

Ask any knitter and he or she will tell you that the only thing better than TV knitting is road trip knitting. I turned the car keys over to Luke again and, pushing aside an explosion of Dream in Color Smooshy, claimed the passenger seat. The circumstances could have been a whole lot better but I have to admit the prospect of a few hours of mindless knit-and-purl made me very happy.

Janice managed to squish herself into the backseat amid the baskets and bags of roving and rolags and fleeces and a very clingy Penny the cat and was three rounds into a Wendy Knits toe-up lace sock by the time Luke angled the Buick out of the Walmart parking lot.

I let myself sink into my default pattern for a three-one rib cuff-down sock. I was using a skein of Noro Kureyon Sock in gorgeous saturated shades of royal blue and purple splashed with hot pink and an understated forest green and as always the chaos in my mind stilled as I anticipated the color transitions and savored the way the yarn felt as it moved through my fingers.

Nobody said a word as we drove toward the highway and left the snow behind. I guess we were all wondering when (and maybe if) we would return. I would have kitchener-stitched my lips together rather than admit it but I was scared. This was the only world I knew. Except for my painfully brief time at Boston University when I was eighteen, I had spent my entire life in Sugar Maple and now it was gone.

I was so far outside my comfort zone that it was downright laughable. The more miles we put between ourselves and Sugar Maple, the less confident I felt that we would return.

What if we never came back?

I glanced toward Luke. He had a life waiting for him in the human world. A phone call or two and he would have a new job in a new town and a new future to consider. He would be back where he belonged, with mortals who went to work every day, who fell in and out of love, who married and had children, who worried about their 401(k)s and whether or not their flu shots were up-to-date. Before long his months in Sugar Maple would seem like a story that happened to someone else.

I knew he loved me. I knew he would want me to share his life. A year ago I might have been able to make it work. But now that I had magick, I wasn't so sure.

And Janice — I couldn't bring myself to

think about what she was going through.

Luke asked if we minded if he tuned into one of the sports talk radio stations. Janice and I lied and said no. We needed our knitting. He needed his Red Sox. We'd cope. He fiddled with the dial but instead of baseball talk, he got nothing but static.

"Your radio sucks," Luke said. "You might want to invest in an antenna."

"I drive three hundred miles a year," I said as I flipped my knitting and continued the round. "I haven't used that radio since gas was a dollar a gallon."

He had a great deep laugh and for a moment things didn't seem so bleak.

"Another year and you'll be able to get historic plates," Luke said. "Lower your insurance rates."

"Another year and she'll be pushing this thing down Osborne Avenue," Janice said and this time we all laughed.

"A little respect," I said. "It's getting us where we want to go, isn't it?"

"I'll give you props for the size of your trunk," Janice admitted. "You could hide three or four bodies in there."

Luke met her eyes in the rearview mirror. "You want to run that by me again?"

"Some people come by their logic watching *Twilight Zone.* I came by mine watching

The Sopranos."

"I'll keep that in mind," Luke said, but a quick smile softened the prime-time cop delivery.

I knew Janice made Luke uncomfortable. He hadn't said anything but his jaw always tightened whenever she was around. Not that I blamed him. Janice had made her feelings about full-blood humans painfully clear on more than one occasion.

But so far, so good. Some of the nervous tension that had locked my shoulders up around my ears melted away and I settled back against the seat and addressed my knitting.

Some people meditated. Some people ran laps around a track. When I was tense, I turned yarn into socks. Lots of socks. More socks than any sane woman with the standard-issue pair of feet could possibly use in a lifetime. Now that Luke was part of my life I had started knitting socks for him (a labor of love when the feet in question wore size twelve shoes) and his sock drawer was already bulging at the seams.

Not that lack of space would stop me. We could always buy him a new sock drawer. At the rate I was knitting we'd need it by the time we hit Salem.

Which was fine with me. Right now the

only thing between me and utter panic was the sock in my hands. I was deeply immersed in all of that purple and blue and green yarny goodness when the snow found us.

"What the hell — ?" He squinted out the window then flicked on the wipers. "That's a blizzard out there."

A wave of uneasiness washed over me.

"Why is it hitting us?" I asked. "I thought we were outrunning it."

Janice wiped condensation off the side window and peered outside. "Not anymore," she said.

"Maybe it was in the weather report for today," I said. "It might have nothing to do with the spell."

I didn't believe a word I said. Neither did anyone else.

Luke muttered something unquotable as the car slid noticeably to the left. He eased up on the gas and we slid back into the lane. "How the hell do you manage up here without four-wheel drive?"

"Easy," Janice jumped in. "Our girl doesn't drive if there's more than an inch of snow on the ground."

I plucked a bit of vegetable matter from my working yarn and dropped it in the unused ashtray. "I have enough trouble driving when it's sunny and dry. Why push my luck?"

"The town council was considering an ordinance to keep her off the road when there's more than an inch of precip anywhere in the county."

I swatted her with my Noro sock yarn. "Excuse me but that was shouted down without a vote."

Janice's grin was thoroughly wicked. "Only because you swore you'd stay off the road voluntarily."

"Thanks a lot," I said. "You made me drop a stitch."

I swear to you Janice gasped so loudly she sucked the oxygen out of the car. "What did you say?"

"I dropped a stitch and it's all your —" Now it was my turn to gasp. I had never dropped a stitch in my entire knitting life. Not once.

Janice squinted at her sock in progress then held it up to the light. "I don't believe this." She rummaged in one of my accessory bags for a ruler then laid it against the knitted fabric. "Holy crap," she said. "I'm not getting gauge."

"Gauge is a good thing?" Luke asked, slowing the Buick down to practically a crawl.

"Gauge is a very good thing," I said. Otherwise that wonderful boyfriend sweater you were working on might be better suited for a toddler.

Sticks & Strings was known as the shop where your yarn never tangled, your sleeves always matched, and you always got gauge. Customers came from all parts of the country to take our weekend workshops and ongoing classes. Fearful knitters cast on, terrified of dropped stitches, miscrossed cables, lopsided sleeves, all of the million and one things that can and do go wrong with a project. But by the time they were tying on their next skein of yarn, they were flying without a net.

It had never occurred to me that my knitting skills might also owe something to good juju and more than a little outside magick. I preferred to think it was great genes.

So much for Wonder Knitter.

Janice slumped back in her seat, mumbling to herself as she frogged her sock and poked around in search of a smaller circular needle.

I was busy fiddling with a steel crochet hook, working my dropped stitch back up the ladder. "Son of a gun," I said as the stitches reappeared. "Guess I'm not such a bad teacher after all."

I knew that in the grand scheme of things a dropped stitch in a road trip sock wasn't a big deal but I was definitely feeling uneasy. When something happened that had never happened before, you didn't need magickal powers to know there was trouble brewing.

Like the blizzard that was now dumping snow on us faster than the windshield wipers could push it away.

"Maybe you should slow down," I said to Luke as the rear end of the car slid left.

"I'm doing twenty," Luke said as he eased out of the skid. "Any slower, we'll be going backward."

"Then go backward," I said, clutching my Addi Turbos in a death grip. "I have a bad feeling."

I felt the car slow down a little.

"Fifteen," he said.

Penny the cat abandoned the backseat for my left shoulder.

"Look," I said, trying to make a joke. "Even Penny's worried."

"Leave the cat out of it and let Luke drive," Janice said. "He's a New Englander, too. He knows snow."

"Thanks," Luke said, glancing at Janice in the rearview mirror. "I owe you."

"Wish I had that on tape," Janice said.

They bantered back and forth, which on

another day might have made me happier than owning my own alpaca farm, but, given a choice, I would have preferred less talking and more driving.

Want to know why I pretty much walked everywhere from November until April? This was it: that sick, out-of-control feeling as you sailed over the icy road trapped in almost two tons of screaming metal.

Okay, so maybe I'm exaggerating a little. It wasn't really that bad; it just felt like it. The second time we went into a mild skid Luke expertly steered us back onto the road in no time at all but the pit-of-the-stomach queasiness took longer to go away.

I have a long history with icy roads. A patch of black ice conjured up by Isadora's son Dane took out my parents when I was a little girl. I was in the car with them when it happened but was somehow thrown clear. I don't have any real memory of the accident. They say that's a good thing but I'm not sure.

I really don't remember much about my life before that terrible night, either. I remember a shadowy human who was my father and the image of my mother, a beautiful sorceress who chose to be with him in another dimension rather than live in this one with me.

So I don't trust cars. I don't trust ice. And I'll always be looking over my shoulder just in case Isadora is gaining on me. I thought I'd banished her forever the night her son Gunnar died saving Luke and me from disaster. I'd inadvertently killed Gunnar's twin, Dane, without a twinge of regret, and then I'd sent Isadora spiraling into isolated entrapment that had been meant to end her influence on Sugar Maple. But she was as resourceful as she was powerful and less than twelve hours ago I'd completed Isadora's banishment in a way that only the cosmos in its infinite wisdom could undo.

Or had I?

An icy road. A human male at the wheel. And the last of Aerynn's descendants sitting next to him.

This wasn't going to end well.

8

CHLOE

Hard to believe but things quickly went from bad to worse.

Penny the cat seemed to sense my unease. Her motorboat purr cycled down into something closer to a low growl and the hairs on the back of my neck lifted in response.

"I hate this," I murmured into the cat's soft black fur. "I can't believe we're driving in a blizzard. We weren't supposed to be driving in a blizzard."

The blizzard that should have stayed over Sugar Maple.

"Take it easy," Luke said in a tone of voice meant to calm a crazed suspect. "I've been driving in snow since I was sixteen years old. We'll be fine."

"It really wouldn't kill you to slow down."

"I'm going with traffic."

I opened my eyes and looked out the

81

window. "There is no traffic. We're the only fools on the road."

"Chloe," he said, "I'm going fifteen miles an hour."

"That's not slow enough."

"I changed my mind," Janice said from the backseat. "Chloe's right. The snow is freaking me out, too. Slow down!"

"Why don't you find a place to pull over?" I suggested. "We can wait for the storm to ease up a little."

"Not a good idea," he said, jaw settling into lines of granite. "Just because you don't see cars doesn't mean they aren't there. We could end up with an eighteen-wheeler in the trunk. It's better to keep moving."

He was probably right. Visibility was less than zero out there. We'd be a sitting target.

I scrunched my eyes closed and poured myself into the knitting.

"You can knit with your eyes closed?" Luke asked.

"I can knit in my sleep," I said and started to tell him about the time I woke up after a nap to discover I'd cast on for a Pi Shawl, when the car fishtailed wildly to the left and we sailed across the oncoming lane, through the guardrail, and over the embankment.

Time slowed to a crawl. The car glided through the air as if we were being cushioned by clouds and I had to remind myself we were falling.

I told myself the snow cover would break our fall and that the tank-sized Buick would withstand the impact. I told myself we'd laugh about it later, but I wasn't buying it.

We were screwed.

My skin went hot, then cold, then hot again. I felt like I was on fire from the inside out. The rush of adrenaline through my bloodstream made it hard to hear anything but my heartbeat.

We were in a flat spin, like one of those fighter planes in *Top Gun* just before it slammed into the ocean. A flat spin that seemed to be going on forever, delaying the inevitable.

Janice would never see her family again. Luke's mortal body would break apart like shattered glass. Our story would end the way my parents' story ended, a half step short of happily-ever-after.

"No!" The word exploded from me with the force of a gunshot. "No!"

Not now. Not here. Not again.

I hadn't come this far to let our lives slip through my fingers.

Unfortunately I had less than a second and a half to keep that from happening.

LUKE

I popped my cherry on my fifth day on the job. The first few days I had pulled scut duty, partnering old-timers who were counting down the days until retirement. Low-crime areas, not much excitement. You could go twenty years out there and never break a sweat.

Near the end of shift on the fifth day, a call came in and we hung a U-turn and headed out toward Langley Crescent near a private high school. It was a bitch of a road: hairpin curve, poorly graded, a drainage ditch with no guardrail.

A kid high on beer and hormones had somehow sailed across the road, over the ditch, and down the embankment to the roadway below.

I was the first to reach him. One look and I was bent over, puking up my lunch. Seventeen years old and his own mother wouldn't recognize him.

So I knew what was going to happen and I knew it was too late to stop it.

The flat spin angled and we tilted from side to side like an amusement park ride. Gravity always won. I knew I wasn't going to walk away from this but maybe Chloe could.

I took that thought and held it tight as the

ground rushed up at us.

CHLOE

Less than a foot before we hit the ground, I remembered the words.

"On the wings of my ancestors, carry us away from danger!"

And just like that we were saved.

No thunder and lightning. No fireworks display. The power of magick simply reached out, plucked us off the path to disaster, and deposited us back on the road as if nothing had happened.

This time I didn't have to tell Luke to pull over. He had no choice. His hands, like mine, were shaking too hard to grip the wheel.

The second we rolled to a stop, Janice flung open the door, leaned out, and said good-bye to her Egg McMuffin. My stomach was in knots, too, but I couldn't do anything more than hang on to poor Penny the cat and wait for the panic to die down.

Luke turned and looked at me. I felt the heat rise to my cheeks as his expression shifted from relief to downright wonder.

"You did it," he said and I nodded.

I did it.

Nobody had ever looked at me like that. I felt embarrassed and proud and totally disconnected from what was passing for reality today.

"You did it," he said again, a crazy smile breaking across his face. "We didn't have a chance in hell but you made it happen!"

"I did," I said with a crazy smile of my own. "My mind was blank, then all of a sudden the words popped out."

The beautiful flowery language of magick. I'd never let anyone poke fun at it again.

Something happened to you when you cheated death. Maybe it was all that adrenaline still racing around with nothing to do once the danger was over, but my senses were on high alert and, judging from the look in his eyes, so were Luke's.

He leaned my way.

I leaned his.

An explosion of white and silver sparks filled the space between us like our own private Fourth of July celebration.

Our lips touched. Our breaths mingled. Tears of relief and joy ran down my cheeks and he brushed them away with his fingertips. We had come so close to losing it all that I wanted to hold on to him and never let go.

"Oh, come *on!*" Janice settled back into her seat and closed the car door behind her. "I feel like I'm in high school again."

We kissed once more just because we could. I could look at his face forever and —

"Your bruises are gone," I exclaimed. "The cuts are healed! You'd never know you'd been in a fight."

He shifted position a few times. "The ribs don't hurt anymore."

We both turned toward Janice. "Hold the applause," she said with a smug but happy smile. "You can thank me when this is all over."

"We'll have dinner at the inn," I said, feeling wildly optimistic. The Sugar Maple Inn was owned by Renate and Colm Weaver, Fae friends who had become enemies thanks to Isadora's influence.

I missed my old friends. I wanted to go back to the way things used to be.

Of course, in order for any of that to happen we had to find the town first.

We sat for a little while in comfortable silence while our pulse rates returned to normal. I guessed that we had finally outrun the storm because the blizzard was no longer a blizzard but an accumulation of semiserious flurries. The county snowplows were probably out in force clearing the highways but it would be awhile before they reached small feeder roads like the one we were on.

The storm might have stopped but the road ahead was still a snowy, icy accident waiting to happen.

Janice and I were in favor of sitting tight until the road was at least salted but Luke disagreed strongly.

"The clock's ticking," Luke said. "We only have a few miles to go until we hit the highway. If we can push through this, the worst will be over."

He readjusted his mirrors. I don't know about Janice but for a second there I considered making a break for it. I caught her eye. She shrugged and picked up her knitting. Good choice. It was either that or a tranquilizer dart. The soft yarn, the bright colors, the slippery slickness of my beloved Addis brought me immediately back to center.

"You really need to rethink the whole toe-up issue," Janice said. "Not only is this way more intuitive, you never have to worry about not having enough yarn to finish the pair."

"I've heard the arguments," I said as I whipped along, "and I agree they make sense but when it comes to everyday socks, I'm cuff-down, heel flap, and gusset all the way."

"I do a gusset with my toe-ups."

"I don't think they look as elegant."

Janice slipped off her shoe and rested her right foot on the console. "Tell me that's not a gorgeous sock."

"Of course it's a gorgeous sock," I said. "You're a fabulous knitter. I just like cuff-down better."

Penny the cat, who had been tracking the conversation from a spot by my feet, apparently reached her limit on knitting conversation and emitted an unearthly yowl.

"Thanks, Pen," Luke said. "I couldn't have said it better."

I ignored him but I couldn't ignore the cat's obvious discomfort.

"Uh-oh," I said. "I think she needs the litter box."

Which, all things considered, was probably not something anyone in the car wanted to hear.

"Why don't you set it up in the backseat?" Luke suggested.

"I don't *think* so." Janice sounded highly put out and who could blame her.

"I hate to say it, Luke, but we need to pull over again."

There was a scenic overlook a half mile ahead and Luke pulled into the tiny rest stop adjacent to it so Penny could take care of her needs.

Janice and I exchanged looks after I set

the improvised litter box down behind the car.

"It's probably gross in there," I said, gesturing toward the shack that called itself a "Unisex Restroom."

"Most likely."

"Still, it's probably not a bad idea."

Janice nodded. "You never know when opportunity is going to strike again."

I reminded Luke to make sure he put Penny back in the car the second she was finished and said we'd be right back.

"Just hurry up in there. It's coming up on eleven and we're not even at the halfway mark yet."

The inside of the bathroom shack was worse than the outside. I found myself wishing I'd worn a hazmat suit.

"Good thing you're a healer," I said as I washed my hands in a sad little trickle of icy cold water. "This place is a bacteria incubator."

Janice was staring at her reflection in the dingy mirror. "Why didn't you tell me about my hair?" she muttered then set to work.

"Can't you do that in the car?" I asked as she ran her fingers through her long wavy hair. "Luke's waiting."

"Be right there," she said, but I knew her idea of being right there was very different from mine.

I rearranged my ponytail and wished once again that I had been born with curly auburn hair instead of stick-straight blond, then hurried back out to Luke.

Who, as it turned out, was up a tree.

9

LUKE

I'm a dog guy. I grew up with dogs. I get dogs. I know what it means when a dog wags his tail or when the ridge of fur at the top of his spine lifts like a line of porcupine quills.

Dogs are simple and direct. Dogs don't mess with your head.

Cats are a mystery to me. Cat signals are like animal cave drawings better left to a student of the species.

You would think the fact that the woman I loved was a sorceress-in-training would be enough to deal with, but fate wasn't through with me yet. She had cats. Lots of cats.

And one of them talked.

Yeah, it freaked me out, too. There really was no way to adjust to a cat that could explain quantum physics to you or turn you into a catnip mouse if the spirit moved her.

The truth is, except for the talking and

the magick and the litter box thing, I liked Penelope. She was a mellow cat. No diva hissing or scratching. No pouncing or swinging from the curtains. She slept, she ate, she slept some more. She was a house cat who'd been a house cat since before we were a loose collection of colonies with an English accent.

In other words Penny the cat wouldn't know the great outdoors if it bit her in her hairy butt.

So what the hell was she doing up a tree?

And the bigger question was, what the hell was I doing up the same tree trying to lure her down with an Egg McMuffin?

"Okay," I said, scrabbling for a foothold on the snow-covered branch, "so I dropped the ball. I shouldn't have turned my back on you."

Penny the cat stared back at me with those unnerving golden eyes.

"C'mon," I said, extending the morsel toward her. "You know you want it."

She didn't say *screw you* out loud but she might as well have. Clearly the cat expected better than fast food.

"Now I remember why I didn't become a firefighter," I mumbled as she inched farther up the tree. Cops didn't do this crap.

For that matter neither did dogs. You

wouldn't find a poodle up a tree or a rott-weiler. Ground level was good enough for a dog.

"Luke!"

I looked down and saw Chloe looking back up at me. "Your cat's up the tree."

"Impossible! Penny doesn't do trees."

On cue Penny the cat gave another of those yowls she'd been unleashing all morning.

"Damn, I wish she'd stop that."

"Penelope," she said, "come down here."

I swear I didn't see the cat move. One second she was looking down at me from the uppermost branch. The next she was wrapped around Chloe's neck like a boa.

And I was still up a tree.

"Are you coming down on your own," Chloe asked, "or do you want me to magick you down?"

I did my best lumberjack impression and landed on my feet next to her.

You wouldn't think a cat could look disdainful but Penelope managed it.

"The cat hates me," I said as we trudged back to the car through the snow. "When was the last time she climbed a tree, sometime around 1712?"

"It's not you," Chloe said. "It's the Sugar Maple thing. She's homesick."

"The cat told you that?"

"The cat will tell you a few things if you don't stop."

Which would have been funny in my old life but in my new life it wasn't funny: it was true.

CHLOE

I settled Penny on the floor near my feet. Luke turned on the heater and she was asleep by the time we exited the parking lot.

"You should've bought one of those cat carriers at Walmart," Janice said as she worked on her sock in the backseat. "Or a leash."

"I'll definitely buy one when we get to Salem."

Until then Penny was staying in the car.

I had trusted that Penny's unusual history made her immune to crazy cat behavior but I hadn't factored in the effect a change of landscape might have on her. Different sounds, different sights, different smells. She was probably as lost without Sugar Maple as I was.

I was halfway down the leg of my sock when we finally reached the entrance to the highway. The sun was shining. The road ahead was clear and dry.

"How long until we reach Salem?" I asked

Luke as he merged with traffic.

"Another two and a half hours, give or take a blizzard or runaway cat."

I'd be able to finish the first sock and take a big bite out of the second. With a little luck I'd fall into the knitting zone where there was nothing but color and texture and the gentle rhythmic click of my needles as they formed stitch after stitch. I definitely didn't want to think about what lay ahead. I'd rather think about the way turquoise bumps up against royal purple.

Luke finally managed to tune into a sports talk station and I tuned out the chatter. In the backseat Janice was already in the zone and was casting on for her second sock.

"Are you knitting for Munchkins?" I asked over my shoulder. "You can't possibly be knitting for adult feet. I still haven't turned the heel on my first."

"Toe-up, baby," she said with a wink. "I told you it rocks."

We chatted back and forth about elastic cast-offs for a while then fell into companionable silence. A radio caller was going on about Opening Day. Luke seemed riveted.

Go figure.

I knitted along in silence for a while. Behind me Janice dropped off into a nap, her head cushioned by a mountain of Manos

96

and Araucania. The heater proved too much for Penny and she arranged herself on the console between Luke and me. She didn't seem any worse for the wear after her adventure in the great outdoors. She did, however, seem unusually fixated on Luke.

"What's up with the staring?" he asked as a big brown UPS truck passed us on the left. "She hasn't taken her eyes off me."

"I guess you two bonded when you were up that tree."

"She made a horse's ass of me up that tree. If you hadn't come along, I'd still be up there waving that stupid Egg McMuffin at her."

Penny stretched out her front paws and inched closer to Luke. She rested her chin on his thigh.

"Too late, cat," he said. "I ate it."

She stretched again then eased her upper body into his lap.

"This isn't going to work," he said. "Not that I don't trust her or anything."

I reached over to pluck Penny from his lap but she was too fast for me. Hard to believe an aged, sedentary cat could move that fast in such a confined space but she went from his lap to his shoulder in an eye-blink.

A cat person wouldn't flinch. A driving

non-cat-person definitely would.

"What's going on?" I said as I unbuckled my seat belt; I leaned over to extricate Penny from her new perch but she pressed her face against his neck. "It's like you used a catnip aftershave or something."

"You want to get her off me?" He sounded a little tense. "The cat breath is getting to me."

Funny how I'd never had to use magick with Penny until I had magick myself. She seemed to up the ante with every new skill I acquired. I cast the same spell I'd cast beneath the tree but this time to no effect.

"No joke," Luke said. "My eyes are getting scratchy and I think I'm going to sneeze."

"From cat breath?" I didn't mean to sound so skeptical.

"Just get her off me, okay?"

"Since when are you allergic to cats?"

"Chloe, come on. Help me out. Use a little of that magick of yours. I feel like someone's pouring salt in my eyes."

"I'm trying," I said, "but the spell is bouncing right off her."

"She's licking my face, damn it. My skin's on fire. Just pull her off me."

I made another effort at prying her from his shoulder but she was stuck like Velcro.

He yelped. "Those claws are sharp."

This was no time to be a wiseass. I bit back my comment and concentrated on how best to reason with a stubborn cat and a ticked-off human.

"Janice bought some Cheese Nips," I said with as much optimism as I could muster. "That might do it."

I knelt on the console and reached into the backseat to rummage through the bags at my sleeping friend's feet for the salty snack.

"I know she bought them," I said, muttering to myself. "Must be in the other bag."

I heard a scuffling sound, a sharp intake of breath, then Luke's voice saying, "Take the wheel."

I scrambled back to my seat. "What?"

"Take the wheel!"

"I don't —"

"Now!"

I grabbed the wheel and held it steady. "What's wrong? What happened? A second ago —"

"I can't see."

I heard the words but my brain couldn't process them through the screaming inside my head. "Start slowing down. I'm going to guide us onto the shoulder. I'll tell you when to stop." We were already in the right-hand lane, which helped our odds.

"What's going on?" Janice poked her head between our seats. "Is something wrong?"

"Luke's eyes," I said, keeping my own eyes riveted to the road ahead of me. "I think he's having an allergic reaction of some kind."

Janice said something unprintable.

"Take Penny," I said. "Keep her away from Luke."

Damn her hide. The cat leaped gracefully onto the swell of yarn next to Janice and settled herself down.

His arms were rigid at his sides. Beads of sweat poured down his face.

"Slow down some more," I said. "No, not the gas pedal! The brake! The brake!"

I wouldn't say my life flashed before my eyes but a few key scenes definitely made an appearance.

The shoulder was wide and clear. I eased the Buick over. Now all we had to do was stop before we hit the thick row of pine trees that marked the point where the shoulder ended and the woods began.

Luke's breathing was raspy, labored. I had the feeling he was on autopilot, relying on muscle memory rather than conscious thought.

"Okay, now more brake," I said. "Easy . . .

full stop . . . that's it. We did it. Great!"

We were safe. I turned my full attention to Luke and a chill iced its way up my spine. His face was red and mottled. His eyes were swollen shut. His breathing sounded raspier and more labored than before.

He was in trouble and my magick was utterly useless against whatever was doing this to him.

10

CHLOE

"He's not breathing right," I said to Janice as I struggled to push down my growing panic. "I think he's in real trouble."

"Don't worry." Janice was an oasis of calm. "I'm here. Let's get him out of the car so I can work."

Penny ignored us while we struggled to pull Luke from the car then stretch him out on the grass adjacent to the shoulder. It was like moving one hundred eighty pounds of deadweight.

He was slipping away from us. I felt it in every cell of my body. I wished with all my heart Suzanne Marsden had never shown up in Sugar Maple. If she hadn't drowned, Luke wouldn't have been given the job as chief of police and we wouldn't have met and fallen in love. And if none of that had happened, he wouldn't be balanced on the knife's edge between worlds right now.

Janice knelt down next to Luke and moved her hands over his chest and along his neck. She splayed her fingers over his face, speaking softly in a language I would never know. Luke lay there motionless. His face was no longer red and mottled; the ghastly pallor of human death was washing the redness away.

I held his hand in mine, grateful for the warmth. His pulse was weak but it was still there.

I had seen Janice work miracles. Her healing powers were strong. If anyone could turn this around, she could. But I was still terrified.

"He's human, Janice," I said. "Have you ever worked on a full-blooded mortal before?"

"Not to this extent," she said, "but right now I'm all he has."

"What if he's in some kind of shock?" I said to her. "Maybe we should take him to a hospital." I watched *Grey's Anatomy*.

"Shock!" Janice sounded elated. "That's it. . . ." Her hands were a blur as they swept patterns over his body. Her voice rose and fell with the strange words.

"Come on," I whispered. "Come on!"

Janice's eyes fluttered closed. Her lips moved but I couldn't hear the words any longer. She had gone somewhere I couldn't follow, deep into the heart of her knowledge and magick.

"What the hell are you doing?" Luke sprang to a sitting position and glared at Janice. The pallor, the harsh breathing, the swollen eyes — all gone. He was big, healthy, and pissed off.

"A simple thank-you would be plenty," she snapped, glaring back at him.

"Janice just saved your life, you idiot." I was laughing and crying simultaneously as I threw my arms around him.

He leaned slightly away and looked into my eyes. "I'm serious: what happened?"

"Your eyes . . . you lost your —" I frowned. "You don't remember?"

He didn't. The episode was a total blank to him.

"Remember what?" he asked.

I filled him in on the details.

"Shit," he said. "Are you kidding me?"

We all knew the question was rhetorical.

He stood up and brushed dirt off his jeans. His color had returned to normal. Even I had trouble believing the last few minutes had been anything but some kind of crazy dream.

"Don't move," I said. "I should have done this hours ago."

I conjured up a simple but effective protective charm then doubled it for good measure.

"Thanks," Luke said. "Does that make me catproof?"

Janice and I exchanged looks. He still didn't understand that cats lived above the rules of law and magick.

I reached for the handle on the driver's-side door.

Luke frowned. "Isn't the guy supposed to open the car door?"

"No offense," I said to Luke, "but so far you've driven us over an embankment and gone temporarily blind."

"You hate driving," he reminded me.

"Yes," I agreed, "but it turns out I hate crashing even more."

"I'm a damn good driver."

"Not today you're not."

"You're blaming me because you have a lousy car with no snow tires and no four-wheel drive?"

"I'm not blaming anyone, Luke, but I'm still driving." Okay, so maybe I did blame him but not in an ugly sort of way. We'd been up for over twenty-four hours. We'd engaged in a fierce battle with Isadora, lost my hometown, pushed our way through a blizzard, crashed through a guardrail and plunged twenty feet to almost certain death, then topped off the fun with temporary blindness.

He was only human and humans had their physical limits. It wouldn't be long before I reached my limits, too, but the magick side of my lineage would carry me through a little longer.

I was still new to the whole male-female dance. Sometimes I could be a little too direct. I loved him. I didn't want to hurt him. "You understand, right? We're going to be busy when we reach Salem. You could catch a nap or something."

I watched as his jaw worked through all sorts of contortions before he spoke. "It's your car," he said finally, then walked around to the passenger side and got in.

"Do I get a say in this?" Janice demanded. "We'd be better off if the cat drove."

"I don't hear you offering to drive."

Janice grunted something nasty about my Buick then climbed into the backseat.

I readjusted the mirrors and buckled my seat belt. I won't lie to you. I wasn't looking forward to merging onto the highway. (I wasn't all that crazy about turning out of my driveway back home.) But I couldn't delay forever.

I shifted into drive and had just started rolling along the shoulder, building speed, when a pine tree crashed to the ground three feet in front of us without any warning at all.

I slammed the gear into park and turned off the engine.

Nobody said a word. When a forty-foot tree missed you by inches, there really wasn't much to say.

You win, Universe. I get it. You don't want us in Salem. Message received.

"What's next?" Janice broke the silence. "Flying monkeys?"

We broke into nervous laughter.

"I thought I saw SURRENDER CHLOE smoke signals overhead," Luke added.

I would have laughed if my attention hadn't been diverted elsewhere. "Look," I said, pointing toward the highway. "They're driving through the tree like it isn't there."

"Holy shit!" Luke leaned forward and stared through the windshield. "That Porsche didn't even slow down."

Janice shrieked as a yellow school bus roared past without problem.

I leaped out of the car and ran toward the fallen tree. Correction: I ran into it, then I fell over it. For me the tree was all too real.

The same thing happened to Luke and to Janice.

"Magic?" Luke asked.

"Oh, yeah," I said. "Definitely magick."

"Party tricks," Janice said with clear disdain. "Amateur crap."

"It got my attention," I admitted.

It also proved Luke was right. If something or someone was trying so hard to keep us away, then Salem was where we needed to be.

But getting there was another story.

"What would have happened if that tree had fallen on the car?" I asked Janice.

"Easy," she said. "It would have killed us."

"No question?" Luke asked.

"Zero," she said. "It exists in our reality and that's all that matters."

"You called it a parlor trick, but it seems pretty sophisticated to me." I'd been studying the Book of Spells for months now and I'd never heard of creating parallel realities. "Who has that kind of magick?"

"Old-school," she said, dismissing it with a wave of her hand. "Impressive, yes, and occasionally dangerous, but way outdated."

"So who used it before?" I pressed.

She shrugged. "Mostly Fae but from what my grandmother told me, it was pretty common around the time the group from Salem settled in Sugar Maple. Everyone seemed to have mastered it to some degree."

"Did Isadora ever use it?" Luke asked.

"Not that I know of. Like I said, it's old-school and kind of cheesy. By the time the country gained independence, it had been pretty much forgotten."

Talk of Sugar Maple's history always made me uncomfortable. Most of my life I'd been a nonmagick half human with no prospects of powers anywhere in my future. My hometown's backstory seemed as dusty and irrelevant as expired supermarket coupons.

"I wish I'd paid more attention to Sorcha's stories when I was growing up," I said. My surrogate mother had been living history and I'd squandered a lifetime of opportunity.

"Can you undo this?" Luke asked, gesturing toward the monster tree.

"No," I said as Janice shook her head, "but I can drive around it."

Which was exactly what I tried to do but somehow the tree was always in the way.

"Let me try," Janice said, quashing her hatred of my poor beleaguered Buick.

She took the wheel while I climbed into the backseat with Penny. "Ouch!" I moved her knitting. "Switch to a single circular, would you? Those double-points are killers."

Janice fiddled with the mirrors, then took

a deep breath and drove straight into the tree.

"Jan!" I yelled while Luke muttered something decidedly uncomplimentary. "What the hell?"

"The tree moved!"

"This isn't good," I said as a canopy of branches appeared overhead.

"You think?" Janice snapped.

"Back up!" Luke shouted. "Now!"

She threw the transmission into reverse and we rocked backward as another tree fell onto the spot where we had been less than a second before.

"Let's get out of here." It was probably the most unnecessary sentence I had ever uttered.

"Come on," Luke said. "Our luck won't hold forever."

What was taking her so long? The way things were going, our luck wouldn't hold another five seconds.

"I'm trying," Janice said. "The gear is locked."

Luke leaned across the console and tried to shift into drive but nothing happened.

I threw myself into the space between them and gave it a try. This time it worked. But instead of hitting the gas, Janice leaped out of the car.

"Drive," she said.

No point arguing. The car made the decision for us. Janice and I exchanged places. I adjusted mirrors, buckled up, then stomped on the gas pedal.

And just in time.

A sinkhole of truly monstrous proportions opened up behind us as we merged back onto the highway. The last thing I saw in the rearview mirror was the trees being sucked down into the void.

I had to fight the urge to slam on the brakes so I could take another look.

"You okay?" Luke asked as I moved into the middle lane.

"No," I said. "I'm scared."

"You'd be crazy if you weren't."

"Every time I think I've got a handle on what's going on, something else jumps up and bites me in the butt."

His beautiful green eyes twinkled for the first time in hours. "Welcome to my world, Hobbs."

In more ways than one.

"Wait a second," I said. "You grew up right near Salem."

"A couple of towns away."

A swirl of conflicting emotions tugged at me. "Is your — is your family still there?"

"I have a brother in San Diego and a sister

111

in Oregon. Everyone else settled near my parents."

"Except you."

The twinkle in his eyes grew warmer. "I have my reasons."

"There's so much I don't know about you."

"We've been a little preoccupied lately."

I laughed out loud. "Now there's an understatement for you."

A theatrical cough sounded from the backseat.

"We didn't forget about you, Janice," Luke said.

"I may be a nosy beyotch but eavesdropping on friends isn't my style."

I opened my mouth to protest.

"Don't you dare! I'm having a moment here." She leaned forward and eyed Luke with open curiosity. "So how many of you MacKenzies are there, anyway?"

"Seven kids," he said, grinning at the look of shock on my face. "I'm the middle kid."

"Do they know where you are?" Janice asked.

"They know I'm up in Vermont."

"Do you ever talk to them?"

He tugged at his seat belt then leaned forward and fiddled with the tuner. "I've been out of touch for a while."

"Is that why you left Boston?"

"Janice!" I glared at her in the rearview mirror.

"What?" Janice asked, all wide-eyed innocence. "My mother flips out if I don't blueflame her at least twice a day." Blueflame was the magick equivalent of a BlackBerry or smartphone. "She'd send a team of house sprites to track me down."

"You don't have to answer her," I said to Luke. Janice knew the story behind Luke quitting the police force and leaving Boston. Everyone in Sugar Maple knew.

"E-mails," Luke said. "An occasional IM. Most of them are on Facebook so I know what they've been up to."

"Your brothers and sisters are on Facebook?" I asked.

"And my nieces, nephews, and in-laws."

"Wish I had my laptop," Janice said and we all laughed.

My thoughts were crazy scattered. Janice came from a big family but it sounded like the MacKenzies had her beat by a mile.

"Do you miss them?" I'm not sure why I asked. The question seemed to have a life of its own.

"I've been on my own for a long time. Hell, my older brother and sisters were gone before I started high school. We've pretty much all gone our own ways."

Maybe so but most of them had stayed in the town where they grew up. That sounded like a close-knit family to me. How could he walk away from that?

Don't push it, the voice of reason inside my head warned me. *He's willing to give them up to be with you. Isn't that enough?*

But family was my Achilles' heel. I couldn't imagine walking away from my own blood, not even for love, and I worried that one day Luke might feel the same way.

Then again, I had no blood relatives. Maybe if I did I would take them for granted the way the rest of the world, both mortal and magick, seemed to do.

But I didn't believe it.

11

LUKE

It was hard to explain family dynamics to a woman who had no family. I'd grown up in the middle of a sprawling clan, both nuclear and extended, and I still didn't know what the hell made them tick.

The truth was I never much thought about it. Family was like air or water or cable TV. Family was a fact of life. Sometimes annoying. Sometimes funny. Sometimes the one thing that made every other thing worthwhile.

When Karen and I married, we both knew exactly what to expect. There was a place waiting for us in the MacKenzie clan, a comfortable place where our newly formed family could settle down and plant roots that would last forever.

Except in this world nothing lasted forever. Not our family. Not our little girl. When life kicked us in the teeth, our marriage went down for the count and took our dreams with it.

By the time I took the job in Sugar Maple all I wanted to do was disappear, and the small Vermont town sounded like just the place to do it.

I disappeared, all right, but not the way I planned.

I'd made a promise to keep Sugar Maple's secrets when I took the job as chief of police and I wouldn't break that promise, not even if Sugar Maple was gone forever. But sooner or later my old life was going to come banging on the door and when it did I'd have to answer.

I hoped like hell it didn't happen today.

CHLOE

We were halfway to Salem when we ran out of gas.

"I can't believe it," I said as the engine started to sputter. "It still shows an eighth of a tank."

"Your car's a hundred years old," Janice said from the backseat. "You can't believe what the gauge says."

I thought about making a knitting joke but it didn't feel like the time.

Luke cocked his head and listened to the sound. "Almost empty but not quite.

There's a rest stop about a half mile ahead. I bet we can make it."

"Bet we can't."

I was right. The engine conked out less than three hundred feet from the gas station attached to a Hungry Camper All-You-Can-Eat Buffet. After battling rogue blizzards, a twenty-foot plunge over an embankment, and killer trees, an empty gas tank seemed like a walk in the park.

"Do you have a gas can in the trunk?" Luke asked.

"You're kidding, right?" I only filled up once a year.

"Stay here," he said. "I'll take care of it."

"When this is over, I'm going to sleep for a week," Janice said as Luke jogged toward the service station up ahead.

"I stopped being tired about two hours ago," I said. "Now I'm in a functional coma."

"You know all those awful things I've said about your human? I take them back. You could have done worse."

"I have done worse," I said, thinking back on my checkered dating history. "You and Lynette set me up with every vampire, werewolf, selkie, troll, and shapeshifter on the east coast."

"I would have run off with that last selkie

if Lorcan knew how to cook for himself." Lorcan was her husband and mate, an Irish selkie who lived part of each year in the depths of Snow Lake.

"You always did have a thing for guys with whiskers," I said and was rewarded with a swat on the head with a ball of Malabrigo.

A car backfired somewhere in the distance and we both jumped as if we'd been cattle-prodded.

"I don't know about you," Janice said, "but I keep waiting for the other shoe to drop."

"Me too, and I'm afraid the other shoe belongs to Forbes the Mountain Giant."

"I miss Forbes," Janice said. "And Lilith and Archie and Midge and —"

"Frank and Manny and Rose from Assisted Living," I continued, "and Lynette and Cyrus."

"They're not coming back," Janice said quietly. "We're doing this because we have to try, because we couldn't live with ourselves if we didn't, but the truth is they're not coming back."

"You don't know that."

"Come on, Chloe. Admit it. Sugar Maple is gone and we're on our own."

"No," I said. "I refuse to believe that."

The fight seemed to drain out of her. She

glanced out the window toward the rest stop. "Luke will be on his way back any minute. There's something I want to say and I don't want you to argue with me or try to change my mind."

"I'm not liking the sound of that."

Janice was usually all fire and sharp edges, but right now she looked more open and vulnerable than I had ever seen her. She reached for my hand and sandwiched it between hers.

"If we don't find the town —" She swallowed hard enough for me to notice. "If we don't find Sugar Maple and my family, I'm going to pierce the veil."

"Janice!" Piercing the veil was the magick equivalent of mortal death. It wasn't as final as mortal death or as dramatic, but the choice was irrevocable. No matter what happened, she would never be able to exist in this realm again. "I won't let you do that."

Some of the flash and fire sparked behind her eyes. "Honey, if you didn't have Luke I would never leave you behind, but your life is settled. You have your powers and your human. You'll miss Sugar Maple and all of us but you'll be okay. You'll survive."

I started to protest but she shushed me with a look.

"You know it's true. I want my family and

119

if I can't have them with me in this realm, I'll be with them in another."

There were so many things I wanted to say to her but I wasn't sure I had the right. She was more than my friend. She was wife and mother and daughter and sister and if she had a chance to be reunited with the people she loved, she had every right to grab it and hold on tight.

Nobody stays, Chloe. Sooner or later they all leave you behind.

Not exactly a line of thought I wanted to explore.

Janice picked up her knitting again and immersed herself in her sock. Her long and elegant fingers manipulated the five double-pointed needles with practiced ease. I knew the exact moment when she slipped into the zone and the real world fell away. Her shoulders dropped, her jaw relaxed, the furrow between her brows smoothed out.

I picked up my own sock, knit three stitches, then put it down again. Normally I experienced a palpable sense of joy when I knit. I love everything about the craft and it never failed to soothe the ragged edges of my soul.

This time? Not so much. I tossed the sock down then looked out the window. No sign of Luke. I glanced at the dashboard clock.

He'd been gone over thirty minutes. How long did it take to walk three hundred yards, buy and fill a gas can, then walk back?

Penny the cat emerged from her woolly cocoon, yawned, stretched, then leaped onto the back of my seat and inched down onto my shoulders.

"Et tu, cattus?" For a moment I felt like Kim Novak in *Bell, Book and Candle* with her familiar wrapped around her shoulders like a feather shawl.

Except Penny wasn't feeling particularly companionable and I definitely wasn't Kim Novak. I made to give her a skritch alongside her muttonchops when she hissed at me then lashed out with her right paw.

"Hey!" I leaned away from her. "Since when do you do that?"

Penny, of course, had no answer for me. She clung to the back of the seat, claws digging into the brittle leather upholstery, and pretty much stared me down.

You're not much help, I thought. Where was all that magickal wisdom she liked to share at the drop of a can of Fancy Feast?

I had seen this cat act as the conduit for my surrogate mother and for Isadora's son Gunnar. The sight and sound of Gunnar's mellow baritone coming out of the same mouth that devoured yarn shop mice like they were M&M's was unforgettable. It was also highly efficient and very effective. When a cat talked, you tended to listen.

So why wasn't Lynette trying to reach us through Penny? Lorcan Meany knew about Penny's abilities and he had the power to access them. So why hadn't he tried?

I didn't like any of the answers I came up with.

The minutes ticked by. Still no sign of Luke.

"How long does it take to fill a gas can?" I asked Janice.

Janice looked up from her knitting. "Depends how long it takes to find a gas can to fill."

"You stay here in case Luke shows up," I said. "I'm going to go see what's taking so long."

Janice lifted her sock-in-progress in salute. "Once more unto the breach and all that."

"You'll still be here, right?"

She nodded. "I'll still be here."

The sun was warm and buttery yellow. The sky was a clear, vivid blue. It had turned out to be one of those intensely gorgeous early spring afternoons that made you glad to be alive. I even heard birdsong ringing out overhead.

Birdsong?

I was walking along the entrance lane to a highway rest stop in north-central Massachusetts. I should have been hearing the sound of trucks rattling down the roadway, the beep of horns as cars jockeyed for a spot at the gas pumps, excited laughter as kids raced each other toward the buffet.

I stopped dead and looked around.

Where was everyone?

The rest stop was a sparkling-clean ghost town. It reminded me of something out of a Stephen King novel, which wasn't a good thing since King didn't specialize in happy endings.

I turned back toward the highway. Six lanes of traffic and not a vehicle in sight.

Including my Buick.

I couldn't breathe. I felt like the air itself was pressing down on me. Either everyone had disappeared or I was trapped in some strangely parallel reality. I wasn't too thrilled with either choice.

I might have watched every episode of *Columbo* and *Murder, She Wrote* but that didn't mean I was a detective. It was easy to sit on the sofa with a bag of Chips Ahoy and some Cherry Garcia and unravel someone else's mess. When the mess was yours, however, there was nothing easy about it at all.

One thing I knew was that standing there

frozen in place wasn't going to get me anywhere. I had to move. I had to do something even if I didn't have a clue where to start.

The doors to the rest stop itself were locked. I peered through the restaurant window. It looked like a movie set waiting for the actors to arrive and bring it to life. I walked around to the rear of the building and crossed the parking lot toward the cleanest gas station on the planet. No oil spills. No smell of gas. The pumps were polished like museum pieces.

"Luke!" My voice rang out across the emptiness. "Luke, can you hear me?"

There was no answering sound at all. Not even the birdsong I'd heard earlier. The nightmarish sense of isolation, of aloneness, was acute. I was having trouble keeping my emotions under control but I knew that if I let go for even an instant, it would be all over for me.

The blue skies darkened to charcoal gray. The buttery sun vanished behind a wall of clouds. Squirrelly mini twisters entwined themselves around my ankles, spinning me like a child's top. By the time the hail started I was seriously tired of weather as metaphor.

"Is this the best you've got?" I yelled into

the icy wind. "It's getting a little old."

The magick side of my lineage was all about whispers and innuendo. The human side wanted to kick ass. Right now the human side was winning.

Don't want us in Salem? Send an e-mail. Try instant messaging. Do something totally insane and materialize and tell me face-to-face.

The hail stopped. But before I could congratulate myself on winning the weather battle, the skies opened up and dumped the Atlantic Ocean on my head. At least it felt like an entire ocean. Rain like that was downright biblical.

Bolts of scarlet lightning shot out from my fingertips. They pierced the downpour with a deafening sizzle. I felt like I was about to spontaneously combust. If I wasn't already at the end of my rope, I was approaching it at Mach 3 and counting.

"Cowards!" I yelled into the rain. "What's next: locusts and frogs? If you have something to say, just say it!"

Hobbs's rule #1: If you ever find yourself dealing with paranormal weather patterns, don't dare the weather wizards. Just grab for an umbrella and a pair of Wellies and roll with it.

Unfortunately I didn't figure that out until

I was already inside a thunderhead, strapped to a bolt of lightning aimed straight for the heart of hell.

"Let's talk it out," I yelled as the high-pitched wail of energy about to be unleashed filled my head. Nothing like a shot of *Dr. Phil* to put things right. "Don't do something you'll regret later."

Even I almost laughed at my threat. Who was I kidding? I was screwed.

You're not going to stop me. You can slow me down but I'll make it to Salem and I'll get to the truth about Sugar Maple. You're not going to win. Not while I'm still alive and —

That might have been the wrong thing to say.

12

LUKE

"I'm telling the truth," Chloe protested. "It was a ghost town out there."

"Was it, Luke?" Janice asked. "You were there, too."

My eyes were locked with Chloe's. "The place was jammed. I finally had to ask one of the state cops for help."

"State cops?" Chloe looked at me in disbelief. "There wasn't a soul around for miles. The restaurant was locked and empty. The gas station was shut down. No people. No cars."

"Chloe, honey, you were dreaming," Janice said. "You were in the car with me the whole time."

"That's impossible. I told you I was going to look for Luke. Don't you remember?"

"You must have changed your mind because you stayed right there behind the wheel."

Chloe's wide golden eyes filled with tears. "I swear I'm telling the truth. I was alone out there when the storm kicked in and —"

"What storm?" I asked.

"There was no storm," Janice agreed.

"I'm not crazy," Chloe said. "I know what I saw." She listed mini twisters, hail, and torrential rain for starters.

"Look at your clothes," Janice said. "They're dry."

"That doesn't mean anything."

"You were out cold when I came back," I told her. "It took both of us to bring you around." For a few bleak moments I thought I'd lost her forever.

"You think I imagined everything?"

"I don't think she imagined anything."

I stared at Janice. "Then why the hell doesn't she look like she's been through a storm?"

"There you go, thinking like a human."

"Are we going to go there again?"

"You're of this dimension," Janice said. "You're hardwired to believe your senses."

"What the hell else can I believe?"

"See!" Janice sounded triumphant. "That proves my point. After four months in Sugar Maple, you still don't get it."

I shut up because she was right. I didn't get it. I tried to, but when push came to

128

shove, the whole damn thing was still a mystery to me.

"Oh, crap," Chloe said. "I see where you're going with this, Janice."

"Fill me in," I said, "because I'm clueless."

I was impressed. Janice let the opportunity for a one-liner pass without comment.

"Parallel dimensions, same as we talked about before," Chloe said as Janice nodded. "Whoever is trying to keep us out of Salem took me on a little magic carpet ride meant to scare me off."

"More than scare you off," Janice said. "I'll bet that trip came with a one-way ticket."

I wasn't liking this much.

"I called them out," Chloe said with a little laugh. "I dared them to quit messing with the weather and confront me face-to-face."

"Is that when you came back to us?" I asked, trying to make sense of her Alice in Wonderland tale.

"No," she said, "that was when I was sucked inside a mini twister that was determined to turn me into a vanilla milk shake."

Another beautiful day in the neighborhood . . .

"So how did you escape?" Janice asked.

"A spell? Snazzy karate moves? Spill!"

"I tried everything: spells, charms, incantations, brute force, begging, pleading, calling in favors from the ancestors. Nothing worked." A slight smile moved across her face. "I was pretty much up the creek without a paddle when I was set free."

"Set free?" That didn't follow the paradigm I'd encountered on the force. "You were powerless and they set you free?"

She nodded. "Next thing I knew I was in the car and you were copping a feel."

I grinned. "That was CPR."

"Says you."

"Hey!" Janice barked. "You can get a room later. I want more information. Who exactly set you free?"

"Okay," Chloe said. "This is the weird part."

Like the rest of the story wasn't Mary Poppins on crack.

She looked down at her hands, examining her nonexistent manicure. "I think it was my mother."

CHLOE

I waited for a reaction but there wasn't one.

Okay.

I'd try again.

"I didn't really see her or anything but I

smelled her perfume."

Come on, people. Give me something.

Luke, who was wearing his cop face, frowned. "You mean, like Chanel?"

I shook my head. "One she created herself. It's my first memory of her." When she died, the formula died with her.

"And you think you smelled it?"

"I don't think I smelled it, I know I smelled it."

"It's been over twenty years since she died. How can you be sure?"

"You're kidding, right?"

His eyes narrowed. "No. I'm not."

"She was my mother. I was a little girl. I idolized her. I remember her smell, her laughter, the way the roving flew through her hands when she sat at her wheel."

"So you think that your mother — the same woman who willingly left you when you were six years old — somehow found a way to help you?"

I'm not going to cry . . . I'm not going to cry . . .

He was in cop mode. He didn't mean it the way it sounded but it hurt just the same.

"I smelled her perfume. I sensed a benevolent presence around me. Who else could it have been?"

Janice made an unpleasant sound. "You

mean besides two dozen other spirits?"

"Janice, don't —"

"It wasn't your mother," she said.

"You sound pretty sure." She also sounded pretty pissed, which got under my skin.

"I *am* sure. There is no way Guinevere could have helped you."

"Gunnar helped us at the waterfall," I reminded her. "And Sorcha helped me before that. Why not my mother?"

Janice looked equal parts annoyed and sorrowful. "Honey, that just wasn't the Guinevere we all knew."

"What the hell does that mean?" My fingertips were beginning to twitch, a sure sign I was going to start shooting angry flames any second.

"It means what it means," Janice said. "You weren't your mother's first priority and Sugar Maple ranked even lower. When she chose to leave you and be with your father, she left all of us. She didn't care, Chloe. Not about you. Not about Sorcha. Not about any of us. And definitely not about Sugar Maple." She reached out her hand to me but the look in my eyes stopped her cold. "I don't mean to be harsh, honey, but even if she had the option, I don't see Guinevere riding in to save the day."

Everything Janice said was true. My

mother had loved me but not enough to stick around for the long haul. And not enough to find a way to ease my pain. The idea that she would suddenly show up in my life in time to save me from meeting an untimely end at a highway rest stop in central Massachusetts was pretty ridiculous.

But the smell of her perfume . . . the sense of being surrounded by love . . .

Nobody could tell me that wasn't real.

From that point on, it was clear sailing.

The Buick drove like a Maserati. The few gallons of gas Luke procured at the rest stop somehow kept the tank filled. Penny the cat slept, yawned, demanded head skritches, and didn't require the litter box.

I handed the driving over to Luke about eighty miles outside of Salem. The traffic had picked up, along with the pace, and since I don't drive over thirty miles an hour unless I have to, I considered it a humanitarian gesture on my part.

I'm not sure whether or not Luke believed my story but he had my back just the same. Which was one of the many reasons I loved him. The whole parallel-dimension thing had to be tough for a literal-minded cop to process. Before my powers kicked in, I would have had a tough time with it, too —

and I had grown up in Sugar Maple, surrounded by magick.

About thirty miles outside of Salem, I lowered the window a few inches and breathed deeply.

"I smell the ocean," I said.

Both Luke and Janice laughed.

"I smell pollen," Janice said.

"Give it another twenty miles," Luke advised. "Then you'll smell the ocean."

"Seriously," I said. "It's all briny out there."

"Lorcan claims he can smell the ocean from our back porch," Janice said. "He says —" Her voice broke and she buried her face in her almost-finished sock.

I unlatched my seat belt and scrambled around to face the backseat. My powerful, beautiful friend looked small and fragile and painfully vulnerable. I rested my hand on her shoulder.

"Damn it," she said. "I swore I wasn't going to cry."

"Nothing wrong with crying," Luke said.

"He's right," I agreed. "Let it out."

She fumbled around for a napkin then blew her nose. "Screw crying," she said. "We'll be in Salem before we know it. What are we going to do once we get there?"

Luke clicked on his left-turn signal and

moved smoothly into the fast lane. "Whip the bad guys' asses and save Sugar Maple."

It sounded like a plan to me.

13

LUKE
A FEW MILES NORTH OF SALEM, MASSACHUSETTS

"There's a Target a few miles ahead," I said. "We'll stop and pick up clean clothes, toiletries, and a cat carrier."

"I don't think we'll need it," Janice said. "Penny's back to her old self."

"Luke's right," Chloe said. "Why take any chances?"

I'd climbed enough trees for one day.

"Anything else?" I asked.

"Disposable cell phones."

"Cell phones?" Janice made a dismissive gesture I caught in the rearview mirror. "We have blueflame."

"Luke doesn't. If we don't have cells, too, he can't reach us."

"I'd ditch the blueflame unless you're sure you're alone." Their method of communication rocked, but speaking into a handful of blue fire wasn't likely to go unnoticed.

Chloe took down her ponytail, ran her hands through her hair, then gathered it up again and caught it in one of those colorful scrunchy things. "How do you know there's a Target coming up?" she asked me.

"I grew up here, remember?"

"I totally forgot," she said. "How close are we to your old hometown?"

"Couple of miles," I said. "About halfway between the Target and Salem." I worked summers schlepping tourists back and forth to Cape Ann for the whale-watching tours.

I waited for the obvious next question but she fell silent. There was no way in hell I could explain any of this to my family, so why try? We were here to see if we could find a way to rescue Sugar Maple, not play Meet the MacKenzies.

After my daughter Steffie died in an accident, I had stepped away from family and all of the baggage, both good and bad, that came with it. Too many memories I wasn't ready to embrace. That was one of the things about big families: it's a hell of a lot easier to disappear when there are five other siblings, five in-laws, and thirty-three grandchildren to keep track of. It would be Thanksgiving before they noticed I'd gone missing.

The Target parking lot was its usual crazy mess of runaway shopping carts, crying kids, and shoppers in search of a spot near the entrance.

"There's one near the door," Janice said, pointing over my shoulder.

"This tank would take out half of the Toyota next to it." I snagged a double spot near the back of the lot.

"You coming, Jan?" Chloe asked as she unbuckled her lap belt.

"I'll stay here and keep an eye on Penelope."

"Is she okay?" I asked Chloe as we crossed the parking lot.

"No," she said, slipping her arm through mine. "She's not okay at all."

She told me about Janice's decision to pierce the veil if we couldn't restore Sugar Maple to its Vermont footprint.

"Would that reunite her with her family?"

"Probably," she said. "Nothing's guaranteed but it probably would."

"Did you try to talk her out of it?"

"I told her how I felt but . . ." She glanced toward a red PT Cruiser angling for a spot. "It won't come to that. We're going to bring Sugar Maple back and everyone will pick up where they left off."

There wasn't anything I could say to that.

She knew the odds were against us. She didn't need to be reminded.

Targets are like Burger Kings and Wal-marts: if you've seen one, you've seen them all. We could have been in Montana.

"I'll check out the cat carriers," Chloe said.

"Better you than me," I said with a quick laugh. "I'll grab some prepaid cells and meet you at the checkout."

She disappeared up the pet supplies aisle. I continued on to electronics, where I went face-to-face with a wall of cell phones. Nobody needed that many choices. I looked for lots of minutes for not much money and grabbed three of them just to be on the safe side.

"Can I pay for these up front?" I asked the teenaged clerk draped over the counter, paging through a copy of *Teen People* with one of those vampire boys on the cover.

"Whatever," she said without looking up.

I headed for the pet supplies aisle, where I'd last seen Chloe. She wasn't there but I had a pretty good idea where I'd find her.

I stopped a middle-aged man wearing a red smock and a badge that read SAM.

"Wool?" I said and he stared at me with a blank expression on his ruddy face. "You know, yarn." I mimed knitting. "Baby booties. Blankets. Sweaters."

He pointed toward the far corner of the store. "Over there with the sewing stuff."

I thanked him and took three steps in that direction, when someone called out my name.

"Luke?"

I would know that voice anywhere. I put my head down and kept walking.

"MacKenzie, wait up!"

Busted.

I turned around and there was my old pal Fran Kelly, the admin assistant at my former station house, who had put the whole Sugar Maple thing in motion for me. She was pushing a cart filled to the brim with toys and kids' clothing and a giant ten-pack of paper towels.

"Frannie!" I laughed as she abandoned the cart and made a run for me. "What the hell are you doing in North Reading?"

She flung her arms around me and gave me a bear hug a WWF contender would be proud of. "I could ask you the same thing. I thought you were still up in the Vermont wilderness."

Definitely not the time for full disclosure. I took a quick look around. No sign of Chloe. I hoped our luck would hold.

"Had a little business to take care of in

140

Salem." I extricated myself from the hug and took a look at her. "Is there something in the water around here? You look great!"

The tough, no-nonsense Fran I had worked with blushed bright red and looked downright girlish. "You're not with the force anymore so you don't have to kiss my ass." She grabbed one of the disposable cell phones I was holding. "What the hell is this? Are you running drugs up there in Maple Sugar?"

"You big-city types are too damn suspicious." I took the phone back from her. "So how is the old gang?"

She filled me in on mutual friends and I was trying to figure out a way to make an escape before she started questioning me about Sugar Maple.

"So what happened with Karen? Did you figure out why she was looking for you?"

If I told her what really happened to my ex-wife, Fran would run screaming for the nearest exit. Lying was the only option.

"She called a few times but we never connected."

"Your brother Ronnie said he heard she headed out west to start over."

"Could be," I said, feeling like a shit. "I'm not on her Christmas card list." I changed the subject. "So what are you doing here?"

"We sold the house and bought into an over-fifty-five complex out on Landingham Road so we could be closer to the grands. Your brother helped us."

"You bought from Ronnie?" My older brother was a successful Realtor with connections all over the area.

"He hooked us up, negotiated a great price, and held our hands the whole way. Great guy."

This was the same guy who had specialized in Atomic Wedgies when I was growing up.

"So tell me about life up in the boonies," she said, a big wide smile on her face.

"Not much to tell. You already know it's a small town, no crime, lots of tourists in season."

She waved a manicured hand. "I don't care about that. Tell me about the woman."

"What woman?"

"What woman?" she repeated. "Your girlfriend, that's what woman."

"Who said I had a girlfriend?"

"You did," she said. "Last time we spoke."

Where were the random bolts of lightning when you needed them? "Early days," I said and hoped she would let it go at that.

"Did she come down here with you?"

"Uh —"

Fran was no fool. She knew a yes when she didn't hear one.

"Where is she?" She did a three sixty in place, scanning the store for Chloe. "I want to meet her."

"You know women," I said, hoping she wouldn't hit me in the head with a box of Legos for the sexist statement. "Retail therapy."

She glanced at her watch and groaned. "It's almost five. Jack's waiting for me at the senior center." She thought for a moment. "I know! Why don't you and — ?"

"Chloe."

Her smile was wider than ever. "Why don't you and Chloe stop by for dinner tonight?"

"That would be great, Frannie, but we have plans."

She pretended to slap her forehead with the heel of her hand. "Going to squeeze in some family time while you're here?"

"You ask a hell of a lot of questions, Kelly."

"Still the best way to get answers."

"Business dinner tonight. How about a rain check?"

Her hazel eyes teared up behind her rimless glasses. "Sure," she said, "but don't be a stranger."

143

I pulled her into a bear hug of my own and that was when Chloe showed up, arms piled high with brightly colored yarn and trailing a cat carrier behind her.

"Holy Mary, Mother of God," Fran stage-whispered. "You're dating Uma Thurman!"

14

CHLOE

Uma Thurman? I could have kissed Luke's gray-haired friend. If she thought I looked like the willowy blond actress, that meant at least part of Aerynn's protective charm was still up and working.

"You're a knitter, too," she said, gesturing toward the pile of Red Heart and Lion Brand cradled in my arms.

"I run a yarn shop back home." It actually hurt to say the words.

"Coals to Newcastle," Luke's friend said, and we both laughed. I knew she was dying to ask me what I was doing buying acrylic.

"I'm Chloe Hobbs."

"Fran Kelly."

My eyes widened. I knew the name. "You used to work with Luke in Boston." He had phoned her for information about Karen when his ex-wife first showed up.

"The stories I could tell you about this

145

boy . . ." She turned to Luke. "I'm going to hold you to that rain check. Chloe needs to be brought up to speed."

She said it with such affection that my normal shyness evaporated. "I'd love it."

The cell phone clipped to the strap of Fran's purse began to play "It's Raining Men."

"My husband is the most impatient man in Massachusetts," she said with a fond laugh. "I'd better get a move on before he trades me in for one of those Botoxed widows."

"He trades you in, give me a call," Luke said, giving her another hug.

She shot me a look and a genuine smile wreathed her face. "Yeah, I'll do that."

"She's great," I said as we watched Fran race toward the checkout lanes.

Luke nodded but said nothing.

"She's really fond of you."

He uttered words usually reserved for cable TV shows.

"You don't like her?" He had seemed so sincere. This was a side of Luke I hadn't seen before and it unnerved me.

"She's like a sister to me," he said as we gathered up some cheap flashlights and extra batteries. "That's the goddamn problem."

Everything I knew about traditional American families I'd learned from watching *The Cosby Show* and *The Waltons*. This did not compute. "I thought big sisters were a good thing."

He shook his head in exasperation. "Frannie bought a house from my brother. She's probably on the cell right now letting him know I'm in town."

"Which means they'll want to see you."

"And you."

"I guess they wouldn't believe we're here to see if we can bring a magick town back into this dimension."

He started to laugh despite his dark mood. "It would almost be worth telling them to see the look on their faces."

And the funny part was we could tell the truth and swear on a stack of Bibles and the Book of Spells and our secret would stay hidden right there in plain sight. There were some truths nobody believed, not even when they were being played out right in front of them.

Janice was bursting with news when we returned to the Buick.

"Some old chick in really unfortunate sweatpants was scoping out the car. She tried to be cool about it but I swear she memorized the license number."

Luke met my eyes. "Told you."

I clued Janice in about Fran and the gossip chain that went straight to the Mac-Kenzie clan.

"I'm one of five," Janice said. "You don't have to tell me."

"What are you going to do about it?" I asked Luke.

He started the engine. "Nothing."

"You're not going to call?"

"No reason to."

"But they'll know you're here."

"So?"

"Won't their feelings be hurt?"

"Yes," he said with a quick smile. "My brothers will slam my voice mail with messages. My sisters will try to catch me in IM and spam my in-box with advice I didn't ask for. If they knew how to blueflame, your hands would be on fire right now."

"Sounds like you know the Big Family drill," Janice said from the backseat.

He nodded. "I know the drill."

I didn't. All I knew was that he had the chance to be with family and he wasn't taking it.

"It's because of me, isn't it?" I asked. "I saw how uncomfortable you were when I popped up while you were talking with Fran."

"It's not you," he said. "It's because I took off after Karen and I split. I've been pretty much of a nonentity for the last couple years."

"They're angry with you."

He shrugged. "Angry, confused, hurt. The whole nine."

That shut me up for the moment. Nothing like discovering that you've turned into a self-obsessed, single-minded moron. Even better if the man you loved was the one who clued you in.

I made a mental note to quiz Janice about intrafamily dynamics. Clearly sitcoms hadn't provided enough information for me to work with. The one thing I believed was that if I had been lucky enough to have blood relatives of my own, I would be devastated to think I'd caused them any distress.

Then again, I also believed knitting goddesses Elizabeth Zimmerman and Cat Bordhi should be memorialized on Mount Rushmore with Washington, Lincoln, Jefferson, and Roosevelt.

Fifteen minutes later we drove past the ENTERING SALEM sign.

"No flying monkeys," Janice said from the backseat.

"That's always a good thing," I said as I

slipped my knitting into the plastic bag the yarn had come in.

We were making light of it but entering Salem's city limits was big for both of us. I kept waiting for the earthquake or blizzard or bolt of lightning that would finish us off but nothing happened.

To be honest, so far it wasn't all that memorable. Twenty-first-century Salem was a nice little city with a dark history and the promise of great fresh seafood. The strong sense of foreboding I experienced years ago had vanished.

"How are you doing back there?" I asked Janice as we rolled past an auto repair shop that seemed to be enjoying turn-away business.

"Not bad," she said. "I'm not hyperventilating and I don't feel like kicking out the back window and running for my life."

"That's something," Luke said.

Probably more than he expected. Definitely more than I had hoped for.

"Now what?" I asked Luke.

"We get ourselves some rooms, establish a base of operations, and figure out what the hell to do next."

We agreed that our lodgings needed to be cheap, clean, and within the Salem city limits. The town was lousy with B&Bs,

which, while no doubt charming, were way too up close and personal for our needs. We needed a place where we could come and go without attracting notice.

"Unless things have changed, there's only one motel in town," Luke said. "The Windjammer out near Cat Cove. It's off-season right now so there should be some vacancies."

"Speaking of cats, what are we going to do about Penny?" I asked.

"Sneak her in," the Sugar Maple chief of police said. "If she doesn't start that damn yowling, we'll be fine."

Penny opened one golden eye then closed it again. Whatever craziness had overtaken her earlier had played itself out and I hoped it would stay played out once we were at the motel.

Salem was a small fishing village that had grown up over the years to be a small city with high tourist appeal. Kitsch vied for space with history, which vied for space with progress, all of which brought visitors in significant numbers. Sure, there were lots of witchy references but the town was more than a glorified theme park.

Janice, however, saw it differently.

"They make money off misery," Janice said, shaking her head. "Lives destroyed and they're offering witch tours."

"I used to drive one of the witch tour trolleys," Luke said easily. "I felt like I was at Disney World."

"You thought it was a joke?" I asked, thinking about the stories I'd heard growing up. Stories that rarely had happy endings.

"The deaths were tragic," he admitted, "but innocent people are killed every hour of every day and always will be. To be honest, nothing about the Salem story ever seemed real to me."

"Because you didn't believe in witches," Janice said.

"One or two of us Irish kids might have grown up believing in ghosts. But witches?" He shook his head. "Only my first grade teacher fell into that category."

Janice's response was pithy and unprintable.

"I don't blame you," Luke said. "If I came from that history, I'd probably hate mortals, too, but remember it was the innocent mortals who were hanged, not the witches."

He was right. The witches and sorcerers and vampires and sprites had all escaped to Sugar Maple.

Janice, however, didn't see things that way and she made her displeasure known.

"Come on, Jan," I said. "It was a long time

ago. You know he's right." Besides, Janice had certainly never tried to hide her aversion to mortals.

"We're on the same side now," Luke said as the Windjammer, a handsome two-story motel, came into view. "That should be all that matters."

15

LUKE

I took note of the changes that had occurred since I worked in Salem as a teenager. Some old favorites had vanished, replaced by interchangeable substitutes. The old barber shop with the red-and-white-striped pole was now a day spa and massage therapy center. My favorite pizza joint had become a sit-down restaurant that took reservations.

The Windjammer, a little older, a tad more weathered, was still there. Our accommodations were located in the back of the building. The desk clerk had offered me ground floor near the entrance but I'd declined. I wanted our comings and goings to occur with as little notice as possible.

Let's face it: a single guy checking in with an Uma Thurman clone and a Julia Roberts lookalike would definitely attract attention.

I grabbed a handful of brochures from the spinner, a mix of tours, attractions, and restaurants, then headed back to the car.

"Any luck?" Chloe asked.

"Adjoining rooms," I said. "We might even have a view."

Janice's room had two double beds; Chloe's and mine boasted one queen. We had a view of the cove but the evening fog was beginning to gather and in another hour we wouldn't be able to see beyond the parking lot.

I wasn't totally comfortable with the idea of separate rooms. Not that I was looking for anything kinky but there was safety in numbers. None of us knew what to expect here in Salem and the cop in me wanted to circle the wagons. But Janice wanted her privacy and, as she pointed out, doors and walls didn't mean a hell of a lot where she and Chloe came from.

I couldn't argue with that.

Chloe had bought all of us new jeans, T-shirts, sweatshirts, underwear, toothbrushes, and other drugstore items. We cleaned up and gathered again in our room looking a hell of a lot more presentable.

"It's almost seven," I said. "If we're going to walk out and get something to eat, we'd better move."

"Guys, I think I'm going to pass," Janice

said. "Just bring me back a lobster roll, okay?"

"Extra mayo?" Chloe asked.

Janice offered a tired smile. "Is there any other way?"

"We've been sitting in the car all day," Chloe said. "A walk in the fresh air would do you good."

Janice shook her head. "I'm fine. I'll watch some bad TV and keep an eye on Penny."

Chloe shot me a look that I don't think was lost on Janice. "Luke, don't you think Janice should come with us?"

Looking at the deep sadness in Janice's eyes, the utter exhaustion, I couldn't push the issue.

"I think she'll be okay," I said after a moment.

"No," Chloe said. "Seriously. We don't know what we're facing in this town. We can't leave her here alone." Her eyes were flashing all kinds of *help me* warnings at me.

"I'm not going to do anything crazy," Janice said, "if that's what you're worried about."

"Yes, that's exactly what I'm worried about," Chloe said, not missing a beat. "I'm afraid you're going to leave us."

"Not until I get my lobster roll," Janice said and I laughed out loud with her. "I'm going to veg out with the television and maybe try blueflaming Lynette or the kids. I don't expect an answer but —" Her shrug said it all.

"Come on," I said, taking Chloe's hand. "If we're going to get those lobster rolls before everything shuts down for the night, we'd better get started."

"You'll be here when we get back?" Chloe asked Janice.

"I swear on Cookie A," Janice said and Chloe grinned.

"Knitting joke?" I asked Chloe as we stepped out into the cool, salty evening air.

"Not if you've ever knitted a pair of Cookie A's socks," she said, squeezing my hand. "They're a religion."

We walked in silence through the parking lot and down the driveway. The air was cool and smelled like home to me.

"I'm going to check out a tour operator tomorrow," I said as we waited for traffic to slow down enough for us to cross the narrow highway.

Chloe looked at me like I'd lost a few screws. "You're going to book a three-hour tour, Professor?"

I ignored the Gilligan reference. "One of the brochures I picked up in the lobby looked pretty interesting." The tour operator specialized in the hidden history of the town without all of the commercial trappings. "It might point us in a direction we hadn't thought about."

"No stone unturned?"

I grinned. "Something like that." You never knew where the next great idea would come from. I was involved once in a murder investigation that swung our way because a detective made a left-hand turn rather than a right one day and stumbled onto the clue that broke the case wide.

Fisherman's Catch had a take-out window so we ordered five lobster rolls, cole slaw, and coffees then started back to the motel.

Every now and then Chloe cast a look over her shoulder or a quick glance to the left or right.

"You okay?" I asked as we walked along.

"Yes," she said then looked at me. "It just all seems so ordinary. I thought everything would make sense when we got here." She fumbled around for words. "I thought there'd be some kind of buzz in the air, some kind of awareness that there was more going on than met the eye."

"Like in Sugar Maple," I said.

"Exactly, but there's nothing. This place is as ordinary, as . . . human as it can get."

The Chloe I met and fell in love with

didn't get depressed. She got sad. She got angry. She got happy. But not depressed.

And never defeated.

"We've been up for over twenty-four hours," I reminded her. "A hell of a lot has happened. A good meal and some sleep and it'll all start to make sense."

"You believe that?" she asked.

"No," I said, "but I was hoping maybe you would."

Back at the motel we tapped on the door that connected our room to Janice's then unlocked the bolt on our side.

"Lobster rolls," Chloe called out. "Come on over."

We heard the answering click of her lock and then her door swung open and a beaming Janice Meany burst into our room.

"You won't believe what I've found!"

"The blueflame worked!" Chloe exclaimed. "You managed to contact someone from Sugar Maple!"

A flicker of disappointment moved across Janice's face.

"No, but we have Web TV in our rooms with high-speed Internet access. The big storm back home was on all the weather reports. They say our area will be inaccessible for at least another three days." She glanced down at the stack of motel stationery in her hand. "Luke, you'd better make a few phone calls and calm things down. One of the stories mentioned that the state was getting worried because they haven't heard from anyone in Sugar Maple."

With all the obstacles we'd encountered on our way to Salem, I'd totally dropped the ball on maintaining communications with the powers that be. If we were going to continue to pull off this ruse, we would need to keep concerns about our safety to a minimum.

"Great job, Janice," I said. "If you ever decide to hang up your blow-dryer, I could use you on the force."

I didn't blame either Janice or Chloe for laughing. A one-man police force deserved a few laughs. But the gratitude was real. Janice had put us back on track.

We divvied up the food and set about reconnecting with the outside world. We all phoned our voice-mail boxes to check for messages and were equally swamped.

"We'd better get our stories straight," I said. We were in Janice's room, which had the extra bed and a fair-sized desk.

"Big storm, bad roads," Janice said with a slight grin.

"No immediate danger," I said. "Plenty of supplies to see our citizens through the next few days. No need for state assistance at this time."

"Chronically ill residents of Sugar Maple Assisted Living were relocated before the bridge went down and the roads became impassable," Chloe offered. "And all classes and workshops at Sticks & Strings will be rescheduled to a later date."

It was all bullshit but I had to admit it was damn good bullshit. If we didn't contradict each other, we could buy at least two more days before reality came calling on what used to be Sugar Maple.

Janice had also discovered a Hobbs Popcorn in the phone book but an online search convinced her there was no link with the Hobbs line to which Chloe belonged. I'll admit I was seeing Salem through different eyes as I watched Chloe's and Janice's reactions to the town their ancestors fled all those years ago.

On the downside, Janice didn't have any luck blueflaming her family or Lynette, which reminded me that there was more at stake than a random collection of quaint shops and picturesque vistas.

Penny the cat was sound asleep on Janice's extra bed and Janice seemed eager for the company so Chloe set up the litter box and bowls of food and water, then we all said good night. It was a little after ten by the time Chloe and I returned to our adjoining room.

"They have one of those hot water thingies in the bathroom," she said, "and some packets of cocoa. Want some?"

"No whiskey?"

She shook her head. "No whiskey."

"I'll pass."

She disappeared into the bathroom to do whatever she did before bed. I was about to settle back with some Red Sox action on TV when my cell phone vibrated against my hip. I'd left at least a dozen call-back pages. Too bad letting it flip to voice mail wasn't an option tonight.

"You're dating Uma Frickin' Thurman?"

I leaned back against the headboard. "Frannie must've called you the second she got home."

"She called me from the car," Ronnie said with a good-natured laugh. "This was too good to wait." I heard him tapping computer keys. "So who is she and when do we get to meet her?"

"Her name's Chloe. She owns a shop up in Vermont. And soon."

"That's all you're giving me?"

"That's all I've got."

"Fran says she's a ringer for Thurman."

"She hears that a lot."

"Fran also says you looked tired."

"Yeah?" I pushed down a yawn. "Lots of meetings, not much time. You know how it goes."

"We've all been worried about you." He paused. My brother wasn't any better at the emotional stuff than I was. "You should've told us you were thinking about moving up to Ben & Jerry country. Ma called your office number one day and they said you'd left. Hell of a way to find out."

The guilt bomb. Where would families be without it? "It all happened fast," I said, which was true. "They had a murder on their hands and needed a chief of police. I was sworn in the day after I got the call."

"They told Ma it was temporary."

"Not anymore."

"You're staying up there?" He sounded surprised.

"Looks like." I heard the sound of keys tapping again. "Who are you messaging?"

"Meghan. She said to tell you she says hi."

Meghan was my second youngest sister and probably my favorite. "Tell Meggie I want my *White Album* back."

More keys tapping. Ronnie's laugh was deep and real, same as he was. "You don't wanna know what she says." A beat pause.

163

"How about breakfast tomorrow? We can grab something in town. Give me a chance to meet Uma."

"Chloe."

"I know," he said. "Glad you're back on track, buddy. It's time."

"Yeah," I said. "It is."

"So how about breakfast? If that's no good, the two of you can come to the house for dinner. Denise would love to see you, and the kids would go nuts."

"Gonna have to take a rain check, Ronnie. Wall-to-wall meetings all day."

"You still have to eat."

"Booked straight through until ten P.M."

I hated lying to him. I hated the fact that he knew I was lying even more. There aren't many good guys in this world and he was one of them. Good guys deserved better.

"You're a busy guy, Chief," Ronnie said lightly. "No problem. We'll catch up some other time."

"Say hi to Deni and the girls for me."

"Will do. Miss you, buddy," he said then disconnected before I could say good-bye.

16

CHLOE

Usually I'm a shower kind of girl but the motel tub was white, deep, and sparkling clean and I couldn't resist it. I filled it as high as possible with water at a temperature just shy of painful and sank gratefully into its depths.

Luke's voice rumbled pleasantly through the paper-thin wall that separated the bedroom from the bathroom as he fielded phone call after phone call. So far my only call-back was from a seriously annoyed knitter from Long Island who held me personally responsible for the twenty-six inches and counting of snow that had blocked her visit to Sticks & Strings.

I couldn't help but wonder what she would say if she knew I really was personally responsible for the storm.

So far Salem was turning out to be a total waste of time. For a town with a reputation for otherworldly connections, it felt relentlessly mortal to me. I had always wondered if anyone had stayed behind when Aerynn led the nonhumans to safety in the Indian town of Sinzibukwud.

I was pretty sure we were going to come up empty tomorrow.

I didn't want to think about the future. I had always known I would live my life in Sugar Maple. That had never been in doubt. I was a descendant of Aerynn and Sugar Maple was my responsibility, same as it had been for the Hobbs women who came before me.

The realization that I might be the one who failed the town and its inhabitants weighed heavily on my heart.

The water was warm and soothing and I felt safe for the first time since Luke and I stepped into the clearing and found out Sugar Maple was gone. I knew safety was relative when you were dealing with the supernatural, but at that moment it was all I had.

My eyes felt heavy and a deep exhaustion pressed me lower into the tub until I was submerged up to my chin. The sound of Luke's voice was as rhythmic and soothing as a lullaby. Sleep was irresistible and I drifted into that delicious state between my breasts. "Where did they go?"

He gave me his patented cop scowl. "Who?"

"The spirits."

"You saw spirits?"

"Two of them," I said as I stood up and reached for a dry towel. "And they weren't very nice."

"Are you sure you weren't dreaming?"

I hesitated. "Pretty sure."

"I didn't see anyone."

"They were ghosts, Luke. They didn't want you to see them." I pointed toward the soggy towel draped over the side of the tub. "Why do you think I was covered with that stupid towel?"

"Part of some kind of girlie bath ritual?"

I ignored him. "Bramford Light," I said. "That's where we'll find the answer."

Except there was one small problem.

Bramford Light didn't exist.

Luke tried every search engine out there and came up empty. We checked the telephone book on the nightstand and the tourist maps stacked up on the desk, courtesy of the visitors bureau.

"I didn't imagine it," I said, leaning against his shoulder as he clicked on every single possible link. "They definitely said to stay away from Bramford Light."

dreams and wakefulness.

"So that's the girl." The voice was light and feminine with an accent that sounded vaguely British.

"She looks like she needs a good meal." This voice was female also but flatter, harder.

I shifted around in the tub and sank down a little deeper in search of more pleasing dream companions. Where was my herd-of-cashmere-goats fantasy hiding? Now would be a nice time for a command performance.

"I'm not terribly impressed," the feminine voice declared. "She hasn't her mother's beauty."

"Envious as always, Tabitha," the flatter, harder voice chided. "She is the spit of Aerynn and that's no lie."

An uneasy chill moved across my exposed skin and I shivered but didn't awaken.

"A fitting end, Dorcas," the feminine voice said. "Here is where she is at last and here is where she'll stay if I have anything to say about it."

Suddenly a pair of weather-roughened hands grabbed my head and pushed it beneath the water. This was exactly the kind of practical joke Janice loved and I despised. I used an old self-defense move from a Jackie Chan film and broke the hold with an upward thrust of my arms and sat straight up, gasping for air.

I blinked the soapy water from my eyes and found myself staring up at two short, plump women in period costumes from a bad revival of *The Crucible*. One wore a bulky gray knitted shawl wrapped across her chest and tied in the back while the other wore a version of a wedding shawl knitted up in a Romney handspun that looked as light as a whisper.

Did I mention I could see right through them?

"Get out!" I pointed toward the door and they laughed. Who could blame them? They probably hadn't used a door since 1692. "I'm not joking. Get out right now!"

"There be no shame in nakedness, child," the younger of the two said in her gently trilling voice. "It is as natural as the changing of the seasons."

"I don't give a damn about naked," I sputtered, grabbing for a towel just the same. "You tried to drown me!"

"Even the temper is like Aerynn's," the older woman said, clearly relishing my distress. "Ever the Hobbs downfall, it is."

"That and the humans," the younger woman said with a knowing nod of her head. "It is as if they are determined to throw away their magick."

"I don't know who you are," I said, "and I don't care. Go away. You're not wanted here."

"You're doomed to failure," the younger woman said. "Better you leave now before it's too late. Had we wanted to snuff out your existence or that of your human consort, there would be nothing you could do to stop us."

"You think Bramford Light is the answer," the older woman said, "but it never was and it never will be. Go back while there is still time."

"I don't know what you're talking about," I said, tugging the bath towel closer. "I've never heard of Bramford Light and if you ever try anything like this again, I will —"

It didn't matter. They were already gone.

"Chloe." The hand on my shoulder was warm and strong. "Wake up."

"Go away," I mumbled. "Why won't you listen to me?"

"Come on, Hobbs. It's pushing midnight. Let's go."

"What the — ?" I opened my eyes and it was Luke, not those two annoyingly critical biddies, looking at me. I was still in the tub with a giant bath towel resting soggily across

Luke, however, said nothing.

"You think I imagined the whole thing, don't you?"

"I don't know what the hell I think." He tossed aside the keyboard and pulled me across his lap. "I'm tired of thinking."

My cheek rested against his thigh. My skin absorbed his warmth and made it my own. After a day of loss and chaos, I was where I needed to be.

His hands moved along my rib cage, my spine, my breasts, leaving silvery white sparks in their wake. He bent over me and I felt his breath against my ear. Warmth swiftly escalated into heat and in seconds we were naked on the motel bed.

The world fell away. I lay back on the soft mattress and opened myself, my heart, to him in a way I never had before and it both scared and excited me. Everything I thought I knew about my life, my future, had disappeared today along with Sugar Maple and now there was only Luke.

This all-too-mortal man.

Luke had been willing to walk away from the life he had known, the family he loved, and build a home with me in Sugar Maple and now here I was, wondering if I would be able to survive anywhere else.

But I wasn't thinking of any of that as we

171

made love that night.

For a little while I wasn't thinking at all.

17

LUKE

If sleeping were a sport, Chloe would be on the Olympic team. Put her within shouting distance of a pillow and blanket and she was a goner.

Come to think of it, she had been asleep when I met her. I walked into Sticks & Strings that first morning and found her conked out on the sofa near the hearth. She was barefoot. Her feet were long and elegant. Her hands were long and elegant, too, but she bit her fingernails. A bright red blanket was pooled on the floor next to her. A fat black cat slept soundly in a basket of what spinners called roving.

They both snored.

And yeah, it was love at first sight.

Tonight she fell asleep minutes after we finished making love, curled up against me as close as she could get. I teased her once about being a heat-seeking missile and the look on her face made me regret opening my stupid mouth. The whole part-human, part-sorceress thing was still a touchy issue for her and probably always would be. I think she was embarrassed by her need for human contact. I had to remind myself that she hadn't grown up surrounded by brothers and sisters who lived to tease each other until they cried or ended up in therapy.

I lay there with her for a long time, listening to the sound of her breathing, the water slapping against the dock not too far from our window, the faint rustle of the sheets each time we shifted position.

This is enough. The thought appeared full-blown and undeniable. If this was all we ever had, it would be enough for me. I was hardwired for home and family. Always had been. I had made the decision to walk away from the world I knew and become part of Chloe's and I was okay with that as long as she was there with me.

Or I would be, in time. I had made a hell of a lot of progress in the four months I had been living in Sugar Maple. Vampire funeral directors and troll librarians and shapeshifters who morphed into parakeets in the kitchen sink. Trust me. You can get used to anything if you try hard enough. And I'd been trying. I wanted this to work. Chloe's destiny had been set centuries ago by forces I would never understand. She had no choice about the life she was living. But I did.

And I chose her.

I chose Sugar Maple.

But now everything had changed. Here I was, back in the world I had left behind and my old dreams back within reach. I could get a job on a local police force. Decent pay. Okay benefits. A pension down the road. And it would be a hell of a lot less dangerous than chasing demons and battling Fae warriors. Maybe Chloe could open up another yarn shop like Sticks & Strings. We'd buy a dormered cape in the suburbs, a couple of cars, have the family over for barbecues on lazy summer afternoons and big Super Bowl bashes every winter.

I'd be lying if I said it didn't appeal to me on a hell of a lot of levels. After years of seeing the worst of my species on the streets of Boston, the surburban dream sounded pretty good. But no matter how hard I tried, I couldn't fit Chloe into the picture. She wasn't ordinary. She wasn't regular. Asking her to be any of those things she wasn't would be wrong.

And no matter how hard she tried to live the life of a mortal woman, she would fail because she wasn't one any longer. In just a few months her powers had multiplied dramatically and there was no reason to think they wouldn't continue to multiply. I had seen what she could do when she battled Isadora at the waterfall and that was only the beginning.

Or it would be, if we managed to find Sugar Maple and restore it to this dimension.

If we failed, the future was anybody's guess.

At around two in the morning, Chloe turned over and hugged her pillow instead of me. I carefully climbed out of bed, hit the john, then stood by the wide picture window for a long time, looking out across the parking lot toward the cove. The beam from a lighthouse glowed softly behind the dense fog that blanketed everything.

I was home.

Chloe wasn't.

It was a long time before I went back to bed.

And even longer before I slept.

CHLOE

I woke up a little after six. I was still tired and groggy but a few cups of coffee would take care of that.

Luke had already been out on a breakfast hunt and the desk in our room was piled high with goodies.

I tapped on the door between our room and Janice's. "Breakfast! Better hurry or the bagels will be gone."

The lock clicked. The door swung open. Penny the cat burst into our room and leaped straight into my arms.

"That cat's crazy," Janice said as she joined us around our makeshift buffet. "She slept on my head all night."

"This is a surprise?" I arched a brow in Janice's direction. "You know cats."

"My cats don't weigh thirty pounds and smell like Egg McMuffin."

Penny swiveled around in my arms and shot Janice a look that would have quelled a lesser woman.

"Stick a sock in it, cat." She dumped four packets of sugar into her coffee and followed it with two containers of cream.

We jokingly elbowed each other as we grabbed for bagels and donuts and claimed the creamers.

Finally Luke and I were settled on the bed while Janice took the desk chair. Penny was off in the corner enjoying Fancy Feast and a piece of bagel with salmon cream cheese.

"The blueflame erupted twice during the

night," Janice said.

I stopped, midchew. "Who was it?"

"Wish I knew. No identifying signal. Just a sputter of flame then nothing." She fiddled with her coffee cup. "I doubt if any Salemites know about blueflame."

I glanced at Luke then over at Janice. "Don't be so sure. I had visitors last night." I told her about the pair of critical wenches who had dropped in while I was in the bathtub.

"So where is this Bramford Light?"

"We googled it but no luck," Luke said. "A couple of subdivisions here and there. That's it." He didn't say it but I knew he thought I'd dreamed the whole thing.

"Shit." Janice leaned back in her seat. Her despair was palpable.

Luke slipped back behind his cop face. "If we're going to make any headway, we'll need to split up."

I nodded. I can't say I was happy about it but the job was big and our time was short.

"Janice?" Luke asked. "Is that okay with you?"

She shook her head. "I can't." Her eyes filled with tears. "I just can't bring myself to go out there."

"That's okay," Luke said, dropping his cop façade long enough to let the real man show through. "You can work the phones and the Internet."

We were looking for any indication that not all the magickal beings followed Aerynn to what became Sugar Maple. In my experience, magickal beings had a great deal in common with their human counterparts. The odds against getting everyone to agree to a plan of action were astronomical. Someone must have stayed behind and left a trail that extended down through the years and it was up to us to find it.

"I want to check out the waterfront," I said to Luke as we walked across the parking lot to the car. "Maybe someone knows about Bramford Light."

"No way," Luke said. "I'll take the waterfront. You start looking around town."

"I'm going to the waterfront."

"Not a great idea."

"I can take care of myself."

"Docks aren't always the friendliest places."

"I'll be fine. I have magick." Humans didn't scare me. The Fae were another story.

"I grew up around here. You're going to have to trust me on this."

Back in Sugar Maple I was the one with most of the answers. I think I liked that better.

"So what do I do in town? Wander around asking where the faeries are?"

"Why don't you try looking for some of those symbols Sugar Maple is so nuts about."

"That's not a bad idea." I shot a conciliatory glance his way. "Almost like you did this for a living."

"Yeah," he said with an answering grin. "Almost."

Clans, families, and individuals all had their own avatars, so to speak. Easy-to-recognize symbols that were woven into our art and our history. Sugar Maple was, not surprisingly, a leaf from the sugar maple tree. The New England Fae were represented by the infinity symbol. My mother's gravestone bore a glowing sun; my father's, a crescent moon.

"Tell me again why we're doing this," I said.

"Because there's a damn good chance not everyone fled to Sugar Maple during the Witch Trials and a lot of knowledge found in the Book of Spells stayed here with them. Maybe as oral tradition, maybe passed along some other way."

I shrugged. "Maybe that and a miracle will bring Sugar Maple back."

"You got anything better?"

"No."

"So we go with plan B."

Luke would search for information about the mysterious Bramford Light while I headed into the heart of town. We would meet back at the motel around lunchtime to exchange notes with Janice.

We drove along Washington Square, looping around Salem Common, where I saw the empty band shell that apparently had served as the model for the gazebo that graced Sugar Maple's village green. It felt both familiar and uncomfortably alien.

"When was that band shell erected?" I asked Luke.

He thought for a moment. "I'm thinking maybe a hundred years ago."

"Not 1692."

He shook his head. "Not even close." His eyes slid toward me. "Why?"

"The gazebo on the green looks exactly like it."

"So?"

"Our founding population fled Salem during the Witch Trials two hundred years earlier."

He was quiet for a moment. "That makes a copycat gazebo a little weird."

I nodded. "That's what I was thinking."

I was also thinking maybe Luke's original

theory about magickal beings left behind might have more merit than I'd first thought.

So where were they?

I willed myself to stay open to whatever might be out there (within reason, of course) but no thought probes or blue-flames or anything else attempted to make contact. I was starting to wonder if maybe the two spirits I saw in the bath the previous night had been the product of exhaustion after all.

Luke left the car on the third floor of a parking garage near the visitor center and gave me the keys as we exited the tiny elevator.

"Drive the car back to the motel when you're finished. We'll meet up there for lunch."

"Be careful." He could handle whatever his world threw his way but my world was a whole other story.

He pulled me into a quick hug. "You have the cell with you. I programmed in my number and Janice's. Use it if you need it."

I stood on the sidewalk and watched him walk away. We didn't have much time. The only way we could accomplish what we needed to accomplish was to split up. I accepted that. But that didn't mean I had to like it.

Especially not in a place like Salem. I walked to the visitor center then along New Liberty and made a right onto Brown, fully expecting the weight of all that tragic history to land on my shoulders. But I felt nothing.

No connection at all to my surroundings.

No sense that magick had ever walked here except maybe on Halloween for the tourists.

I didn't care about Salem. Long may it thrive but it meant nothing to me. What I did care about was the fact that I was afraid we had been played. Dorothy and the Scarecrow hadn't faced half as many obstacles on their way to Oz as we'd battled on the drive to Salem. Pissed-off trees lobbing apples at your head? Piece of cake. I'd take that over crashing through a guardrail any day.

So what was all that drama about? Had someone or something been screwing with our heads for the fun of it or was it really trying to keep us away from Salem? I was more confused than ever.

For all the good I was doing, I might as well have been in Boise. I had no sense of the ancestors at all. It was pretty clear that

Aerynn had left no blood family behind.

When it came to Salem, I wasn't feeling the love.

But if there was one thing Luke and all my years of watching *Law & Order* had taught me, it was to keep on looking.

Even if the whole thing seemed pointless.

18

LUKE

Detective work is a hell of a lot easier when you know what you're looking for. Not only didn't I know what I was looking for, I didn't know where to start looking.

The waterfront was a long shot but it was as good a place as any to begin. Salem's early history was largely seafaring. If any of Aerynn's ancestors remained behind, the waterfront was most likely where they would gather. It was away from the center of town where most of the population lived and the sea would provide an easy escape route if trouble erupted again.

It wasn't much but at the moment it was all I had.

Lighthouses had been on my mind since I got out of bed. I'd walked over to the window to enjoy the view of the lighthouse I assumed was out there beaming its light through the fog.

At least that was what I thought. The morning fog had lifted. The visibility was great. And there were no lighthouses visible from our window. We did, however, have a great view of the New Pinky's Crab Shack but I don't think that was what kept me up last night.

Then again, anything was possible.

I wasn't crazy about splitting with Chloe but there was no choice. I set off at a reasonable pace, trying to keep the cop vibe under wraps and a more benign local vibe front and center. It wasn't hard to do. I pretty much was a local. I'd put myself through two years of community college working in this town. I ate my weight in chop suey sandwiches and rolled my eyes with the rest of the summer workers at the tourists who blew their vacation looking for things that didn't exist.

Irony.

You gotta love it.

One thing about Salem: you were never far from the water. I started near Central Wharf and worked my way toward Derby.

It was still too early in the year for the pleasure boats to be out. Here and there rowboats thumped against the docks where they were tied. A RENT A KAYAK sign was posted over the window of a shuttered sporting shop.

The sun was rising higher in the sky. The morning chill was turning warm. The smell of fish was strong but not unpleasant. Spring in this neck of the woods was capricious — especially by the water — but the signs were good.

I stopped in at the usual conglomeration of businesses you would see along a waterfront.

"Any idea where I can find Bramford Light?" I asked the manager of a boat rental place near the Maritime Historic Site.

He looked up from his *Sports Illustrated*. "Bramford? Never heard of it."

I tried the mechanics at the engine repair shop. "Bramford Light?"

"You sure you're in the right town?" the oldest of the group asked.

"Thanks anyway," I said and moved on.

I nodded at two young guys in T-shirts and leather wristbands who were leaning against an abandoned shack across from the House of Seven Gables. The words BAIT AND TACKLE were painted over the door in faded white letters. A Harley was catching its breath ten feet away. If I were on the force in Salem, I'd stop for a moment, make a comment about the hog, make sure everything was the way it should be, then continue on my way.

But I wasn't a cop here so I stopped and said instead, "Bramford Light?"

Maybe they didn't hear me.

"Bramford Light?" I asked again.

Dead-eyed stares a cop would envy. I took the look as a no and moved on.

It was hard to believe Salem had once been a thriving fishing village. Now it was more a shore community with great seafood and lots of tourists.

And, as far as I could tell, no magic.

CHLOE

As it turned out, Salem had been waiting for the right moment to let me know I wasn't welcome.

It happened first at the Witch House. The building was undergoing renovations and visitors were instructed to go around back. I attempted to follow the path but it was like being on a treadmill. No matter how hard I tried, I got nowhere.

Even stranger was the fact that nobody around me noticed. Other people came and went with no problem. Small children dashed past me like trained athletes while I metaphorically treaded water.

Not being a big fan of humiliation, I dashed across Washington Square North to

188

Salem Common with the purpose of checking out the band shell that had been duplicated in Sugar Maple. Great plan, right? Too bad I couldn't seem to get in.

"Not funny," I muttered under my breath, to the consternation of a jogger stretching near me.

Who needed the common anyway? A few trees. Some scruffy, winter-pale grass. Some sad-looking joggers and dog walkers. Nothing I could use there.

A steady wind blew in from the water. I shivered and wished I had worn one of the sweatshirts I'd picked up at Target. I had spent most of my life feeling lonely but the sensation of actually being alone was a new one. Where were the tourists? I had expected to see scores of them dashing up and down the streets and alleyways, snapping photos and filming videos and generally soaking up all of the witchy lore they could.

And, while I was asking questions I couldn't answer, where were the townies? The place seemed — no pun intended — more like a ghost town than a tourist mecca.

Then again, so did Sugar Maple much of the time. It was only the beginning of April, I reminded myself. Most of New England was still looking over its collective shoulder, waiting for the last snowfall. If Salem was anything like Sugar Maple, tourist season wouldn't kick into high gear for another month or so.

I followed the Red Line (which really was a red line painted down the middle of the sidewalk) deeper into the heart of town. The homes ranged from magnificent two-story brick edifices to clapboard cottages badly in need of fresh paint and roof repairs. They had been laid out haphazardly over the centuries. Some were a sneeze away from their neighbors. Some had been set kitty-corner on their tiny lots. Others nestled gracefully atop a small rise. No matter how hard I tried, I couldn't relate any of this to the plight of Sugar Maple.

Did you ever dream that you were naked at the supermarket and all of your neighbors had picked that day to dash out to buy milk? I felt more self-conscious than I had as a gawky twelve-year-old and that was saying something. It wasn't that I felt like I was being watched exactly, but a vague prickly feeling settled itself between my shoulder blades and wouldn't leave.

I spotted a café on Washington near Lynde. It wasn't that I was hungry exactly but the thought of a butter and sugar transfusion was irresistible.

The first problem was I couldn't get

through the front door.

The other problem was nobody seemed to notice.

For a moment I wondered if I was invisible but an old man with a walking stick glared at me as he pushed his way out of the shop. I grabbed for the door but yelped as an electric shock knocked me back a step.

Are we having fun yet?

Luke thought I had a combustible temper but I really didn't. Those flames that suddenly shot out from my fingertips were just a coincidence.

Kind of like the fact that every shop in Salem seemed to be turning its back on me.

I was starting to feel like a five-foot, ten-inch ant at a picnic.

So far the Red Line hadn't been working out too well so I veered off down another side street where I hoped the welcome would be a bit friendlier. I strolled past a hair salon, a kitschy tourist shop that specialized in sparkly glass witch's balls in every color of the rainbow, three candle shops, and a quilter's paradise and was about to continue on past a dusty-looking antique shop, when I saw it.

There in the window was a late-seventeenth-century wheel. Tall, graceful, originally created to spin flax and look utterly beautiful while it did. It looked so much like the wheel that had been handed down from Aerynn that I had no doubt it had been made by the same craftsman.

The modern wheels were wonderful — fast and quiet and unfailingly efficient — but I was a sucker for the moody, romantic wheels of the past.

You didn't see an Irish castle wheel every day. I was lucky enough to have learned to spin on one but most spinners wouldn't know where to start.

I had to see the wheel up close. I had to touch it, run my fingers along the smoothly polished wood, see it do what it was made to do: spin floss into gold just like magick.

I braced myself for involuntary electrotherapy and reached for the door handle. It didn't shock me, bite me, or turn me into one of those kids on *Jersey Shore.* It actually opened the door.

Now here was where it might get dicey. An invisible tidal wave might rise up and throw me back into the street on my bony butt. Or maybe I would be turned into a giant ice cube. And there was always the chance that I could be struck dead.

Scratch that. No use putting ideas into people's heads.

Again nothing happened. I stepped into

the quiet shop and breathed in the wonderful scent of beeswax, potpourri, and history. I'm a big fan of clutter but this place was crowded even by my seriously deranged standards.

Fancy-schmancy antiques vied for space with kitschy 1950s throwaways. A pair of cigar store Indians flanked the archway to the next display room. A wax figure of Teddy Roosevelt leaned against a player piano across from me. Cups, saucers, teapots, and china display plates saluted from row upon row of maple shelving that blanketed the wall to my left. A ratty-looking basket the size of a Mini Cooper occupied the center of the room and it was piled high with knitting needles that were clearly from centuries past.

I had found my people.

"Hello," I called out. "Is anyone here?"

No answer.

"Anyone?" Leaving a glorious antique wheel unattended wasn't a bright idea. A roaming band of knitters just might spirit it away.

Still no response. Was Salem so devoid of crime that the owner would take off on a coffee break without locking the doors behind her? As far as I knew, only Sugar Maple had that particular demographic and even I locked the doors of Sticks & Strings against knitters in search of Wollmeise.

But there was no law against touching, was there?

I had a Sleeping Beauty moment when I drew my hand along the satiny wood. Sugar maple, to be precise. What were the odds? I felt a lump in my throat as I absorbed its essence and felt the pull of home. I half expected to prick my finger (I never did figure out exactly what a fairy-tale girl could prick her finger on, but it definitely moved the plot along) but I didn't expect to see lemon yellow glitter pooled at the base of the wheel. Or the small infinity symbol carved on one of the legs. How had I missed them?

I think I might have stopped breathing for a moment or two. My heartbeat was so fast and deep that my chest hurt.

Glitter was the Fae equivalent of human fingerprints. No two glitterprints were alike. The subtle variations in color might not be perceptible to the non-Fae population but they identified areas of origin, clans, and families within clans more precisely than DNA.

One more thing. Glitterprints had the shelf life of a ripe banana.

In other words, those prints were new.

And that meant the Fae community was alive and well and living in Salem, Massachusetts.

And that I'd walked straight into a trap.

19

Luke

I was getting nowhere fast. This whole Bramford Light thing was a dead end. It was time to move on again.

I checked the time on my cell. A little after ten. According to the brochure, Holly's Day Tours should be open for business. I walked west on Derby, past In a Pig's Eye, then spotted the tiny store front.

The biggest part of detective work was asking questions; the most important part was asking the right questions of the right people. At that point I would have been happy if Holly just talked to me. So far I hadn't found Salem residents to venture past monosyllables.

A bright blue OPEN sign was turned face outward. I took it at its word and swung open the door. A bell tinkled somewhere in the rear of the storefront as I stepped over the threshold.

So far, so good.

A calico cat watched me from the top of a bookcase situated against the back wall. The shelves were crammed with obviously old volumes, some cloth bindings, some leather. They were jammed into any available spot. Spine out. Straight up. Flat on their backs. Whatever worked.

Clearly Holly of Holly's Day Tours was interested in information, not the antiquarian value of the books, which, considering the proximity to the ocean, was probably a good thing.

"Just be a second," a very young and feminine voice called out. "Don't go away!"

The cat leaped to the ground and glided over to check me out. The calico pressed its nose against my left ankle, my right ankle, then turned and stalked back to its perch atop the bookcase.

I wasn't sure if that was a pass or fail.

"Just another second," the musical voice rang out. "Please don't go!"

"I'm not going anywhere," I answered.

Waiting isn't always a bad thing. It gave me a chance to check out the photos and paintings on the walls, the awards, the framed clippings. Holly's Day Tours didn't follow the usual Salem paradigm. From what I could see, there was little or no emphasis on the Witch Trials and the usual paranormal stuff that was the town's bread and butter. Holly's specialized in history, architecture, and seafaring lore.

Holly was at least forty years older than her voice led me to believe. She was a tall, handsome woman with an abundance of white-streaked red hair, broad shoulders, and the kind of smile that transcended age.

Cops never like anyone immediately but for me Holly was an exception to the rule.

"So what can I do you for?" she asked. "The One-Hour Overview, the Gilligan Three-Hour Special, or Holly's All-Day Extravaganza?"

I laughed out loud. There was no escaping Gilligan today. "How about the ten-minute Getting to Know You Offer."

She laughed with me. "I come on strong, don't I? It's just that there's so much to see around here that doesn't have to do with a pointy witch's hat. Not that there's anything wrong with the pointy witch's hat, but when I get a live one in here, I can't help myself." She extended her hand. "I'm Holly."

"Luke."

"So what's on your mind today, Luke?"

"Not the usual Witch House tour. The people I want to impress have seen just about everything." No lie there if you included magical anacondas, enchanted waterfalls, and flying Buicks.

"That's excellent because I don't do the usual Witch House tour. I pride myself on revealing new facets of the rare diamond that is Salem, Massachusetts."

If anyone else had said that, I would have run for the exit. From Holly, it seemed sincere.

"So you don't believe in all that witch and sorcery stuff."

"Now don't go misquoting me, Luke. I never said I don't believe. I just said the story is a whole lot more interesting than wax museums and animatronic witches would lead you to think."

I decided to take a chance. "So you probably know about Bramford Light."

Her eyes widened. "*You* know about Bramford Light?"

Finally someone who didn't look at me like I was nuts.

"My friend heard about it from a business associate who grew up around here."

She narrowed her eyes in my direction. "How much do you actually *know* about the light?"

"Not close to enough."

"Honey, I can't give you a tour of Bramford Light. It's been gone since the War of

Independence."

Fifteen minutes and fifty dollars later, I was standing with Holly at the edge of the dock near the motel, looking toward the area where I'd seen that eerie glow.

"It was situated one hundred yards out," Holly was saying as she pointed to the same spot I had calculated earlier that morning. It just kept getting better and better. "They say the old man built it himself on a little spit of rock then tore it down in grief after he lost the woman he loved. Now even the spit of rock is gone."

"One man built a lighthouse?"

Holly gave a little shrug of her impressive shoulders. "Legends have a logic all their own."

"So how much of this legend do you believe?"

"All of it; none of it." She sighed. "The lighthouse was first mentioned in contemporaneous accounts some five years before the first hanging. It disappeared somewhere between 1776 and 1780."

I took a leap of faith. "I saw a beam out there last night."

"Join the club," Holly said. "Sailors have been seeing that light from Marblehead up to Rockport since the old man took it down.

But come daylight, there's never anything there."

"So how do they explain it?"

"They don't. I could show you hundreds of captains' logs that mention a strong beam of light that appeared just in time to save them from disaster then disappeared."

"Divine providence?"

"Or just plain good luck."

"Kinda makes you believe in magic, doesn't it."

"Honey," Holly said, "if you live in this world long enough and you don't believe in magic, there's something wrong with you."

"So who was the guy? Does he have a name?"

"The man who built the lighthouse was called Samuel."

"No last name?"

"Think about it," she said with a wink.

I groaned. "Bramford."

"Bingo."

"What else do you know about him besides the tragic love affair?"

"I know he came under scrutiny during the worst of the persecutions."

That caught my attention. "They thought he was a witch?"

"He was a healer," Holly said carefully. "That alone was enough to attract considerable attention during perilous times."

"But there's more."

She nodded. "There's more. I have a hard drive filled with more."

We drove back to her storefront in her faded blue Jeep. She locked the door behind us and flipped the sign to CLOSED.

"I'm taking up a hell of a lot of your time," I said. I tried to hand her another fifty but she refused. I was right. Holly was the real deal.

"This one's on me," she said. "My own private obsession, if you will. I'd like somebody else's take on it."

We sat down behind her desk and she booted up her computer.

"I have everything scanned," she said. "Some of the originals are in my possession; some are public domain; others are the property of various museums and private collections."

"You have my attention," I said.

"I thought so." She clicked a few times and a faded line drawing of a young man filled the screen.

I leaned closer. "Samuel?"

She nodded. "Around the time he began constructing the lighthouse."

She clicked the screen again. An oil portrait, good but not great, appeared.

"Samuel," I said. "Maybe fifteen years later." And they hadn't been good years. His eyes held a look of almost unbearable sorrow. I knew that look. I saw it in my mirror for years after Steffie died.

"You have a good eye."

"I'm a cop," I said. "I get paid to notice things."

"That would explain the questions." She distanced herself slightly from me. "Is there anything official about this visit?"

"No," I said. "Strictly personal."

She relaxed noticeably. That was the thing about being a cop. Guilty or not, most civilians immediately put up their defenses when we're around. Holly was no exception.

She clicked forward to another line drawing pulled from a newspaper published in early 1750. "Notice anything?"

I leaned as close to the screen as I could without distorting the image. "He hasn't aged."

"Now here's where the ride gets interesting."

Holly set a slide show in motion that took us through the eighteenth, nineteenth, and twentieth centuries. There he was on the docks with a group of fishermen and their daily catch around the time of Lexington and Concord. And there he was in the crowd celebrating a bank opening right after the Civil War. A church social around the turn of the twentieth century. A World War II bond drive.

Forrest Gump was alive and well and living in Salem.

"Anything more recent?" I asked.

"His image showed up in a tourist's blog post a few weeks ago but it's still in my To Scan file."

"We both know it can't be the same guy."

"Of course not," she said, "but there he is anyway." She aimed a smile in my direction. "You've already made the Forrest Gump analogy, haven't you?"

"About ten seconds ago."

"Logic says it's coincidental but my eyes tell me something else."

"How about your gut?" I asked.

"My gut says it's Samuel Bramford in all the pictures."

"Which is impossible."

"Honey," she said, patting my hand, "when you reach my age, you'll know nothing is impossible."

20

CHLOE

Most spinners agree that different wheels have different personalities. Some are smooth. Some are slow. Some fight you every inch of the way but produce sublime yarn.

But I never once heard about a wheel that hauled off and knocked the spinner off her feet.

I didn't see it coming. I was so busy staring at the yellow glitter and the infinity marking that everything else in the room faded away. The walking wheel in the far corner saw an opportunity and hit me in the head with its flyer.

Fortunately for me it was only a glancing blow but damn. You just don't think a spinning wheel is going to turn on you.

"Not funny," I said, refusing to rub my temple where the flyer made contact. "I saw the glitter. I saw the carving. I might as well see you, too."

I heard a scratching noise and turned to see the walking wheel moving in my direction. And it wasn't alone. Wheels of every era and style dropped from the ceiling, popped out of the walls, marched in from the hallway.

"Knock it off," I said, feigning more courage than I actually felt. "I've got matches and I'm not afraid to light them."

I turned around. Six Scottish castle wheels were lined up behind me like prison guards.

"This is old-school," I said, striving for a blend of scorn and laughter. "What's next: the poison apple?"

A long exasperated sigh filled the room. "Snow White bit the apple, child. Didn't those people of yours teach you anything? Sleeping Beauty pricked her finger on the wheel."

"Didn't your people teach you any manners?" I shot back. "Anonymity is the coward's way out."

The room erupted in raucous female laughter. Bursts of light encircled my ankles and wrapped themselves around my legs, twining their way up my torso like a kudzu vine. I batted away a phalanx of lights that were trying to turn themselves into a necklace.

Don't get scared, I warned myself. *Get angry.*

Fear diminished my powers. Anger made them stronger.

Strands of bright lights like a Christmas tree string with attitude slashed through the air in front of my face, leaving a trail of heat behind.

Oh, crap. I suddenly realized what they were. Fae drones acting as a scouting party for a clan leader. They were mapping my body, determining strengths and weaknesses, and reporting back.

And, if memory served, they wouldn't hesitate to inflict a little collateral damage along the way.

One of the Scottish wheels bumped me from the back. Before I could respond, another bumped me harder. Then a third bump and a fourth.

"Knock it off," I warned. "You really want to stop doing this."

Which led to being knocked to the ground again by the last two Scottish wheels.

I scrambled to get up but an Ashford sailed across the room and slammed into my right shoulder. A moment later, a Louet slammed into my left. Kromskis, Schachts, Lendrums rained down on me like giant hailstones. I was crouched on the floor with my arms protecting my head like someone in one of those Cold War–era end-of-the-world movies. I never understood how your back could save you from an atom bomb but my back was doing a pretty good job absorbing the blows from the attacking wheels.

And in case you didn't know it, wheels are ferocious fighters. Sure, they look all fragile and unassuming, but, trust me, they kicked my ass pretty good.

The only thing more embarrassing than having my clock cleaned by a spinning wheel would be getting mugged by a harp.

Where was my anger? Where was my fire? I had nothing. The more the spinning wheels pounded me, the deeper I sank into submission.

This wasn't like me at all. Exhaustion turned my arms and legs to rubber. I was having trouble keeping my thoughts together. I felt like the Scarecrow in *The Wizard of Oz* after the Wicked Witch of the West scattered him across the cornfield.

"No wonder she lost Sugar Maple," a disembodied female voice said. "She's utterly incompetent."

"Stupid, I'd say." Another female voice. "Look at her lying there like a mollusk."

"Poor thing can't help herself," a third

female voice added. "She lacks courage."

"So true, sister," a fourth female intoned. "She lacked the courage to claim her town before it was too late."

"It's in the blood. Look to her clan to see the reason," said a fifth.

"She chose the side of the humans, same as her mother, and her human blood will be her downfall," the first voice said. "And after all these centuries, we will be here to watch it happen."

Their voices rose and fell, and new voices joined them, jumbled and filled with both scorn and amusement. I couldn't listen. I refused to listen. They were wrong. I loved Sugar Maple. I had done everything in my power to save it from being dragged beyond the mist. I might not know exactly what did happen but I could tell you with certainty that the town hadn't entered the Fae portal at the waterfall.

I felt a surge of anger and looked at my fingertips, expecting to see them start to redden before shooting out flames that I hoped would torch this place to the ground.

But there was nothing.

I had the sense that the life force was leaving me but I didn't know where or how. My legs were wobbly. My vision was starting to blur. I sensed that my thought processes weren't as clear as they'd been ten minutes earlier. I hadn't battled demons and walked away triumphant so I could die buried beneath a pile of mass-produced spinning wheels.

If I'd had the energy I would have laughed out loud at the thought. I mean, stabbed by Addi Lace circular needles, maybe. Or trapped in a web of sticky Outback Mohair or even driven insane by dropped stitches in a five-hundred-plus-stitch bind-off. At least there would be some knitterly dignity involved.

Then get up.

The baritone voice was rich and compelling and it seemed to be centered deep inside my chest.

You can do this, Chloe. You must or Sugar Maple will be doomed forever.

My ribs vibrated at the sound.

Who are you? I sent the thought out into the universe but it bounced straight back to me.

Do it now! Trust your heart to know the truth.

Now what was that supposed to mean? If I ever became Queen of the Other Dimensions I was going to permanently ban fortune-cookie talk.

Trust my heart to do what? Quit speaking in

riddles, Voice, and tell me what to do.

I felt the answer before I heard it.

You could start by getting up.

Trust me to harbor an uninvited inner wiseass.

One of the Scottish castles reared back and rolled into my side like a battering ram. Damn those fragile wheels anyway. They could really pack a wallop. What was I going to do, lie there until I finally succumbed to a vindictive travel wheel while those invisible harpies took bets on how long it would take Luke to find someone else?

Well, yeah. That was exactly what would happen if I didn't do what the Voice said and get off my sorry butt and fight back.

I shook the pile of wheels off my back the way a dog shakes off water after a bath. They flew across the room and smashed into the walls, sending splinters of wood flying in all directions. The spinner in me felt a sharp pang of regret but the sorceress thought it was kind of cool. My legs were wobbly but I managed to stay vertical as I blocked a dive-bombing electric drum carder with my forearm.

The drum carder was followed by a phalanx of niddy-noddies, which were followed by a barrage of spindles that made me feel like London during the Blitz. I swatted them away like mosquitoes. Flames shot from my fingertips. Arrows of lightning shot from my eyes.

And then it was over.

No trumpets blaring. No cheering crowds.

Wheels rolled back up the hallway. Wheels slid back against the walls. Drum carders, niddy-noddies, spindles, and combs settled themselves back where they'd come from. In the blink of an eye, I found myself standing near the Irish castle wheel once again with my hand resting lightly along the satiny wood. The heady scent of beeswax and potpourri and history was everywhere.

So was the feeling I was being watched. Suddenly I had to get out of there.

I turned toward the door but the door wasn't there and then the wheel wasn't there and suddenly the shop lifted up and up and up and sailed off into the blue sky like a birthday balloon and left me standing alone on a rock on an island in the middle of the ocean.

The only thing missing was the massive tidal wave with my name on it.

I looked behind me and saw a tornado of water whipping my way.

Who said you couldn't have it all?

21

LUKE

I said good-bye to Holly a little after one o'clock and only because she had a tour group waiting for her in town.

"Take this," she said, handing me a thick brown envelope. "I printed off some of the scans for you. Maybe you'll put your cop instincts to work and figure this all out for me."

I thanked her for her time and tried once more to pay her for her expertise but she was having none of it.

"I should pay you," she said. "You're the first person who's ever shown the slightest interest in poor old Samuel."

"I like a good mystery," I said, feeling a little shitty for withholding the truth from her. "And you're one damn fine storyteller."

She glanced at her watch. "But not much of a businesswoman. My tour awaits." She kissed me on my left cheek and then on my right. "Let me know about a tour and I'll block out the time."

I owe you one, I thought as I watched her hurry off. With a little luck, I'd have the chance to pay her back soon.

Thanks to Holly, I had the Sugar Maple version of the Holy Grail and I couldn't wait to tell Chloe what I'd uncovered about Samuel Bramford and the lighthouse that bore his name. I couldn't prove anything, not in the human definition of proof, but my gut told me I had stumbled onto the key we needed to unlock a few doors.

I was deep in thought when a small woman with long, shiny white hair appeared in my path and stopped me cold.

"Sorry," I said, dodging around her. "I wasn't watching where I was going."

She was in front of me again.

"Sorry again," I said and dodged the other way.

I swear she didn't move, didn't take a single step. She was just there.

Her eyes were light gray, so light they were almost devoid of color. The hairs on the back of my neck lifted.

"I've been waiting." Crystal earrings, pale as her eyes, swung with the nodding motion of her head. "I never gave up hope."

Apparently crazy wasn't limited to big cities. I nodded politely and tried again to get around her. She was a little old for the goth thing and I was a little old to care.

"Tell her." A slender alabaster hand snaked out from under one enormous sleeve and gripped my forearm. "Tell Chloe he's waiting."

She was gone before I could say a word, which was probably a good thing because I couldn't have come up with anything coherent if I tried.

Except: "Who the hell is *he?*"

Kind of took the edge off being right about Salem.

We'd agreed to meet at noon and I was over an hour late already. I jogged back to the motel and let myself into the room I shared with Chloe.

"Chloe!" I called out. "You here?"

Not many places in a room-plus-bathroom to hide.

I rapped on the connecting door to Janice's room. "Anyone there?"

The lock clicked and the door opened.

"I hope you brought food," Janice said as Penny the cat burst into the room. "I've been eyeing the Fancy Feast."

"I thought you could go days without eating."

She ignored my comment. "Any bagels

215

left over from this morning?"

I pointed to the desk. "Help yourself."

She grabbed one and tore into it. "So where's Chloe?"

"I thought she was with you."

I shook my head. "We were going to meet back here."

"No sign of her."

"She didn't call?"

"I would've told you."

I raised my hands palms outward. "No problem. I'm just asking."

"Sorry," she said, looking as contrite as it was possible for the redoubtable Janice Meany to look. "I get cranky when I'm hungry."

"No luck working the phones?"

She tore off another piece of bagel. "I tried to link into the Wiccan and pagan communities but I kept getting voice mail. I left messages but no call-backs."

"Why not try blueflame?"

"If I blueflamed a human I'd be arrested for arson."

I kept forgetting the difference between magic and the Wiccan religion.

She popped the bagel into her mouth, chewed, then swallowed. "How'd you do?"

I gestured toward the thick brown envelope on the bed. "I'll tell you when Chloe gets here. Too much to go through twice."

"Not even a hint?"

"How about a couple of questions instead?"

She nodded.

"Was Aerynn pregnant when she left Salem?"

Janice gave a bark of laughter. "That was over three hundred years ago! How would I know?"

"I thought you knew all the old stories and legends about Sugar Maple's early years."

"Lilith is the real expert," she said modestly, referring to the beautiful Norwegian troll who served as town librarian and historian. "But I can hold my own."

"Haven't you ever wondered who fathered Aerynn's children?"

"I never much thought about it."

"It wasn't an immaculate conception."

"And it wasn't happily ever after either," Janice shot back at me.

"And you know that how?"

"The fact that Hobbs women are notorious losers when it comes to love. That's part of their heritage."

They loved only once and not always wisely. Janice didn't say those words but I heard them just the same.

"It'll be different for Chloe and me," I said.

Janice just gave me a *we'll see* kind of smile.

"So was Aerynn's first child born in Sugar Maple?"

"First child?" Janice's look changed subtly. "You mean, her only child."

"I didn't know she only had one child."

Now she looked downright uncomfortable. "Hobbs women always have only one child," she said. "A girl."

"You're kidding."

"Historically proven fact."

"Is it something biological?"

"That would be one hell of a coincidence, don't you think?"

She had me there. One child. Always a girl. The link remained unbroken.

We dropped the subject by unspoken mutual agreement. I put the information aside for some other day.

Janice applied herself to the task of eating her way through the remaining bagels. I dialed Chloe's cell phone but it flipped immediately to voice mail.

"I'm at the motel with Janice," I said. "It's twenty after one. Call me."

I checked for messages. Returned a few. Ignored the rest. The ice-eyed woman's message repeated itself on an endless loop inside my brain. Better than an endless loop of Janice's revelation about the Hobbs women and their reproductive pattern. I turned on the television then turned it off again. Janice was standing by the window, looking out at the water.

Penny the cat was —

"Where's Penny?" I asked.

"Asleep on the bed," Janice said.

"Not on this bed."

"She was there a minute ago."

"Check your room," I said. "I'll check the bathroom."

Janice was looking under her bed when I walked into her room.

"Shit," I said. "She's gone."

"She can't be gone," Janice said as she stood up and brushed dust off her jeans. "The doors are closed and so are the windows."

"She's still gone."

"Chloe's going to kill me," Janice said.

"Probably," I said, "but Chloe's not here either."

"You think there's some kind of connection?"

"We're in Witch City looking for a way to bring a magic town back into our dimension. I think everything's connected."

Her gaze drifted to the sliding doors and her brown eyes widened.

"What?" I asked. "Is something wrong?"

She dashed across the room and bent down in front of the doors. "Do you see that?" she asked, pointing toward the metal runner that held the doors in place.

"The floor? The door frame?"

"The glitter."

"Shit," I said. "Tell me you're kidding."

"I'm not kidding. The floor is thick with spruce green, chartreuse, and burgundy glitter." She stood up and ran over to the closet. She flung the door open. "More burgundy. This place is infested with Fae."

"With talk like that, it's no wonder there's a problem between you."

"You don't really think you're being funny, do you?"

I did, but this didn't seem like the time to explain my family's penchant for black humor. "Can you identify anyone?"

She shook her head. "These colors are all new to me. It has to be locals." She stood and tugged at the hem of her hot pink T-shirt. "You know what this means."

Hell, yeah. I was a cop, wasn't I? "Either the Fae reestablished here after the witch troubles faded away —"

"Or some of them never left to begin

with," she finished for me.

"And now Chloe's gone."

"And Penny," Janice added.

"I don't give a —"

"Yes, you do."

She was right. I did. Penny the cat was inextricably linked with Chloe and Sugar Maple and probably to Salem as well.

"Grab your stuff," I said. "We need to find them now."

"I'm not going out there."

"You can't stay here alone."

"You can't force me. In case you forgot, I have magick."

"Go for it," I said. "Like it or not, we'd better stick together." I softened my tone. "You know I'm right, Janice."

Her eyes brimmed with tears. "I don't know anything."

I rested a hand on her shoulder for a moment. "Me neither," I said.

We agreed that we needed to concentrate our efforts on finding Chloe. It wasn't like Penny had shimmied through a pet door or slipped out while we were getting the mail. The cat had made an escape worthy of Houdini. She'd be found when she wanted to be found and not before.

And unless I missed my guess, she'd be with Chloe.

"You're the detective," Janice said. "How do we start detecting?"

"Try blueflame," I suggested. "See if Chloe answers."

Janice cupped her hands, focused deep, then yelped as blue flames shot up her arms all the way to the shoulders.

I didn't know whether to pour water over her or arrange an exorcism.

"That's a first," she said, waving her arms around like a windmill.

"On to step two," I said to Janice. "Clock's ticking."

She dashed into her room, gathered up a big bag full of stuff, then slung the bag over her shoulder. "Ready."

Except there was one problem: I couldn't open the door.

"Shit," I said, jiggling the doorknob. "The damn cat locked us in."

Janice struggled to suppress a grin. "You don't really think the cat did it."

"The hell I don't. We're here. She's not. Do the math." Another thing your average dog would never do.

"Let me try." Janice grabbed the doorknob, jiggled it, then let loose a string of curses.

Okay, there were two doors. We'd use the one in her room.

Except that door was locked, too.

"We could go out the sliding door. The balcony's about ten feet off the ground." A pretty easy jump.

Janice looked appropriately horrified. "Wait here," she said and in a puff of deep purple smoke, she disappeared.

Two seconds later the room door opened and I saw a black and white needle-nosed bird standing on the other side. The bird looked smug.

"Janice?" This stuff never got old.

A few feathers were lost in the process but she managed to resume her normal packaging. "That's how you open a door," she said.

"Beats the hell out of using the key," I admitted. "But why didn't you just magic me out with you?"

"Not part of my skill set. I'd probably scramble your atoms and send half of you to Poughkeepsie."

The staircase was at the far end of the walkway. We were almost there when a yowl split the air and I saw Penny the cat balanced on the railing that overlooked the parking lot.

Janice made a move toward her but I held her back.

"Wait," I warned her. "It could be a trick."

"It's Penny."

"Probably," I said, "but that cat had it in for me yesterday. I'll bet this is part of her scheme."

"All she did was climb a tree, MacKenzie. Get over it."

"She put me in some kind of damn coma, Janice."

"And you're fine now. What's your point?" She got in my face. "This is Penny we're talking about. Put your human limitations aside and think about it. If something happens to Penny, Chloe will be devastated."

"She's a thousand years old." I was exaggerating but not by much. "She's survived wars, pestilence, you name it. An afternoon in the Salem sun won't kill her."

But what if it did? Since I met Chloe, I had seen the impossible happen every day. Just because something had never happened before didn't mean today wouldn't be the day that it did.

"Okay," I said. "We'll get the cat."

Another yowl right on cue. I looked over at Janice and did my best Spock eyebrow lift.

There was nothing worse than being played by a cat.

"You've had your fun, salmon breath," I said, moving slowly toward her.

She hissed softly.

Janice reached into her pocket and pulled out a piece of bagel. "Come on, Pen. You know you love it."

If she did, she'd forgotten. She began a slow, stalking kind of prowl along the rail.

Another reason why I was a dog person. Dogs didn't tightrope walk along railings fifteen feet above the ground.

"Here, kitty kitty." I felt like a jerk but whatever worked. "Here, kitty."

The look of scorn on Penny's face made me cringe.

"Do something," I said to Janice. "You're the one with powers. Cast a spell on her."

"I can't."

"What do you mean, you can't?"

"Penny's powers are stronger than mine at the best of times. Besides, that whole key business drained my reserve. I've got nothing right now."

Just what I needed to hear.

Penny shot me a look, hawked up a hairball that would do a mountain lion proud, then leaped from the railing to the grassy slope below. She shook out her fur, examined her right front paw, then ambled slowly toward the cove beyond.

"I don't believe it!" Janice dashed toward the hairball balanced on the railing.

"She hawks one up every day," I said, adding that to the list of things dogs don't do. "I don't think we need to alert the media."

"I forgot you can't see it."

"I see enough."

"You don't understand." She peered down at the disgusting lump of wet fur like it was a rare diamond. "There's glitter all through it."

It took me a second. "You mean, like Fae glitter?"

"Exactly like Fae glitter." She met my eyes. "They were using Penny to stop us."

"Past tense?"

"We can hope."

"I'm going after her."

"I'm right behind you."

I scaled the railing, lowered myself as far as I could, then jumped.

"Never mind," Janice called after me. "I'll take the stairs."

Penny was faster than she seemed. What looked to the eye like a casual saunter was actually hauling ass. I broke into a sprint but no matter how fast I went I couldn't seem to gain any distance on her.

Where was she going? Cats hated water. If she kept running like that, she'd be in for a major dunking.

I accelerated.

So did she.

Another fifty yards and she'd be in the water.

Correction: She wasn't in the water, she was on the water. Sitting on the water, to be precise, licking her left front paw between lazy yawns.

Damn, that cat was good.

I hit the water hard. It was New England cold, which meant cold enough to snap a few bones. The depth went from ankle to over my head in a single step and I quickly started treading water. Penny, still casually grooming herself, paid no attention. I broke into an easy crawl. I wasn't exactly sure what I would do when I reached the cat but first I had to get there.

Another twenty feet . . . ten . . . five . . .

Penny stopped grooming.

"Come on, girl," I whispered. "Don't get spooked. Timmy's trapped in the mine."

A dog would have gotten the joke.

Penny stood up. She stretched. I moved closer, angling so my left shoulder was pressed up against her. Cats loved sitting on shoulders. I'd seen Penny riding around on Chloe's shoulder a million times.

Her nails were razor sharp as she climbed aboard. She really did smell like salmon.

"Thought about Jenny Craig lately?" I murmured as I struggled to keep her above the water level.

She swatted at me with a lazy paw.

"You've got her!" Janice yelled from the shore. "Don't let go!"

I felt something moving beneath me. The way things were going, it was probably a great white. I tried to move out of its way but it came closer, tugging at my legs. In fact, I was pretty sure there were more than one of whatever was down there.

"Come on!" Janice bellowed. "What's taking so long?"

Damn. What the hell was going on? I tried kicking free but a hand — at least I thought it was a hand — grabbed my right ankle and pulled. I kicked out with my left foot but a hand grabbed that ankle, too.

I was starting to feel like a wishbone on Thanksgiving.

Good thing I had something your average wishbone didn't: the protective charm Chloe had woven around me back on the highway. Maybe all I had to do was roll with the punches and see where I ended up.

And maybe I still believe in Santa Claus. . . .

The hands on my ankles tugged harder and I sank beneath the waves. What the hell? My eyes were open and through the salty murkiness I saw mermaids floating beneath me while Penny flailed desperately above, clawing at the water with her mouth open wide in a silent howl.

The mermaids grabbed at my legs, which in another context might not be half bad. I squinted into the dim light and saw Janice struggling a few feet away from Penny with a look of total panic in her eyes. She was wrapped head to foot in a fisherman's net.

I kicked out at the mermaids but they were tenacious. They wrapped themselves around my legs like barnacles and started pulling me deeper into the water. Penny had attached herself to the netting around Janice and the two of them were looking toward me, the resident human, for help.

Cultural conditioning is a tough thing to break. I'd never struck a woman in my life and, if the curve factor was any indication, the mermaids who surrounded us were definitely female. But when the females in question were trying to kill you, all bets were off.

I kicked hard. Two mermaids, a brunette and a blonde, loosened their grip and that was all I needed. I launched myself through the suddenly warm, murky water toward where I'd seen Janice and Penny. My lungs were screaming for air. My brain was seaweed. I kept pushing forward, praying the first thing I bumped into was a red-haired witch from Sugar Maple and not a shark with a taste for B negative.

My fingers grazed something thin and ropelike. Fisherman's net! I wrapped my arms around a struggling Janice and ignored the fact that Penny was being turned into a cat sandwich between us because suddenly those mermaids got behind me and pushed.

You know that feeling you get when you stand at the edge of a cliff and look down?

This was worse.

Janice, Penny the cat, and I rocketed down toward the ocean floor like we were jet-propelled. The glide was eerily smooth, as if we were being cushioned within a tube of air.

Which, as it turned out, we were. I didn't know how long the pocket of air would last, but my lungs gulped in as much as they could take. I tapped Janice and showed her I was breathing, then ran a finger along Penny's whiskers. She opened her mouth in protest and the look of surprise on her feline face when she started to breathe again was priceless.

"Luke!" Janice's voice was weak and raspy. "What's happening?"

"Don't know," I said and warned her not to waste oxygen talking.

When you found yourself rocketing across the ocean floor in a tunnel of air, things were pretty much out of your control.

It was like going to Sea World except that you were the one in the big tank. It was too early for striped bass but cod and big-eyed black oreo dory and serene haddock peered in at us. Somehow I didn't think Penny would ever look at her can of Fancy Feast seafood special the same way again.

I was beginning to wonder if this was going to end up with us being shoveled into a whale's mouth, when the trajectory suddenly angled up and the tube was flooded with brilliant white light and, like it or not, we were heading straight into it.

22

CHLOE

Nothing prepared a girl for being swept up inside a waterspout. I don't care how many times you've seen *Twister:* watching Helen Hunt and Bill Paxton cower under a bridge won't help you one bit.

I mean, who would have expected the impact to be softer than a whisper? Or that the sensation of piercing the funnel would be like stepping into one of those fancy multijet showers like Janice had installed in the spa section of her salon? The water was silky soft, fragrant with lavender and a touch of pine. Warm . . . buoyant . . . deeply relaxing. If Janice could harness this sensation for her spa, she would rule the world.

The fight left me in a giant whoosh and I settled back into the cocoon of warmth that happened to be a giant waterspout. Nobody sane wanted to spend even a second in the eye of any storm, much less one as poten-

tially deadly as a water-fed tornado, but the sense of peace I experienced was narcotic. I wanted as much of it as I could get.

The words **Don't worry** resonated inside me like a mantra. My anxieties about Luke and Janice and Penny the cat, about Sugar Maple and the friends I loved and our combined future, all vanished.

I suddenly realized I was being held aloft by an army of knitters, dozens of them, all in period dress, kindred spirits from across the centuries. Hippies and flappers, Gibson Girls and Civil War belles, Colonials and rustic early settlers. They laced their hands together and kept me from going under. They whispered my name like a litany in tones that were warm and loving and strangely comforting. I tried to speak but no sound came out. There was only the soft rush of their voices filling the spaces where the water wasn't.

My sense of direction was suspect in the best of times even with landmarks and street signs and GPS to help me out. Put me in the middle of a churning steel-blue sea and I might as well be on Mars. Land was nothing but a memory. The sky melted into the ocean. The ocean was absorbed into the sky. I didn't know if I was flying or drowning. I only knew that I was safe.

I was drifting away, in danger of disappearing altogether, when a beam of silvery light pierced through all of that nothingness and a small white and black lighthouse rose up in the distance.

My mind turned into white noise. My heart skidded into my ribs. My breath caught deep in my throat. All of the adrenaline that hadn't flooded my veins when I saw that funnel of water broke free now. I felt like I'd consumed two pots of espresso on an empty stomach. I wasn't exactly scared but I was alert in a way that was almost painful.

The lighthouse grew closer. Except for the size differential, it was identical to the kitschy ten-foot-tall replica that resided in the center of Sugar Maple. I had always wondered about the significance but chalked it up to another simple homage to Salem, same as the names we'd chosen for our streets and bridge.

A shimmering gold and silver pathway unfurled from the base of the lighthouse. I rose to my feet, balancing effortlessly on the foamy waves, and stepped onto it. I wished Luke was there with me and at the same time I was glad that he wasn't. I don't remember walking but somehow I found myself standing in front of a whitewashed

door with a tarnished knocker in the shape of an anchor.

I rapped twice, feeling like I was in the middle of one of those movies where everyone but the heroine knew what was waiting on the other side of the door.

You don't have to do this. You can use your magick and leave.

I would be lying if I said I didn't consider it. I've never been a big fan of the unknown. If I had my way, the future would come with a trailer so you could check out the coming attractions.

I lifted the knocker to rap again, when I heard a shuffling sound on the other side of the door and a crackly voice mumbling something that sounded like "Hold your horses. I don't have wings on my feet like others I know."

The door swung open. At first I didn't see anyone but then I looked down and my eyes landed on a very small, very round woman with a rosy, wrinkled face and spiky hair the color of buttercups.

"Takes you three hundred years to show up and you expect me to run to the door the second you knock. Well, girlie, that's not how it works around here."

"Sorry," I said, bristling at her tone, "but this wasn't my idea."

"Oh, a fresh one you are." She looked up at me with enormous deep brown eyes. "Not exactly what Himself is expecting."

Himself? "So you didn't bring me here?"

Her laugh was a cross between a cackle and a crow. "I'm not one for bringing trouble in when there's enough to be found close to home. It was Himself and he may regret it."

"May I come in?"

I found myself standing in a foyer the size of a postage stamp.

"I'm Chloe," I said, extending my right hand.

She dismissed it with a look. "I know who you be. You're lucky it's not too late."

"Too late for what?"

"As if you didn't know."

"I don't know."

"You wait here," she said, "and don't you be touching anything what isn't yours."

Which pretty much took in everything but the clothes on my back.

I had never been inside a lighthouse. The smell of the sea was strong and a faint mist glazed the exposed brick walls. A circular staircase dominated the area and I laughed in surprise when the old woman swirled around it like smoke up a chimney.

I stopped laughing a second later when it

was my turn to be swirled sideways through a whitewashed wooden door into what looked like an eighteenth-century dentist's waiting room.

A moment later the side of the wall unzipped and Luke, Janice, and Penny tumbled in on a frothy wave of seawater that spilled across the floor and lapped at my ankles.

"Luke!"

The look in his eyes almost made me forget we were trapped in a lighthouse in the middle of the ocean.

He held me so tight I could barely breathe. "I was afraid I'd lost you."

"Impossible," I whispered into his ear. "Never happen."

Penny, who had been watching us, chose that moment to hawk up a hairball of truly monumental proportions.

"Editorial comment," Janice said. "Better watch out or I'll do it, too."

Luke and I separated reluctantly.

"Anyone have any idea what's going on?" I asked.

"We were going to ask you," Janice said. "How'd you get here?"

I gave a casual shrug. "Just your usual tidal wave and a squad of female naval operatives."

"We can beat that," Luke said with a grin. "How about a half dozen knockout mermaids."

Janice shot him a look. "Knockout mermaids?" she asked. "What ocean were you in?"

"You saw them," he said. "Playboy centerfolds with flippers."

This time Janice couldn't stifle the laughter. "Hello. Bea Arthur with fins? Angela Lansbury topless with a tail? The Wicked Witch from *Wizard of Oz* without her —" She peered at him closely. "Did you ever actually see their faces?"

"No," Luke said. "They had their backs to me."

Janice waved her hands around in the air in a kind of figure eight pattern and a screen opened up between us. "Take a look."

I wasn't about to miss this. I positioned myself in front of the screen right next to Luke.

There he was in crystal clear HD, struggling against the current as he tried to save Penny, when six supple, sinuous mermaids appeared out of the murky depths then pulled him beneath the surface. It was easy to see why sailors crashed their boats on the rocks just to be near them. The allure crossed all boundaries. I felt the nasty pinch of jealousy.

Are we having fun yet?

"Keep watching," Janice said with a wink for me. "You don't want to miss the big reveal."

"This isn't going to end well, is it?" Luke mumbled as the mermaids spiraled toward the camera.

"Oh, I think it ends just fine," Janice said, starting to laugh again.

She was right. The mermaid with the long mane of golden hair was a Bea Arthur lookalike. The redhead could have been Angela Lansbury's twin sister circa now. I thought the brunette looked suspiciously like old news clips of Mamie Eisenhower but I would have to Google to be sure.

"Don't go feeling too sorry for yourself," I said, trying very hard not to laugh, "but the spirits have a sense of humor."

"I'm not sure how funny this is," Janice said, "but the motel rooms showed signs of Fae infestation."

My laughter quickly stopped. "I saw glitter at the antique shop." I told them about the Attack of the Spinning Wheels.

"Did you recognize any of the glitter-prints?" Janice asked.

I shook my head. "Did you?"

"Nobody," Janice said, "but I'm pretty

sure I recognized two branches: the Weavers and the Olivers."

The Weavers owned the Sugar Maple Inn and up until Luke came to town, I had counted the family among my closest friends. "The Olivers are the new family who moved down from Ottawa, right?"

Janice nodded.

"I know them," Luke said. "Are you saying the Olivers might be ringers?"

"I'm just saying there's a link between the Olivers and these Salem glitterprints," Janice said.

A quick survey of the room revealed nothing.

"How long have you been here?" Janice asked me.

"A few seconds longer than you," I said. "Did you see that ancient yellow-haired gatekeeper?"

"Only Luke's mermaids," Janice said with a broad wink.

Luke stood up and I realized we were all somehow clean and dry again. I'd worry about the how of it later. Right now I was relieved to have one less problem. His gaze traveled the room in that methodical way he had as he filled us in on the information on Bramford Light that he'd gathered from the tour operator in town.

"Do you think that's where we are?" Janice asked.

"Pretty safe bet." He paced the small waiting area. "You'd think somebody would come out and tell us something."

"You wouldn't say that if you'd met Buttercup." I told them a little about the curmudgeonly housekeeper and her concern for Himself.

"Himself?" Luke said. "What the hell? Did we wash up on the shores of Massachusetts or Ballycastle?"

"Who knows," I said. "We could be anywhere."

"We're still in Salem," Janice said. "I can feel it all around us."

"Are we alone?" Luke asked.

Janice hesitated. "Not quite."

"Not the Fae," I said, feeling my adrenaline surge.

"I don't think so," Janice said, glancing around at our surroundings. "Not unless they've come up with invisible glitter."

"Then who?" Luke asked.

We didn't have to wait long for an answer.

23

LUKE

Chloe was the first one to disappear up the spiral staircase. A second later Janice swirled around the curving structure in her wake. Penny scampered after them under her own power.

Then it was my turn.

I'd been transported before. I knew I was going to feel like a fry pan of scrambled eggs by the time it was over. But take away the whole surprise-slash-fear factor and it was actually kind of cool in a Harry Potter sort of way.

A little grinch of a woman was waiting at the top of the staircase. Her face looked like a dried apple. Her hair was crayon yellow. Her personality made some perps I'd known seem like Mr. Congeniality.

She had Chloe separated from the herd on the other side of the round room. Janice and I stood awkwardly at the top of the staircase.

"What did I tell you?" the crone scolded Chloe who was motionless. "Don't you even think about moving a muscle, missy."

I stepped forward. "What the hell are you —"

Bad idea. A jolt of electricity shocked its way through my body, knocking me flat on my ass at Janice's feet.

Chloe whirled on the gatekeeper. "Touch him again and I'll blast you into the next dimension." Bolts of fiery lightning from her fingertips punctuated her threat.

"He's human," the crone said. "He has no place here."

"I'm half human," she shot back. "Do I have a place here?"

The old woman opened her wizened mouth to speak but stopped suddenly.

That's all, Elspeth. You can go now.

The voice was baritone and it filled the room. I looked around for speakers but wasn't surprised to find none.

Janice made a small noise and wrapped her arms across her chest. Penny leaped to her feet and ran a circle around the room. Chloe's eyes widened slightly as she locked gazes with me over the crone's frizzled yellow head.

She didn't know what was going on either. Damn.

"Don't be telling me what to do after all these years," the crone declared. "I won't be bringing a human close unless I know the reason why."

That's enough, Elspeth. The voice seemed to push out the walls with its power.

Angry Elspeth sizzled like a hot pan of bacon. I could feel the heat from ten feet away. Chloe stepped between us, almost daring the crone to make a move.

"You have no business here, missy," Elspeth said, shaking a gnarled finger in Chloe's direction. "Don't be thinking you can take advantage of Himself just because you lost Sugar Maple and need —"

Elspeth! The room shook with the force of his voice.

The yellow-haired crone was gone before the sound faded from the room.

Penny sniffed cautiously at the spot where the old woman had been standing then quickly backed away.

"She's not really gone," Chloe said, bending down to scratch Penny behind her right ear. "Listen."

It took a moment but I heard the woman's voice, creating soft eddies of sound without meaning.

"She's cloaking," Janice said. "Wow!"

"I know," Chloe said. "I'm years away from even attempting it."

"Cloaking?" I asked. "You mean like the Klingon Bird of Prey in *Star Trek*?"

Chloe nodded. "But we thought of it first."

Another reminder that we weren't in Kansas anymore.

"How long do you think they're going to keep us waiting?" I asked Janice and Chloe.

"Who knows," Chloe said. "It's all up to them now."

Calm, patient Zen master Chloe? That would take a little getting used to.

Chloe wandered over to the huge gray-blue wingback chair that was angled near one of the three visible windows. A book lay open and facedown on the seat cushion. A basket of lemon yellow yarn sat between the chair and the wall with a pair of long ivory knitting needles stabbed into the center of the woolly mass.

"That's just so wrong," she said, removing the needles and laying them across the yarn.

"What makes it wrong?" I asked. "Seems like the logical place to stow the needles."

"If you want to split your yarn and destroy a friendship."

"And deplete the rain forest?" I asked.

"I'm serious," she said. "If you ever start

245

knitting, don't do it."

Not much danger there.

Curved bookshelves hugged an expanse of wall. Chloe hurried over to investigate.

"*Moby-Dick.* Leather-bound first edition," she said, running a finger along the spine. "Don't you love that?"

I shrugged. I was more a Tom Clancy/ Robert B. Parker fan myself.

She continued along the shelf. "Hemingway's *Old Man and the Sea.* Sebastian Junger's *The Perfect Storm* in hardcover *and* paperback. A stack of captain's logs from who knows when." She bent down and grabbed a huge stack of magazines from the bottom shelf.

"Janice!" Her voice was practically a squeal. "Knitting magazines! Including —"

"*Interweaave Knits,* Spring 2004?" Janice said. "The one with the Marilyn sweater on the cover?"

"The very issue."

Chloe and Janice broke into the knitter's version of the happy dance, which, considering the fact we'd been kidnapped to a lighthouse that may or may not be real in the middle of an ocean that may or may not be real, seemed a hell of a lot like slow dancing to the *Titanic* orchestra.

But maybe that was just me.

I pulled one of the magazines off the shelf. "What's with the red sticker on the spine?" At least six of the stack had been labeled that way. Mine also had a yellow Post-it flag affixed to a page near the back cover.

Chloe pulled another one from the stack. She flipped to a middle page with a yellow Post-it flag.

Janice did the same.

All three pages contained glowing references to either Chloe or Sticks & Strings.

"I'm not sure if I'm creeped out or flattered," Chloe said, sliding the magazines back onto the stack.

"Depends who's keeping track," I said.

Chloe forced a laugh. "I'm pretty sure old Elspeth isn't keeping a scrapbook for me."

Too bad old Elspeth had uncloaked and was standing next to Chloe with a rolled-up parchment clutched in her left hand.

"If I had my way, missy, you'd be sent back where you came from and no two ways about it."

"Go for it." Chloe didn't bat an eye. "Send us back to Sugar Maple and save my Buick some heavy mileage."

Janice's eyes were watchful as Chloe assumed a confrontational stance. Penny oversaw everything from an extremely narrow windowsill to my right.

Elspeth made a sweeping motion with the tube of parchment and a soft line of light unspooled toward the rear of the room. Or the front. Or maybe one of the sides. It was hard to tell when the room in question was round.

"Follow it," Elspeth said, motioning with the paper, "but know this: Harm one hair on his head and know my wrath, missy. Make no mistake."

"I don't even know who *he* is," Chloe said. "Why would I want to harm him?"

"I know your kind," she said, shooing us along. I had the feeling she would bite our ankles if we weren't quick enough for her. "Now go. He's waiting."

She said *he* the way other people said *Your Majesty* or *Your Holiness.*

"Who is he?" Chloe asked as we followed the line of light around the curve. "A name would be nice."

The crone clamped her plump lips shut and made another shooing motion with her apron.

We rounded the staircase. Natural light spilled through the window and splashed across the wide-planked pine floor.

"Over here, Chloe." The baritone voice again, but closer. I detected the slight raspiness of age scuffing up the mellow tones.

The light in this part of the structure was shaded by an opaque ivory curtain and my eyes took a moment to adjust to the change. The room was sparsely furnished with a dark pine table, a spinning wheel, and some baskets filled with wool.

"Come closer, Chloe," the man with the baritone voice said.

I sensed rather than saw him but that was enough. I worked in a world where control was everything. Lose control and you would probably lose your life. This situation was out of our control. A disembodied voice held all the cards and once Chloe took her first step toward him, the game was his for the taking.

The old man was seated in a wooden rocker near the window. The cop side of my brain registered the details I would process later. He wore faded gray pants, heavy workman's boots, and one of those heavily cabled fisherman's sweaters Chloe loved to knit. She said every fisherman's sweater told a story. I wondered what his was.

The guy looked the way an old salt should look. His skin was deeply wrinkled and permanently tanned from the sun. He boasted a full head of white hair that fell like a lion's mane to his shoulders. His eyes were deep and hooded. I couldn't make out the color from where I stood but my money was on blue.

In his portraits, Samuel Bramford's eyes were blue.

I heard Chloe take a long, shuddery breath. She straightened her shoulders then stepped forward and introduced herself.

"Look what you've done!" Elspeth pushed past me and ran toward Chloe. "He shouldn't be up! He *knows* he shouldn't be up! He's showing off for you."

Elspeth pressed her palm to his forehead and clucked. She poured him a tumbler of water from an earthenware jug then handed it to him but his eyes never left Chloe's. He said something to his manic nursemaid in a low voice. She turned and glared at all three of us then with a wave of her apron swirled down the open staircase to the main floor.

He whispered Chloe's name and his eyes closed. His head fell back against the rocker. A tear slipped down his weathered cheek.

"Who are you?" Chloe asked. "Why did you bring us here?"

He opened his eyes and looked straight at Chloe. "I'm Samuel Bramford," he said, "and I am Aerynn's mate."

24

CHLOE

I heard the words but my brain couldn't process them.

"I am Aerynn's mate," he repeated and this time I understood.

The air rushed out of me like I'd been punched. I doubled over at the waist and closed my eyes against the wave of dizziness threatening to drop me to the floor like a bag of rocks.

Aerynn's mate . . . her lover . . . father of her child. . . . He's my blood . . . my blood!

He reached out a hand to me but I couldn't move.

"This isn't how I wanted us to meet," he said, "but circumstances made it necessary."

My brain started to make the calculations. "You're my great-great-great-great —"

"Too many to count, child, but the link is strong and it endures."

Again that feeling of dizzying wonder.

"You are Aerynn's image." His voice broke as he said the words. "I've waited a long time for this moment."

"You knew about me?"

"From long before you took your first breath."

"You knew what happened to my parents?"

He nodded. His eyes never left mine.

"And you never —"

"That decision was made many years ago and it could not be broken."

"What decision?" I demanded. "Someone decided I would grow up without parents? Someone decided I'd be alone? I'd like to know more about all of those decisions."

"I had hoped the transition would be an easy one but we have no time to waste."

"Transition?" I could hear my decibel level rising. "What transition?"

He looked at me as if I were a beloved but backward child. "The leadership that will pass to you when I finally pierce the veil."

"Which he would have done by now if not for you, missy!" Elspeth's voice could be heard from downstairs.

I had heard those same words years ago when my surrogate mother, Sorcha, sacrificed piercing the veil to stay in this world and raise me to adulthood. I would carry the weight of that sacrifice with me for the rest of my life. I refused to carry the weight of this stranger's sacrifice as well.

"Elspeth, that's enough." It wasn't what Samuel Bramford said but how he said it. I could actually feel Elspeth remove herself from the situation.

"I didn't want to come here," I said, almost daring the old man to contradict or interrupt me. "I wanted to stay in Sugar Maple. This was Luke's idea. Salem means nothing to me."

His faded sailor-blue eyes were focused on mine. "I know that."

"You didn't" — I waved my hand in the air — "send out any messages or anything to influence us, did you?" As a human, Luke would have been highly susceptible.

"Had I the power, I would have discouraged the three of you."

"Swell," I said. "That's good to know."

"You're defensive."

I said nothing.

"That's understandable. You've made mistakes."

I've made mistakes? I still said nothing.

"You are drawn to humans and that was your undoing."

"I'm half human," I snapped. "I share their blood."

"We are alike in our compassion for the species."

"It isn't a question of compassion," I said. "It's a question of blood."

His sigh made the room shiver. "You know so little of your heritage."

My face burned in response to his criticism. "My mother and father weren't there to teach me." *And neither were you, for that matter.*

"My parents were magick but I never knew them," he said. "I was raised by a human couple who took me in as their own."

"Did they know your truth?"

"My birth parents had sheltered the Bramfords during an Indian uprising years earlier. The bonds of affection between them were strong."

I didn't want to feel anything for Samuel but I couldn't help myself. "That must have been incredibly dangerous for them." Given what we all knew about the seventeenth-century mindset, possessing magick was akin to consorting with the devil. The discovery that they had taken in a magick child would have been a certain death sentence.

"I didn't understand how dangerous until the troubles began and Salem split apart into factions."

"Meaning humans against magic," Luke said. I could hear the faint tinge of resentment in his voice.

"That battle is ageless," Samuel said with a glance toward Luke, "and most likely will never be resolved. But our problem, then and now, was magick against magick."

"The Fae," Janice said. "I think my grandmother told me something about that."

Bramford gave her a warm smile and, to my surprise, I experienced a stab of jealousy. I curled my fingertips into my palms to keep the flames from shooting out and singeing the old man's mane of white hair. What was that all about anyway?

"One of the reasons I like humans is they don't speak in riddles." I sounded like a world-class bitch but couldn't stop myself.

"And *you* speak before you think," Samuel said. "You are much like Aerynn in every way."

I knew that was a compliment but I clung to silence. It was safer that way.

"She was headstrong and impulsive."

Okay, maybe it wasn't a compliment after all.

"I have no magick to make you believe me, Chloe, but if you hope to restore Sugar Maple, you'll listen to my story."

"Go ahead," I said, folding my arms

across my chest. "I'm listening."

"Aerynn is the reason Sugar Maple came to be," he said, "and you are the reason why it is gone."

If you want to put it that way . . .

"Hold on," Luke said, stepping forward. "You were up here in a lighthouse while we were fighting Isadora in Sugar Maple. You don't have a clue what happened."

I shot Luke a warning look. Samuel Bramford might be old but I had the feeling his powers went far beyond anything we'd ever encountered.

And there was the fact that, blood relative or not, I still wasn't convinced he was on our side. It was hard to tell friend from foe around here without a scorecard.

"I made mistakes," I admitted. "But the Fae didn't pull the town beyond the mist. I know that for a fact."

"And who said they did?" Samuel's words seemed to require enormous effort on his part and I found myself almost feeling sorry for him again. "Nobody stole Sugar Maple from you, Chloe. Your commitment was not strong enough to keep it, so the town was taken from you for its own protection."

"Not strong enough?" I laughed in his face. "Nobody loves Sugar Maple more than I do."

My life up until now had been played out within the township limits and I hoped the rest of my life would be as well. In what crazy world did that constitute danger?

"Think, Chloe," Samuel said as he rested his head against the back of his chair. "Know the truth so the path will be illuminated."

I groaned out loud. "Spare me the fortune-cookie wisdom, if you don't mind."

"Temperance," he warned. "Think before you speak, child, or you will never achieve all that is within your power."

Now he sounded like Mr. Miyagi from the original *Karate Kid.* Why did everything have to be larded with metaphor and deep-fried in self-help speak?

"You said I'm not committed to Sugar Maple," I said with as much restraint as I could muster. "I want to know what you mean."

Samuel leaned his head against the back of his chair again and closed his eyes. I exchanged looks with Luke and Janice. Janice pointed toward the staircase but I shook my head. We had come here for answers and I wasn't going to leave until I had them.

We waited. Then waited some more.

"Is he breathing?" Janice whispered.

I wasn't sure. I stepped closer.

"I'm still of this dimension."

I jumped back at the sound. His eyes were closed. He hadn't moved a muscle. But his voice filled the room like a philharmonic orchestra in a concert hall.

"Aerynn was as wise as she was powerful," he continued. "Long ago she understood that the ultimate safety of Sugar Maple depended upon the strong, undivided commitment of its leader."

The man could say more by saying little than anyone I had ever met. I instantly felt small and foolish but not contrite. A girl had to draw the line someplace.

"There was fatal dissension within your town," he continued. "You allowed yourself to be distracted by matters of the heart."

"I fought Isadora," I said. "I was there at the waterfall to keep her from taking away the town."

"When you saw the child, you lost sight of everything beyond her tears."

So he knew about Luke's late daughter, Steffie, and the battle for her spirit. Interesting.

"I reacted to the problem at hand."

"While Sugar Maple slipped away."

"I didn't know it was slipping away."

"The true leader would have."

For once I kept my mouth shut, but the truth was I would do the same thing over again. The lonely little girl who still lived inside of me would choose to help Steffie every time.

"You have nothing to say in your defense?" he asked after a few moments passed by in silence.

"Do you?" I retorted. "You ignore me for almost thirty human years then do everything you can to keep us away from here —"

"He didn't do it," Luke broke in.

"Luke's right," Janice said. "It was the local Fae."

I spun around to face them. "Where did you get that idea?"

Janice explained about Penny and the glittered hairball.

"The second she got rid of all of that gunk she headed down to the water and we followed her."

"It was deliberate," Luke said. "The cat had a plan."

Samuel laughed. "In truth I had the plan. Penelope helped me to execute it. I needed to bring you to me and this was the only way at hand."

"So you gin up mermaids and tidal waves to get me here? Why not just summon me here for a family reunion without all the drama?"

Ha! I thought. *Try to weasel out of that, Mr. Wizard.*

"The old magick is strong and I am old. I'd used my resources to break Penelope free and, beyond releasing you from the rest stop, I couldn't protect you from random mischief. You had to find your own way through it."

Random mischief? That was one way to put it. Wait a second —

"You're telling me that *you're* the one who broke me out of the rest stop?" *He's lying, Chloe. You know he's lying.*

"You believed it was your mother, didn't you?" He sounded regretful. "That was unintentional."

He relayed some convoluted story about getting my subconscious to share one of its most powerful happy memories in order to relax me enough to break the Fae's hold on me.

"I am sorry if you read more into it, Chloe, than was actually there."

You mean like thinking that maybe my mother actually loved me and watched over me?

Janice had been right. I should have known better.

260

I forced my thoughts away from the past. I had more than enough bones to pick with him right here and now. "So why didn't you contact us as soon as we were in Salem?" I demanded. "Why all the cloak-and-dagger nonsense? Janice and I could have whipped up a spell that didn't involve underwater highways and waterspouts."

"Warning you would have opened up a conduit for thought probes."

"Thought probes don't require conduits."

"Remember, we use the old magick here. I couldn't risk another obstacle placed along your pathway."

I had to hand it to the old guy: He had an answer for everything. "And you believe staying on my pathway will help me restore Sugar Maple."

"Staying on your pathway will help you to claim what is yours."

"My hometown."

"Your heritage."

"Sugar Maple is my heritage."

"No!" His eyes blinked open and an explosion of light illuminated the room. "Without this, you have nothing."

25

CHLOE
SALEM, 1692

The cottage smelled of hay and sheep, salt air and wood smoke. I moved through the door with a spirit's ease and settled myself on the trestle table against the roughly plastered back wall of the keeping room.

Heavy snow pelted the closed shutters but the fire roaring in the enormous hearth made the dwelling surprisingly toasty and bright. Near the hearth a round black cat slept peacefully atop a basket of yarn.

"Penelope?" It couldn't be. Penny had been sprawled across Samuel's bony shoulders when I took my leave.

The Penny clone lifted her head at the sound of her name and winked one enormous golden eye then settled back to sleep.

A shiver ran up my spine as I realized what was going on. *This is really happening,* I told myself. *I'm here where it all began.*

That was my Penny and yet it wasn't and it was clear I wasn't the only one who knew the difference.

Samuel hadn't enough strength to accompany me on this trip into the past or to send Luke or Janice with me. But what magick he had at his command was seamless. I moved from the twenty-first century to the end of the seventeenth in the space of a single breath without any of the car-crash aspects that usually went hand in hand with astral transport.

I sensed, rather than saw, the landscape beyond the small whitewashed cottage. The harbor clogged with fishing boats preparing to head out toward Stellwagen. Dirt roads that led to the center of the small New England town we now knew as Salem. The silence was rich and deep, unbroken by the incessant hum that marked the years after the Industrial Revolution that still lay ahead.

Two young women, teenagers really, swept into the room, arms piled high with fleeces and roving. They wore plain dresses of light brown wool with white aprons tied over full skirts. One girl was tiny and dark and beautiful in the way only a member of the Fae could be. Her eyes were wide and sea green, framed by thick dark lashes that cast a shadow on her sculpted cheekbones. A narrow trail of bluish purple glitter followed her as she walked.

The other girl was tall and skinny with long arms and legs and unruly blond hair that poked out from beneath her starched white cap. She had a big laugh and wide golden eyes and for a moment I thought my heart had stopped beating inside my chest as I realized who she was.

Aerynn Hobbs.

Aerynn, who had led the hunted from Salem to Sinzibukwud.

Aerynn, who was the mother of us all, a sorceress whose magick remained legendary and unequaled.

The sorceress whose blood ran in my veins, whose legacy shadowed every breath I took, every decision I made, the sorceress I would become.

I wanted to touch her hand. I wanted to look into her eyes and see myself reflected in them.

She exists only as a reflection. Samuel's voice rumbled against my breastbone. ***You can't make contact with her.***

But Penny saw me, I said deep within myself. *She winked at me.*

Watch and learn, child. Aerynn sat down at her wheel, the same wheel that had been my mother's and her mother's before her.

The same wheel Janice had saved before she fled Sugar Maple in my Buick.

"Are you most certain, Da'Elle? I could brew the indigo once the wool is spun and achieve a most pleasing effect."

The tiny brunette shook her head. " 'Tis plain I want. With the troubles afoot, plain is best."

My mother Guinevere had been the most gifted spinner I had ever seen. Even as a little girl I had known I was in the presence of something very special. But watching Aerynn at her wheel was to see magick happen right before your eyes.

The roving raced through her fingers in a spray of silver and gold sparks I knew very well and was transformed into yarn as fine as a spider's web in the blink of an eye. I could have sat there, perched on the heavy pine table, and watched her forever.

You are her image. Can you see it?

I nodded, unwilling to break the spell I was falling under.

"The meetinghouse is no longer safe," the dark-haired Fae said as she settled down on the long bench with her needles and ball of yarn. "Mary Hopson passed word to Willem that we need to go underground."

"It is time." Aerynn's eyes never left her wheel. "We need to leave quickly, Da'Elle," she said, and my heartbeat quickened. "The madness is knocking at the door."

"Humans have a limitless capacity for evil," Da'Elle said. "They drove us from our homes across the ocean and now they are driving us from our homes in the New World. Our only recourse is to slip beyond the mist where we belong and leave this world to them."

"We belong here in this dimension," Aerynn said. "Our ancestors decreed it to be so."

Da'Elle's lovely face darkened. "And they have long pierced the veil." Her knitting was all sharp angles and stabbing motions. "There are those who would sweep down upon the humans and kill them as they sleep."

"Then we would be no better than those who have oppressed us."

"But we would survive," Da'Elle said, tugging hard at the yarn as she formed a stitch. "Is that not what we are striving toward?"

Aerynn shook her head and said nothing as she applied herself to her spinning. A ripple of apprehension moved between my shoulder blades. There was something about the way Da'Elle looked at Aerynn that chilled my blood. I knew that look. I had felt the edge of its sharpened teeth.

Isadora, I thought, and knew the truth of it in my bones. Isadora was one of the beautiful young Fae's descendants. Was I seeing the beginning of the war between our families?

"How is your Samuel?" Da'Elle asked in a casual tone of voice.

"He is well, thank you. He will be home from the sea any day."

Da'Elle's mouth tightened. "You are in love."

Aerynn's cheeks reddened. I smiled to myself. So it was hereditary after all. "We have not tried to hide it."

"And how do his human parents feel about it?"

"Samuel was taken in by his human parents when he was a baby," Aerynn said carefully, "but they knew from the start that he is full-blood magick and welcomed him as such."

Da'Elle's laughter held the sound of breaking glass. "And you believe that."

"They have moved among us every day since we first came to be. You know this to be true, same as I."

"You know because that is what Samuel wishes you to know."

Tiny flames of anger danced from Aerynn's fingertips. She curled them closer to her palm and continued spinning.

"He clearly has you bewitched," Da'Elle said. "There is no other reason for you to cling stubbornly to your idea of migrating northward."

Aerynn's laugh was uncertain. "I am most certainly not bewitched."

"And that is part of bewitchment," the beautiful Fae said. "He has ensorcelled you and yet you remain unaware."

"I love him," Aerynn said simply. "Magick plays no part."

Da'Elle's laugh held a bitter edge. "Samuel may be magick but in many ways he is more human than sorcerer."

"Thanks to Joshua and Rebecca Bramford, he has seen the best the race can offer."

"And now we are seeing the worst."

Aerynn inclined her head in agreement. "And that is why we will go north in the spring. It is but a few weeks, Da'Elle."

"The hangings will continue. We could be dancing on air long before the thaw."

"I believe we have time."

"We need to be of one mind," Da'Elle said, glitter spilling from her fingers and toes. "Our unity is our strength."

"And our strength will only grow if we remain in this dimension," Aerynn said.

"We'll build our own town to the north where we'll be free from persecution." She stopped spinning and looked at her companion. "All of us together, as the ancestors want it to be, sharing our wisdom and our riches."

"The community must be of one mind," Da'Elle repeated. "It has been so from the beginning in the Old Country."

"They'll follow us," Aerynn said. "North is the promise of freedom."

Da'Elle put down her knitting and met my ancestor's eyes. "And the Fae can promise that and more beyond the mist."

"You can make many promises, but only I have the power to bring a town to life."

"That may not always be so and as long as you draw breath in this dimension, you will always be at the mercy of the whims of humans," Da'Elle said. "You will take our people and walk them into bondage."

"Never!" Aerynn cried. "My magick is strong. I will find a way to protect our new home down through the ages, a spell that will remain unbroken as long as our town exists."

"Your magick is new. Your powers are yet untried." Da'Elle gestured beyond the cottage. "In the end it will be up to them to decide our fate."

And in the end, that was how it happened.
Samuel's voice filled my head. **But that moment of truth still lay in the future.**

What about you and Aerynn? Why didn't you go with her?

As you will see, that was not my destiny.
He exhaled slowly. **Nor was it hers.**

I don't believe that. You could have found a way to be together. You were both magick. Your powers dwarf anything I've ever encountered. Don't tell me there was no way for the two of you to spend your lives together.

The old man was good. No doubt about it. I'd barely finished my sentence when I found myself perched in an enormous maple tree behind the meetinghouse. The night was dark and star filled. Without the ambient sounds of the twenty-first century, I found myself readjusting again to the depth of silence they enjoyed. The distant hoot of an owl sounded like a clap of thunder.

Young Samuel arrived first. He was tall and strong and dazzlingly handsome. Magick shimmered from him like starlight as he waited for Aerynn. His serious face broke into an unguarded smile as she appeared around the side of the meetinghouse. No words were spoken. None were needed. I felt like a voyeur as I watched them melt together in the shadows.

I tried hard not to listen but the soft sighs and gentle laughter painted a picture that broke my heart. Sometimes it was better not to know what the future held.

"The worst is upon us," the young and handsome Samuel said as he held Aerynn close. "The town elders will come for you and for all of us two nights from now and we cannot stop it."

But you can, I thought. What else was magick for if not to protect the ones you loved?

I heard Aerynn's sharp intake of breath followed by a prolonged silence.

"We'll leave tomorrow after dark," she said finally. "That should give us time to gather everyone."

"Da'Elle will not go easily."

"But she'll go," Aerynn said. "Our tribes have been united down through the centuries. Our knowledge springs from the same source."

"She will go beyond the mist with her sisters."

"She'll come with us," Aerynn said with more confidence than I would have felt in her place. "She is as much of this world as we are." I felt, rather than saw, her smile. "Besides, you have something she values as much as we do. She will follow where it goes."

"The talisman?" Samuel asked.

"We are bound to it, all of us. The Fae feel its mighty pull same as we do."

"But will it pull them into the north lands?"

"Where the talisman goes, we go. It gathered us together here in the colonies and it will gather us together at our new home up north."

Talisman? I thought. *What talisman?* Nobody ever told me about a talisman.

"Building a town is a difficult task," young Samuel said.

"But we can do it," Aerynn said. "Together we can build a sanctuary where we will all be safe from harm."

"Humans are not the only danger we face. Our biggest danger may yet come from within."

"I am not a fool, Samuel. I see clearly what lies ahead but we will create the sanctuary I dream of and even my most outspoken foe will be won over to our side. I know this."

"I am not sure such a place can exist in

272

this world or any other."

"It can," she said. "It will! That is our destiny."

The plan was simple: Aerynn's clan would gather at the outside of town the next night when the moon was new. With Aerynn in possession of the talisman, Da'Elle and her people would have no choice but to follow.

"If something happens and I am not there by the hour before dawn —"

"Shh!" Aerynn pressed her fingers to his lips. "Do not say that. You will be there with me."

"They are watching me closely, Aerynn. I will not lead them to you."

"I need you and I will not leave without you."

"Yes," he said. "You will." He pulled a small pouch from inside his cloak. "To travel safe from harm, this is all you need."

She peered inside. "The talisman," she said, her voice breaking. "It was to remain with you 'til we started up north. You'll be vulnerable."

"Only if I am delayed," he said, his voice betraying no fear.

"Is this the end for us?" she asked. "Is this your way of saying good-bye? For if it is —"

He silenced her with a kiss. "I will never say good-bye," he vowed. "What I feel for you is eternal."

She pushed the pouch back toward him. "Then bring this with you when we meet again."

"I would have you keep it for me."

Finally Aerynn acquiesced, but her fear showed clearly on her face. "You will be here at the appointed hour," she said. "That is our true destiny."

"If I am not," he continued, "you must leave without me."

"I would never —"

"Yes, you will because I ask you to."

"Samuel." She sounded a warning. "Do not —"

"Hear me out. If I am not there, the reason will be serious. Use the time to put miles between us. Head north along the route we have planned and I will find you as soon as I am able."

"The wilderness is vast. How will you do that?"

"Use the power of the talisman to summon me and I will follow the scent of magick until we are together again."

My heart ached for the two foolish young people. I wanted to believe they would find their way to Sugar Maple and grow old together but I knew otherwise. Sugar Maple

was Aerynn's destiny but not Samuel's.
They would discover that fact soon enough.

26

LUKE

Chloe had been gone from the room for less than a minute but when she returned I knew everything had changed.

The old man was still deep in the meditative state that he had entered moments before Chloe vanished.

"Spill," Janice said, racing to Chloe's side. "Where did you go? What did you see?"

Chloe had the dazed look of someone who had seen things the rest of us could only imagine.

"Give her a break, Jan. She just got here."

Chloe looked at Janice then at me. I could see her struggling to focus in on us, the room, this dimension of reality.

"Aerynn," she said in a hushed voice. "I saw Aerynn." She described the woman in detail, right down to the yarn she had been spinning at her wheel.

"Holy shit!" Janice exclaimed. "Blue-faced

Leicester! Are you serious?"

The two knitters burst into laughter and I saw some of the nervous tension leave Chloe's body.

"There's more," Chloe said, and told us about Isadora's ancestor, Da'Elle, and the beginning of the feud that ultimately shaped Sugar Maple.

Janice peppered her with questions about Da'Elle's hair and clothes and knitting skills but Chloe's focus was on other things.

"They loved each other," she said, referring to Aerynn and the old man who was now dozing in the rocking chair. "Deeply, honestly loved each other."

"That surprises you?" I wasn't sure where she was going with it.

"Aerynn and Samuel loved each other and still ended up apart. My parents loved each other and my mother chose human death to be with my father." The look of sorrow in her eyes hit me like a punch to the gut. "Looks like we're fresh out of happy endings, MacKenzie. The Hobbs girls really are congenitally unable to get it right."

"I don't scare easy."

Her eyes welled with tears. "Maybe you should."

"Chloe is right." The old man was awake and taking it all in. "There is reason to be scared."

"There are always reasons to be scared," I said, meeting his eyes. "It's the human condition. You learn to work around it."

He nodded. I would have given my bank account to know what he was thinking. It wasn't every day a man went eye to eye with a wizard.

"I will tell you what I know about your situation." His voice had the resonance of an old-time radio announcer. "Then I will tell you what you need to do to recover Sugar Maple."

"Not now you won't!" Elspeth spun up the staircase like a bright yellow dervish. "Rest!" she cried. "You need rest! They made their bed, let them sleep in it. 'Tis no concern of yours now."

"Elspeth is my oldest and dearest friend," he told us as the crone touched the back of her wrinkled hand to his forehead. "She's a healer who has brought great comfort to me while I wait for my time."

"And it's well past his time," Elspeth clucked. "If you hadn't kept him waiting all these years, he would have pierced the veil long ago."

"Sounds a little harsh," I said. "Don't you want him around anymore?"

Elspeth ignored me. Apparently humans

were beneath her notice.

"Janice is a healer, too," Chloe said to the crone. "The most powerful healer in Sugar Maple."

"Like that be something special," Elspeth muttered. She turned her gimlet-eyed gaze on Janice. "You descend from my sister Rebecca's line."

Janice's jaw dropped open. "Get out!"

"I'll do no such thing," Elspeth snapped.

"That's an expression of surprise," Samuel said, his blue eyes twinkling.

Janice stared at the old woman with a mixture of horror and excitement. "Are you saying we're related?"

"What is wrong with your people?" Elspeth said with a shake of her bright yellow head. "Did they teach you nothing? A child should know her lineage to the last fourth cousin three times removed before her seventh birthday."

I had to hand it to Janice. She didn't give the old woman an inch. "Maybe they were embarrassed by some of the branches in our family tree."

Elspeth considered Janice carefully.

"Is your magick serviceable?" she asked.

"Depends what you have in mind," Janice said.

The two women eyed each other specula-

279

tively. There was no family resemblance that I could see but in spirit they were cut from the same bolt of cloth.

"Hold my apron," Elspeth commanded, and they were gone.

"Should I worry?" Chloe asked Samuel.

"Elspeth's heart is tender. She values family above all. Janice will not come to harm."

Chloe nodded. "Tell me about the talisman."

"What talisman?" I asked.

She recounted the conversation between Samuel's younger self and Aerynn.

Samuel's eyes never left us. "The talisman is at the heart of our clan and the New England Fae clan as well."

I knew that the magick clock and the human clock operated independently of one another but no matter how you looked at it, time was running out. Back in Vermont, the snow was going to melt and all hell would break loose. The one thing we didn't have time for was a walk down paranormal memory lane.

"Our first home, millennia ago, was in northern Wales. Where we were before that is lost to history but it was in Wales that we grew together and formed a community."

"Including the Fae?" Chloe asked.

"We were as one," he said.

They were also the keepers of a gold mine that was discovered somewhere near the midpoint of the European Bronze Age.

"There's gold in Wales? I thought they only mined coal."

"Our gold was legendary for its beauty and scarcity," Samuel said. "Traders came from faraway lands to barter their goods for our treasure. The Romans, however, had other ideas. They marched in with their armies and their legions of slaves and before long our peaceful, prosperous community was driven out. The world was changing. The old religions were being replaced by the new. Magick was viewed with suspicion. We traveled the length and breadth of the British Isles in search of sanctuary. We settled in town after town, only to be driven out again by humans who feared what they could not understand. But through it all, we stayed together."

"The talisman," Chloe prompted. "What does any of this have to do with the talisman you and Aerynn talked about?"

"Each member of our community carried away a small nugget of gold from our ancestral home in Wales. During a long treacherous winter in Sweden, one of our artisans melted down the nuggets then fashioned the ore into a disk that featured our two clans, magick and Fae, connected by an overarching canopy of sky. A symbol, if you will, of the special bond we shared and would always share."

"No magick?" I asked.

"There is always magick," he said.

"So what's the problem?" Chloe asked. "You had the disk. The disk had magick. Every single one of you had powers that mortals couldn't imagine. Why did you ever leave the Old World for the New?"

"At first our powers weren't strong enough to defeat the humans."

"Not even with the disk?" I asked.

He shook his head. "In time our clan came to the realization that the human race was evolving into a more tolerant, adaptable species and would continue to evolve. So they refused to fight."

"But they still left the Old World for the New," Chloe said.

"Their world was ablaze with fervor for the new ways. Those accused of witchcraft were being burned at the stake across the continent. Our elders, fearing the worst, left the talisman with my parents for safekeeping and either chose to pierce the veil or slip beyond the mist."

"And their wisdom went with them," Chloe said.

Samuel nodded. "Without the wisdom or an heir apparent, our clan lacked the leadership we needed to survive."

"How did they escape?" I asked, pulled into the story despite the ticking clock. "Did they use their remaining powers?"

"Their powers at that time were not up to the task of transporting the clan across the ocean," he said with a rueful shake of his head. "They bartered their way on board a ship headed to the New World and put their destiny in the hands of the winds and sea."

Which turned out to be the right choice.

The years in the Massachusetts Bay Colony were good ones. The two clans lived and worked in harmony and they grew prosperous. The artisans among them turned their talents to the fiber-related pursuits favored by the locals. They became spinners and weavers and spawned knitters who turned out the fisherman's sweaters Chloe loved so much.

Chloe cautiously leaned forward and touched the old man's sweatered arm. "Did — did Aerynn knit this for you?"

His laugh was surprisingly full and hearty. "She spun the yarn but I knitted the sweater."

I was surprised to see Chloe's golden eyes fill with tears. "It's beautiful."

He pointed to an intricate cable that ran down the center of the sweater. "This represents the braiding of the Hobbs clan with the Bramfords."

Chloe zeroed in on the design. "A panel of eighteen stitches flanked by two panels of six." She looked up at him and smiled for the first time since they'd met. "You're crazy."

"I was young and my hands were more flexible," he said with an answering smile. "Your skills far surpass mine."

Chloe blushed and shook her head. "Not even close."

I was all about family bonding but we had a town to recover. I steered the conversation away from knitting and back to why we were there in the first place.

"When did things start to change?" I asked.

Bramford looked over at me and again I had the feeling he knew my thoughts before I thought them. "Like human families, we had our disagreements but our commitment to the greater good of the community always took precedence."

The Royal Charter of Massachusetts had been canceled in 1684 and the future was cast in shadow. Not that anyone had much time to worry about things like charters: the native Indian tribes had erupted into violence that spread to the coast of Maine.

But things would get quickly worse when the daughter and niece of Reverend Parris showed signs of what the Puritans claimed was demonic possession and the hideous era of the Witch Trials was under way. *Nothing new here,* I thought. I could have recited the information in my sleep.

"Instead of uniting us even closer, the old mistrust of humans drove us further apart. Aerynn wanted to pick up stakes and move north into the wilderness while most of Da'Elle's Fae wanted to pull our community beyond the mist into their realm." He sighed deeply. "And then there were the ones who believed that Salem was our home and as such was worth fighting for."

"And you?" Chloe asked.

"I understood their feelings but my heart was Aerynn's and always will be. I had made my peace with the fact that I would leave this place behind and together we would build an oasis for our band of magickal outcasts."

I don't know how it happened but suddenly his words had color and dimension. I saw a woman, who looked enough like Chloe to be her twin, in the arms of a man who was clearly a younger Samuel Bramford. Their love was real. It was palpable. He felt about her the way I felt about Chloe, an emotion that went so deep it scared the hell out of me.

He had been willing to follow Aerynn into the unknown for the same reason I was sitting in a wizard's lighthouse: love.

"What went wrong?" I asked. I knew he hadn't changed his mind. His love for Chloe's ancestor was as constant as the tides beyond the lighthouse.

His eyes closed again and around him the colors deepened. The sound grew more resonant. Once more his words came to life and I could smell the fear as Aerynn and her followers and Da'Elle and most of hers waited in the shadows for Samuel. Finally, just before first light, she gave a signal and they blended into the fog and headed on their way north.

And then I saw Samuel suspended over acrid flames that licked the soles of his feet and made him cry out in pain. Bone thin, semiconscious, but still he resisted his captors' demands.

"I know nothing about it," he said as they pressed for information about Chloe's disappearance with the talisman and over fifty followers. "My life is here in Salem. *I* am here in Salem."

"Where is the talisman?" The flames rose higher, up his calves and winding around his knees in an attempt to destroy flesh and spirit.

His high, keening cry filled my head. But he still told them nothing. The orange and red and black flames enveloped him. The stench of sulfur made my head spin. "Tell us!" they cried. "Tell us now!"

The images faded then disappeared. I doubted the memory ever would. The human race had done terrible things to the magical creatures but what the creatures had done to themselves deserved equally harsh judgment.

"You saw the worst of those who were my friends but the truth of their actions was far from simple," Samuel said, opening his eyes again and meeting mine. "The Witch Trials did terrible things to everyone in this town, turning friend against friend, parent against child. We were not immune to the insanity that fear and suspicion can generate."

"Why didn't you use your magick against the Fae?" Chloe asked. "Fight fire with fire."

"For me it was still early days. Aerynn was by far the most powerful of our clan. Without the talisman my magick was not strong enough to fight on the night I was captured."

"What about later?" Chloe persisted. "Obviously the damage wasn't permanent. Why didn't you reach out to the talisman and use it to find where Aerynn had settled?"

"I was filled with the pride of youth and burgeoning powers," he said after a long silence. "When I gave the talisman to Aerynn, I made no provision to communicate with it."

If he had tried to locate the talisman, he would have revealed its whereabouts to those who had chosen to stay behind and by doing so compromised Aerynn's control.

"Home and family," I said. "The only two things worth fighting for."

Samuel nodded his agreement. "The Fae blamed Aerynn for Da'Elle's departure." The Fae had seen power in Da'Elle unlike anything they had encountered before. They had put their hopes for the future in the young woman, only to have her turn away from everything she knew and head north with Aerynn and her followers. "Some of the Fae believed Aerynn had cast a spell over Da'Elle using the talisman and they were willing to do anything necessary to break the hold."

Including murder Aerynn, if necessary.

Chloe sank back in her seat, her face a

mask of anguish.

"So you let her go," she said.

"She was carrying our child. I was not willing to endanger either of them."

"You let them go," she repeated.

He turned to me. "Time, to us, is not the same as it is to a human. We would wait and one day we would be together again."

But time, human or magick, was not on their side. The Fae community in Salem was small but their anger at the loss of Da'Elle was large. Aerynn became the focus of their bitter rage.

"They monitored my every move," he said, shaking his head sadly at the memory. "Probes violated the sanctity of my thoughts on an hourly basis. In order to protect my soul mate, I had to banish her from my thoughts, my heart."

"But you couldn't," I said.

"No," he replied, "I couldn't. At least, not completely."

Now and again he monitored the progress of Sugar Maple through the eyes of Penelope the cat, who had been Aerynn's familiar from the cradle. The seasons changed and the memory of the troubles grew fainter, less charged with passion. He consoled himself with the thought that each year brought them closer to being together. The day would come when the old problems would disappear and the need for secrecy and caution would disappear with them.

Until then, he could only wait.

Time passed. Too much time as it turned out.

One day the unthinkable happened and Aerynn pierced the veil.

"How did you know she was gone," I asked, "if you hadn't been in communication with her since she left Salem?"

His smile was bittersweet. "She came to say good-bye."

27

CHLOE

It would take a week to explain the traditions that surrounded piercing the veil. I struggled to condense it enough so I could bring Luke up to speed.

"Your essence — your soul, if you will — travels about this dimension prior to piercing the veil and bestows blessings on the ones you love." I looked over at Samuel. "Do I have it right?" Very few townspeople had left us during my time on earth so my experience was minimal.

The old man nodded while Luke looked like he was rapidly approaching magick overload. Who could blame him? I felt like I was drowning in it myself.

"But it's always your choice, right?" Luke asked. "You determine when you pierce the veil."

"Even we have an allotted span," Samuel said. "Mine is longer than most." And

Aerynn's had been considerably shortened when she sacrificed some of her own life force to empower the talisman.

I had grown up knowing that the odds were against me. No Hobbs woman had ever managed to get the guy and keep him. Forever wasn't in our DNA. The only thing we could do was cherish every day we had with the man we loved and not be surprised when destiny had its way. I hadn't kept this fact a secret from Luke but knowing it and understanding it were two very different things.

I would outlive him. Probably by a very long time. The day would come when he would breathe his last and I would be forced to go on without him, moving down through the years cloaked in the old loneliness I knew all too well. That was the flip side of the magick I had claimed when I fell in love.

He understood it now and the look in his eyes broke my heart. I wanted to reach out and reassure him that it would be different for us but the truth was I knew it couldn't be. My half-human lineage would even things out a little bit but not enough to matter. Sooner rather than later it would be our turn to say good-bye.

"Why didn't you join her?" I asked the old man, not caring that the question was insensitive. "If you loved her the way you claim you did, what kept you in this dimension if you could have been together in hers?"

I had to hand it to him: he didn't flinch or look away. "I stayed because we knew the day would come when you would need the help of family."

I couldn't help laughing out loud. The word *family* wasn't even in my vocabulary.

The bitterness in my voice was unmistakable. "You believed I would come to Salem to find you even though I didn't know you existed until twenty minutes ago."

"Yes."

"I told you this wasn't my idea." That fact bore repeating.

"But you are here just the same."

In the movies I loved, the books I reread a thousand times, this was the point where the wise old grandfather would open his arms wide and the needy young granddaughter would run into them and all of her problems would be solved in one homily-filled fireside chat. But even though I'd spent my life longing for exactly that, I didn't have a clue how to make the first move.

Or even if I wanted to.

"I want my town back," I said to Samuel

Bramford, "and I need your help to get it. That's the only reason we're having this conversation." I told him exactly what had happened and how I had tried and failed to access the Book of Spells for help.

"The Book does not contain the answer you seek."

"Then what does?"

"You should have figured that out by now."

"And you should come with a translator," I snapped, "because I don't understand a word you're saying."

"Chloe." Luke sounded a warning but I was beyond worrying about anyone's feelings.

"Do *you* understand him?" I challenged Luke. "Do you understand one single word he's said since we got here?" I waved my arms in the air like a frustrated windmill. "You're the one who said the clock was ticking. We're wasting time, Luke." I aimed a deadly stare in Bramford's direction. "*He's* wasting our time!"

What did it take to anger the old man? The patient look he gave me was filled with something that looked an awful lot like love.

Which was totally ridiculous. We didn't know each other. We would never really know each other. You couldn't possibly love

someone you didn't know. They said blood ran thicker than water but you couldn't prove it by me. I had never really had the opportunity to love or be loved by someone with whom I shared familial blood.

And yet I felt an answering rush of emotion that I would rather die than acknowledge.

"You do not need the Book, Chloe." Bramford's voice seemed to emanate from every part of the tower room. "You need only what is in your head and in your heart."

"That's a big help," I said, with even more snark than I'd intended. "If you tell me life is like a box of chocolates, I'm out of here."

He laughed out loud, a rippling rumble of a laugh that snapped my head back in surprise. "You got the reference?" I asked.

"I have been waiting for you a long time," he said. "DVDs and knitting are a grand pairing."

Poor Luke. Knitters were hard enough for civilians to understand. Sorcerers who knit while they watched *Forrest Gump* were probably impossible.

But again I refused to allow emotion to cloud my purpose. I didn't want to feel anything for this stranger who claimed to be Aerynn's soul mate and the father of her child.

"So how do I retrieve Sugar Maple?" I zeroed back in on the matter at hand and I would keep on zeroing back until I got an answer out of him.

"How did you lose it?" he countered.

"We went through this before. I didn't lose it," I said with deadly calm. "It vanished."

"Because your commitment was not strong enough to keep it. Your loyalties were divided. Your love for Luke made you blind to the dangers facing Sugar Maple."

"That's not true! Why do you think we were at the waterfall? I was there to prevent Isadora from pulling the town beyond the mist."

"The child's welfare became your priority. The safety of the town was a very distant second."

"The child's soul was Isadora's priority. Do you have any idea what Isadora had planned for that little girl?" A yawning black dimension of eternal loneliness that should be reserved as a hell for the worst creatures who ever walked the earth. Luke's daughter deserved better than that.

"You are wrong. The child was merely Isadora's tool for prying Sugar Maple out of your control and moving it beyond the mist, but you saw yourself in her plight and acted from your heart. It is your commitment to

Sugar Maple that wavered."

My eyes flooded with tears I struggled to blink back. Like I said before, the lonely girl inside me was never far from the surface.

"For a moment I committed my heart and soul to saving Steffie. How could that possibly cause Sugar Maple to vanish?" I asked Samuel.

"The talisman observed your loss of commitment at a time when Sugar Maple's residents needed your leadership most and took it from you."

I looked over at Luke but he was in full cop mode and his expression gave away nothing. I took the plunge alone.

"So you're saying that the talisman — an old piece of jewelry, a keepsake — took over the town?"

I had to hand it to the old man. He didn't bat an eye as he launched into an explanation.

"Since its creation the talisman has been sought after not only as a symbol of unity but as proof of strength. It began with Aerynn, who imbued it with the ability to protect Sugar Maple, and each of her descendants added to its powers, further ensuring the supremacy of the Hobbs clan."

"My mother didn't," I said. "She left this

dimension only a few earth years after her own mother pierced the veil."

"A rare exception to what had been the rule," Samuel agreed, "and one that weakened the chain. The years between Guinevere's leave-taking and your assumption of your powers were fraught with peril."

I frowned at him. "Peril? The town thrived!"

"That is what the residents of Sugar Maple wanted you to think," Samuel said. "You were struggling to find your way in the world, battling loneliness, waiting for the day when your powers would finally come to life. They didn't want you to know that with every day that passed, the talisman swayed closer to changing allegiance to Isadora."

Now that was just plain crazy talk. "But the talisman belonged to Aerynn's descendants. Even if Isadora stole it away, it would still respond only to a Hobbs."

Samuel shook his head sadly. "Before Aerynn and Da'Elle left Salem, their powers were nearly equal. The talisman gave Aerynn the edge that conferred leadership upon her. Da'Elle only followed her to Sugar Maple because she hoped to capture the talisman then return to Salem and rebuild the community the Witch Trials had

decimated. Over time, going beyond the mist replaced going back to Salem in the hearts of Da'Elle's descendants, but the hunger for the talisman only grew stronger."

"I thought Sugar Maple was my destiny and my mother's before me and her mother's, all the way back to Aerynn." This was like finding out there was no Santa Claus but worse.

"Aerynn's line has thus far proved wise and strong but do you believe the Fae would willingly play second fiddle to her descendants if there was no chance they could one day ascend to power?" He paused for a second to catch his breath. "The answer is no, Chloe: the leadership of Sugar Maple has always been determined by possession of the talisman and always will be."

"So nothing ever changed," I said. "We have the same problems with Isadora and her followers as Aerynn had with Da'Elle and hers."

"The bitterness runs deep and long," Samuel said with a quick glance toward Luke. "The treatment they received at human hands instilled a mighty distrust that time only served to intensify. When your mother Guinevere fell in love with your human father, the battle lines were drawn. Their deaths, however, only served to cool the flames for a moment because you posed an even bigger problem."

"They hated the idea of a leader with human blood," I said. "It's their worst nightmare."

"No," Samuel said, "their worst nightmare is the thought of the child you and Luke will one day have."

A child whose blood was three-quarters human and only one-quarter magick.

"The thought that the day would come when a leader who was more human than magick would assume control with the power of the talisman to enforce her rule had Isadora's clan teetering on the edge."

It took the arrival of Luke's ex-wife to bring everything tumbling down around us.

"Aerynn wasn't a seer but she understood the nature of her community. The only way they would survive in the mortal world was if the magick and Fae clans could continue to live in harmony. She knew that there would come a time when the tug-of-war would begin again and the sanctuary she had built in Sugar Maple would be in danger of toppling."

And so Aerynn reached for the talisman, the disk of Welsh gold that Samuel had placed in her care on the night she fled Salem, and imbued it with powers of its own

that would far outlive her own stay in this dimension.

"I thought the talisman already had magick," Luke said.

"You listen well," Samuel said, nodding his leonine head. "But Aerynn had something else in mind."

"The talisman would become an entity, a living thing with intellect and judgment and a strong sense of responsibility toward the future of Sugar Maple. No longer an inanimate object acquired to enhance an individual's power. The choices it made would be with the village's best interests at heart. Everything else would be secondary to that.

"If the talisman ever sensed that a Hobbs woman had lost control of the two factions and a coup was imminent, a fail-safe mechanism would be activated and Sugar Maple would be put in lockdown."

"Lockdown?" I imagined a high-security prison with guards and iron bars.

"Isn't that the modern terminology?" Samuel asked. "I heard it on *Law & Order*."

Luke assured him his terminology was correct.

"The town would be relegated to an alternate dimension," Samuel continued, "until if or when the problem resolved itself."

I felt like I had been kicked in the gut. Losing the town in battle to Isadora would have been easier to accept than this. I had lost it the moment I fell in love and let it slip through my fingers.

"My mother turned her back on Sugar Maple when she joined my father in mortal death. Why didn't that trigger a lockdown?"

"Despite the upheaval your mother's passing created, the town still thought as one. Fae and magick lived peacefully together as Aerynn had hoped. Sorcha was there to guide you into adulthood and the villagers were willing to wait for your powers to finally bloom. Those were good years for Sugar Maple. Happy ones."

"And then I grew up and blew it by falling in love with a mortal instead of a good-natured werebear from Ohio or a selkie from Maine." Someone who would bring more magick into the Hobbs genetic equation.

Samuel held my gaze. "We don't choose our destiny, child, not in this dimension or any other I have encountered. Our destiny chooses us."

"So tell me what to do," I demanded. "Don't give me stories. Don't show me home movies. Tell me what to do so I can get my home back."

"Stake your claim," he snapped, his temper obviously rising. "If you believe Sugar Maple is your destiny, then stand up and fight for what belongs to you."

"All I've done these last few months is fight for Sugar Maple. I wasn't raised to be a warrior!" The only thing I liked to fight was a balky cable crossing in an Aran sweater.

He rose to his feet. He towered over me. Anger radiated from him in waves of red and black that reared up and battled like cobras above his head. At least now I knew where my temper came from.

"You're not a warrior yet," he bellowed. "You don't know the meaning of the word. You fought to save your mate. You fought to save his child. But not once have you ever fought to save your home." He fixed me with a look that almost brought me to my knees. "Are you woman enough to do battle, Chloe, or will you be the Hobbs who loses everything?"

28

LUKE

We were going home.

According to Samuel, the Salem Fae had been in our old neighborhood since Sugar Maple disappeared, which was how they had managed to take control of Penny the cat and manipulate her actions during our road trip from hell. He was reasonably sure they were planning to stake claim to the town as soon as they could find the talisman.

"Mortals believe they have long memories," Samuel said as a pine table laden with steamed lobster, crabs, shrimp, ears of yellow corn, and snowy white potatoes appeared in the center of the room, "but the Fae will hold a grudge for millennia and beyond."

"The talisman wouldn't turn the town over to the Fae," Chloe said. "Would it?"

"If the talisman deemed the Fae the best

caretakers for Sugar Maple, then yes, it's possible."

"They tried to kill us," Chloe said. "They sent us plunging off a cliff. They blinded Luke. If the talisman is half as smart as you say it is, how could it possibly hand Sugar Maple to creatures like that?"

"The Fae fight for what they believe in," Samuel rebutted. "They are willing to risk all to achieve their goal."

"So did the Nazis," Chloe shot back. "So did Pol Pot. There has to be more to the equation than ferocity and focus."

Samuel smiled as Elspeth and Janice materialized next to him. I had the feeling he was responsible for the timing.

"Sit down," he said. "Enjoy the feast. We will all need nourishment for what lies ahead."

Chloe did as told. High color splotched her cheeks and her eyes were unnaturally bright. She wasn't finished with Samuel yet. Not by a long shot.

Me? I was scared shitless. I had battled the Fae twice before and I would have bought the farm both times if first Gunnar, then Chloe hadn't come to the rescue. My odds weren't looking too good.

Although Samuel had assured me that we were not living by the human clock in the

305

lighthouse and only seconds had passed in the real world since our arrival, I felt the urgency to get back on the road.

"He is as jumpy as a bug on a skillet," Elspeth observed, looking over at me. "It must be a human trait."

Janice laughed and whispered something that made the old crone cackle as she cracked a lobster claw with her twisted fingers.

"You two are getting along," Chloe observed. "So blood really is thicker than water."

Janice ignored the edge in Chloe's voice. "I've made a decision," she said, neatly placing her empty crab shell in the waste bowl next to her. "You're not going to like it, but I've decided to stay here with Elspeth and Samuel until Sugar Maple . . ." Her words trailed off.

"Stay here?" Chloe leaped to her feet. "Why in the world would you want to stay here?"

I placed a warning hand on Chloe's arm but she jerked away. Janice's family was gone and they might not be coming back. Elspeth was her blood. There was a place for her here. It was something even a human could understand.

Janice's eyes flashed but somehow she

306

maintained her cool. "Elspeth is the finest healer I've ever encountered. There's a lot I can learn from her."

"And she can help me with Himself," Elspeth said, jerking her bright yellow head in Samuel's direction. "He requires a lot, he does. An extra pair of hands would go nicely around here."

I had the feeling there was nothing Elspeth couldn't handle on her own. Her unexpected act of kindness toward Janice surprised the hell out of me. Then I caught the look of concern in her eyes as she looked at Samuel, who was drooping slightly in his captain's chair, and remembered her words from before.

Samuel had commented that clan leadership would pass to Chloe when he pierced the veil and Elspeth, in high dudgeon, had said: "Which he would have done by now if not for you, missy!"

I suddenly realized she hadn't been lying. Samuel was hanging on by sheer force of will. Only his determination to bring Chloe closer to her destiny was keeping him in this dimension.

I looked over at Chloe. Did she know how close Samuel was to leaving this dimension? I wasn't sure. I also wasn't sure how much she would care. Right now only Sugar

Maple mattered.

We finished eating and Elspeth magicked the dishes away with a flick of her apron. She took up her post next to Samuel and practically dared any one of us to question her right to be there. None of us was that crazy.

"I'll need your help finding my car," Chloe said to Samuel. "I think it's still in the parking garage near the visitor center."

"You won't need your car," Samuel said. "I have arranged for other means of transportation."

Her eyes widened. "I thought you lacked the power to effect a long-distance transport."

"But I don't lack the resources to patch together an alternative," he said. "You will be safely and swiftly carried to your destination."

"Both of us?" I asked, just wanting to make sure.

Chloe met my eyes. "You're staying here."

"The hell I am. I'm going with you."

"That's not happening."

"Nonnegotiable," I said. "We're in this together."

"Talk some sense into him," she said to Samuel. "He's mortal. He doesn't stand a chance against an army of Fae."

"Chloe is right," Samuel said. "Entering the battle would be an act of suicide."

I turned to Chloe. "Would you let me go into battle alone?"

Her expression softened. "That's different."

"How?"

"You know how." She lowered her voice. "I'm magick, Luke. I understand what we're facing. I have the tools to fight it. They would mow you down in the first ten seconds."

"Then they mow me down," I said. "We're in this together."

She looked at Janice for help. "Say something, Jan. You know what we're going to be up against." But Janice shook her head and said nothing. "Damn it, Luke! I don't want to see you die."

"Your courage is admirable," Samuel said, "but foolhardy. Is there nothing we can do to sway you from your course?"

"You could kill me," I said, "but I'm not sure that would stop me."

Samuel considered me for a long moment. "You feel strong hatred toward the Fae?"

I held his gaze. "I feel strong love toward Chloe."

"Then I will give you the tools to even the playing field."

Even I knew this was no time for macho crap about not wanting any help. I needed all the help I could get.

"What kind of tools?" Chloe asked. She didn't sound too thrilled.

"Magick," said Samuel. "That's the only thing that will save him."

Holy shit. I was picturing a superhero costume like the guy wore in *Iron Man*.

But the old man's plans were bigger than that. He proposed to give me temporary powers that would enable me to not just survive the battle at hand but to help win it.

"Twenty-four hours at most," he said. "That's all you will have."

"No problem," I said. "That's all the time we'll need."

The old man and I both knew the battle would never get that far.

CHLOE

"Do something," I begged Janice. "Luke doesn't know what he's getting into."

"He knows," Janice said. "That's why he took Samuel up on his offer."

"Cast some type of spell on him. There has to be some way to keep him here where he'll be safe."

"He's *your* human," Janice said with a shake of her head. "Haven't you learned anything about him? Even I know that nothing short of a bomb will keep him from you."

"Then drop a bomb. He can't go back with me, Janice. Something terrible will happen."

Or maybe it was happening already. Samuel had warned me about this. I felt my focus shifting away from Sugar Maple and zeroing in on Luke, which was a surefire path to losing my hometown and everyone in it forever.

"He's a grown man," Janice said. "He knows what he wants. Let him make his own choices, Chloe. It's his life."

Samuel had bestowed twenty-four hours of magick on Luke and given him a crash course in how to use it. Luke was crouched next to Samuel's chair, taking in everything the old man had to say as if his life depended on it.

Twenty-four hours of magick and maybe ten minutes to learn how to use it.

I didn't like the odds.

Elspeth handed me a small pouch of herbs that she guaranteed would keep me focused on the job at hand.

I hugged Janice tight. "Watch Penny for me," I said. "Don't let her try to follow me."

"With all the lobster around here, she

won't even notice you're gone."

"And take good care of the Buick."

"I was thinking about letting high tide take it out to sea." She grinned even though her eyes brimmed with tears. "After I saved your stash."

It felt good to laugh. I had the feeling I wouldn't be doing much of it in the near future.

Elspeth was watching me with a little less hostility. "You young ones know nothing about the old magick," she said. "Beware the expected: that is where the true danger lies."

"Elspeth speaks the truth," Samuel said as we joined him and Luke. "Old magick relies on your most basic fears. They won't hesitate to tap into your memories. Strive to empty your mind of all but the battle at hand. Don't let them lead you astray or they will weaken and then destroy you."

The room fell into silence. What more was there to say?

"So how do we get back to Sugar Maple?" Luke asked.

Okay. There was that.

"You have magick now," Samuel said. "We'll use astral transport."

We were going to battle New England Fae for control of a magickal town. Taking a puddle jumper out of Logan just didn't cut it. I wasn't about to tell Luke but the thought of being beamed from Salem to northern Vermont made driving on ice sound like a walk in the park.

And, considering what was waiting for us, that was pretty funny.

Finally we were ready to go.

I hugged Janice, kissed the top of Penny's head, returned Elspeth's grave nod, then went eye to eye with the man who had been Aerynn's mate.

"You understand what is needed?" he asked.

"I understand."

"Full commitment," he reiterated. "Anything less and they will find a way to destroy you."

"You need to work on your motivational speeches," I said. "That one makes me want to jump out the window and swim to shore."

"In your world, those remarks are considered witty."

I shrugged. "Snarky might be a better word."

"I know that they provide cover for your emotions."

"I'm not sure you know anything at all about me, Samuel," I replied calmly. "But I appreciate the help you've given us."

I refused to acknowledge the quaver in my voice. The fact that this man was my blood filled me with the kind of sadness that lies beyond words. How different my life would have been if he had reached out to me ten or twenty years ago. But it was too late now.

"I wish you good speed," he said, touching my hand with his and for an instant my bitterness fell away and acknowledgment took its place.

We are one, I thought as I met his eyes. *I know that.*

And I will be with you always.

I started to smile. "You're better than a ventriloquist," I said and, to my surprise, he laughed.

Out loud.

In a way that touched the human side of my heart.

And then, just like that, we were gone.

29

LUKE

Samuel's baritone was still ringing in my ears as I landed headfirst in the notch of a snow-covered maple tree.

Guess I had my answer to "Are we there yet?"

"Luke!" Chloe's voice sounded from somewhere nearby. "Where are you?"

"Up a tree," I hollered. "Where are you?"

"In a snowdrift."

"Are you okay?"

"Freezing," she said. "I think we did it."

I righted myself and let myself down to the snow-cushioned ground. "You're right," I said. I knew exactly where we were.

I spotted Chloe some twenty feet away as she muscled her way out of the snowdrift. I pushed my way through and met her halfway.

"You look like hell," she said with a small laugh.

"You don't look so great yourself," I shot back, laughing with her.

We had just traveled hundreds of miles in the span of a breath. The fact that we weren't splattered globs of protoplasm seemed pretty amazing. Nothing broken, not even a tree branch.

"He's good," she said, glancing around.

"Pinpoint accuracy."

"He didn't have enough power to do it himself." Her voice broke unexpectedly and she coughed to cover it. "Elspeth told me he called in favors from friends in other dimensions."

"He gave me his powers, didn't he?"

"And more," she said. "Otherwise you probably wouldn't have made it through in one piece."

"Let's hear it for magick powers."

"Last chance to change your mind," she said. "Why don't you use those magick powers of yours and go somewhere safe like Afghanistan or Iraq."

"Because I love you," I said, "and I'm in this for keeps."

The look in her beautiful golden eyes said it all.

There was no way we could lose.

We were standing at the edge of the clearing where we had stood the night we battled

Isadora at the waterfall. In the waning moonlight we looked at the dense forest that stood in the place Sugar Maple used to be. Except for the mountains of melting snow, nothing had changed.

"I think it's still there," Chloe said, "but we won't know for sure until we get through that memory foam barrier the Salem Fae set up."

"Any idea how we can do that?"

She outlined a simple plan that had at least one or two chances in hell of working.

According to Samuel, this was the first time the talisman had executed the fail-safe plan so there were no historical references to help determine where it had taken Sugar Maple. The old man's best guess was that the town was still in the same physical location but in a different dimension of time. That theory explained a couple of questions that had been nagging at me: Janice's time-delayed appearance in the Buick and the untouched, almost primeval look of the forest.

"Don't overthink it," Chloe warned me. "That's what always screws me up. Samuel said they'll be using old magick."

"Which means what?" Old magic, new magic. The difference wasn't clear to me.

"New magick transported us from Salem

to Sugar Maple. Old magick trapped me in an empty rest stop."

"I don't get it."

"Old magick is more personal. It preys on your fears, so do whatever you can to keep your mind clear. Don't give them anything to grab hold of."

"Shouldn't be a problem. I'll be too busy trying to keep from turning myself into a basset hound."

She smiled but I could see the nerves behind it. "Let your powers be an extension of yourself and your abilities. That way you won't get into trouble."

"When this is over —," I began.

She pressed a swift kiss to my mouth. "— We'll still be together."

We started across the field toward the forest that dominated the place where Sugar Maple once thrived. One step . . . two steps . . . on the third I was walking across the top of the melting snow, not sinking into it. A loud laugh of surprise and wonder broke free and echoed around us. Chloe, eyes dancing, motioned for me to take it down a few notches. But hell, how many times in your life do you get to levitate?

Because that was what I was doing. I was walking on air at least three inches above the snow. The last time I felt this pumped

I'd just taken down two perps in a home invasion sting. And let me tell you this was a hell of a lot better.

I took bigger steps, faster and faster, sure that I could take off and fly if I wanted to.

"Luke." Chloe sounded a warning. "You've got to pull it back."

She was right. Too bad there was no time to enjoy it.

We reached the stand of maples in a handful of seconds and this time we gained a foothold and began scaling the invisible wall. I'd expected a straight vertical climb but instead it felt gently curved, almost domelike.

When we were about twenty feet off the ground Chloe stopped climbing. "No point going any higher," she said.

She took a long slow breath, repositioned herself, then let go with her right hand. She flexed her fingers twice then pointed toward a spot about five feet away and closed her eyes.

At first I sensed rather than saw the heat. A faint hissing sound was followed by a spray of sparks spilling from her fingertips. I watched, impressed, as her eyes opened and she focused in on the spray, refining it, focusing it, until the sparks burst into flames worthy of an industrial-strength blowtorch.

319

A hole the size of a half dollar appeared. A faintly sulfurous smell wafted toward me. Chloe's concentration didn't waver. The flames grew hotter. The hole grew wider and wider still until it could accommodate a grown man.

Which was a damn good thing since a second later we were both sucked through it and plunged straight into hell.

CHLOE

Nothing prepared me for the darkness as the opening we had been pulled through closed behind us. Moonless nights fell hard in northern Vermont. Far away from big-city lights, the deep velvety blackness absorbed everything it touched.

But this was different. This darkness had weight and dimension. The silence was profound.

"Don't move," I warned Luke and he grunted his assent. We could be standing above a river of piranha or poised at the edge of a cliff. It was anybody's guess.

Seconds passed. I had hoped that our eyes would adjust to the intense darkness but no such luck.

"Maybe we're in a cave," Luke said.

My stomach clenched at the thought of bats. I instantly pushed the image out of my head. No point giving our opponents extra ammunition.

"We're not in a cave," I said with more certainty than I felt. "Caves smell cool and damp."

And this was anything but cool. In fact, it was getting downright steamy.

I wasn't getting a good feeling.

And neither was Luke. "Can you burn another opening for us? I'm starting to feel like a burger on a grill."

I tried but nothing happened. "Damn," I whispered as waves of heat closed around us. "Nothing's happening."

I tried again. Still nothing.

"Did you hear that?" Luke asked.

"You mean that sloshing sound?"

"And what about the stench?"

I sniffed the superheated air. "Rotten eggs and tar." And something darker, more malevolent.

"Shit," Luke said. "I'm burning up."

"So am I." Sweat stung my eyes and poured down my back. "It must be one hundred twenty degrees in here."

"This is worse than Phoenix in July," he said.

I wouldn't know. I had never been anywhere but Sugar Maple in July.

I tried to burn us a way out but whatever

firepower I had was dwarfed by the heat bouncing off the walls. Even the soles of my feet were starting to burn.

Imagination is a powerful tool. Most of the time what you imagined was far more frightening than anything reality could dish up.

Not this time.

The walls surrounding us began to glow a faint orange and with the light the details came clear. We were standing on an outcropping of rock overlooking a bubbling, steaming pool of golden red molten lava that overflowed the sides of its enclosure and spilled down into the bowels of the earth. Every few seconds a huge plume of lava erupted from the center of that pool and scalded our faces with its unbearable heat as it shot up past us in a shower of multicolored sparks.

This wild sea of lava stretched as far as the eye could see and was punctuated by more than a dozen boulders of varying sizes that had yet to vanish beneath the molten flood.

"I've seen this on Discovery Channel," Luke said. "We're inside an active volcano."

Which we both knew was impossible because we would have been turned into toast within the first nanosecond.

"This isn't real," I reminded both of us. "This is an illusion." Old magick specialized in illusions.

Still, I had to admit it was a good one.

And, if I remembered what Samuel had told me about old magick, it was every bit as deadly.

It didn't seem possible, but the heat had intensified to the point where I was having trouble standing upright. The sweat that had been running freely dried up. My mouth felt parched as desert sand. I was dizzy, chilled and burning at the same time. Framing a sentence became a challenge.

If possible, Luke was suffering even more. Not even the overlay of magick was enough to shield his mortal body from the onslaught.

"I changed my mind," he managed with a wobbly gesture toward the inferno beneath us. "This isn't just a volcano: this is hell."

Luke had spent eight years in Catholic school. The notion of hell as a specific place had been ingrained in him from an early age. It would have been easy for them to grab his memories and shape them to their own advantage.

"Empty your thoughts," I begged. "Don't give them anything to use against us."

I wondered what fears I had already given

away. Driving over thirty miles an hour, driving on ice, driving in general, snakes, spiders, rabbits, creepy crawly insects, enclosed spaces, splitty yarn, slasher movies —

Stop! I willed my brain to go blank, which was a whole lot easier said than done. Why hadn't I paid more attention to Janice when she tried to teach me how to meditate? *Take a deep breath,* she always began.

But every breath I took made me feel like my lungs were being scalded from the inside, which made the extreme dizziness even more fun. I wasn't sure if the world had suddenly tilted on its axis or I had. I also wasn't sure which was worse.

I had to sit. I didn't care how hot the rocks beneath me were. If I didn't sit down in the next ten seconds, I was going to fall headfirst into the deadly magma.

Get out, a voice inside my head urged. *You don't need this. You could make a life in Salem with Luke. Open a new yarn shop. Start all over without all the old Sugar Maple baggage. This is the twenty-first century. Don't be mired in decisions made hundreds of years ago.*

The logic was hard to argue. No more fighting. No more struggling to prove myself. No more apologizing for my mother's decisions. Everything would be all shiny and new again, including me.

All I had to do was take Luke's hand, admit defeat, then slip back into the mortal world where I would be Chloe Hobbs, knitter and spinner and shop owner. A tall gawky blond human female who would be living only half a life without magick.

And wasn't that exactly what they wanted me to do: start doubting my resolve? Start doubting my love for Sugar Maple, my deep and abiding connection to everyone who lived there? If you lost your past, you lost everything. Samuel had warned me about this and he had been right. They were trying to wear me down with the ancient weapons of fear and physical pain. I needed to stay focused or I would lose this battle before it began.

But how did you fight what you couldn't see?

I could feel entities all around me but so far they hadn't showed themselves. Every now and then I heard a faint rustling, caught an unfamiliar scent in the superheated air, sensed a presence near enough to touch, but whatever it was remained cloaked against us.

Luke's face was the pale beige of over-milked tea. His beautiful green eyes were glazed and red rimmed. I touched his forehead and was shocked by the icy feel of his skin, such a marked difference from the unbearable heat in this domelike enclosure.

"Sit down before you pass out," I said to him. "You look like hell."

"I'm fine."

The macho male was alive and well.

"You don't look it," I said.

"It's hot," he snapped. "What do you want from me?"

I couldn't force him to sit, not without expending precious magick I would need later. Besides, he had magick now and he wasn't afraid to use it.

Next to me his body stiffened.

"What?" I asked. "Do you see something?"

"Straight ahead, eight o'clock position."

I looked where he directed.

"Any ideas?" he asked.

"You can see them?" I asked, surprised.

"Can you?"

I nodded. Two pudgy crones sat at spinning wheels, floating in midair, oblivious to the flames dancing all around them and the gusher of molten lava erupting beneath them every few seconds.

Then again, why would they care?

Ghosts Tabitha and Dorcas, my old bathtub buddies, were already dead.

ced ten feet away from the heart
e volcano.

that mean I had to stand there
up on a log and not do anything
n?

d up a lifeline that would be vis-
o him and anchored it around the
ost I'd also conjured that was now
ched to the ledge. All I had to do
s attention, then throw him the
the magick contained within
he rest.

nately the Fae had other ideas.

npricks of light emerged from the
nd danced along my arms and
stomach. They twined themselves
e lifeline with eerie accuracy and
ies of synchronized movements
ning into nothingness.

ts on a hot summer night the Fae
arty was out for blood.

y magicks were immune to their
ut my half-human heritage made
able. None of the Fae in Sugar
ever exploited my weakness. I'm
d ever seen a Fae scouting party
incident in the antique shop.
dora hadn't liked me, she had
e with the deference I deserved
o mayor and leader of the town

CHLOE

"They're the ghosts from the tub," I said as they stopped spinning and started staring. "The ones who tried to drown me."

"They're not real." It was his turn to do the reminding. "Blank out your mind and they'll disappear."

I went all white noise but the two crones didn't budge.

"Crap," I said. "They should've vanished."

"*Should have* butters no parsnips," the crone named Dorcas called out.

"We warned you," Tabitha trilled. "I do not know why you chose to make your life so difficult."

"Stubborn like her mother," Dorcas agreed. "Right down to the human she took as consort."

Tabitha nodded and resumed spinning. "This one is stronger than the last. Death was a blessing for Guinevere and her mate."

"Shut up." My hands were curled into fists by my sides. "I won't let you talk about my parents that way."

"Let it go, Chloe," Luke said calmly. "They're baiting you." The color seemed to flow back into his face. "Don't let them distract you."

"You should be worried," Dorcas said in a pleasingly gentle voice. "Your human cannot possibly survive what is to come."

"Your threats don't scare us!" I called out as I gauged the distance between me and the nearest boulder. "You tried to keep me from Samuel, my only family!"

"Let it go," Luke repeated, this time with more heat. "They're chumming. Don't take the bait."

"They tried to drown me back at the motel," I shot back. "How do you know they're not the enemy we came here to defeat? You're human. You don't understand the way they think. You can't possibly —"

You know that old saying, Leap and the net will appear? That was all I could think about when Luke suddenly launched himself into midair and landed on top of the nearest boulder. Then again *landed* might not be the right word. He crashed into it and was now clinging to its surface as he struggled to gain purchase and position

himself on top.

A hideous chai[n]
words spewed from
the top, balanced
the next one. He
powers and no e
could only hope S
not even magick c

He leaped to the
and then the next,
spirits, who had a
yet again and wer
sardonic glee as th
feet away from whe
the glistening rock.

And then I realiz
Dorcas and Tabith
temporary powers
your average gard
male staking out h
the price. The two
seat to the impen
that they believed v
the talisman spinn
ever.

Luke was doing
tion away from me
to face the real cha
Sugar Maple. Whic
the fact that the on

was bala[n]
of an acti[v]
But did
like a bur
to help hi
I conjur
ible only t
hitching p
firmly att[a]
was get h
rope, and
would do
Unfortu
Little pi
shadows
across my
around th
with a se
sent it spi
Like gn[a]
scouting
Normal
mischief,
me vulne
Maple ha
not sure
before th
While Is
tolerated
as pro b[o]

and I had returned the respect.

The Salem Fae didn't much care about deference and respect. I was the enemy and they were going to use everything at their disposal to take me down, including body-mapping me and turning my own biology against me.

The pinpricks of light encircled my head like a wreath. I could feel the heat pressing against my temples, my forehead, my ears. Had they already gleaned information or did I still have time to stop them before they could upload my secrets?

I reached back into my Book of Spells training, visualized a page of information, then said, "Encircle, entangle, entrap," three times and was rewarded with the sight of those annoying little beasts being gathered up in a black velvet pouch, then tossed into the heart of the volcano.

I'd have time to congratulate myself on averting catastrophe later.

I shrank back into the shadows and struggled to clear my mind. More than anything I wanted to send help Luke's way but each attempt at sending him a lifeline resulted in a rise in the lava that was already threatening to sweep him away.

Dorcas and Tabitha were floating free of their parapet, laughing uproariously as he clung to the high point of another boulder. Their abandoned spinning wheels were lying on their sides. The rock wall behind them shimmered with some kind of glaze. In spots it glowed red-hot.

With only the spinning wheels to provide scale, I had difficulty determining how big a space we were in but I assumed it encompassed Sugar Maple's footprint. Height and depth? Infinity was a good guess.

Cloudlike bursts of white light randomly dotted the darkened sky. They were too big for a scouting party but too small for stars. I held my breath as ropes of glittering silver chains snapped and whipped their way toward Luke, who was now balanced on the last remaining boulder.

No fear, I told myself. *No fear.* I filled my mind with nothing but hanks of pure silk dyed in jewel tones of ruby and sapphire and topaz.

The ropes of silver chain sizzled through the air as they swung toward his head. He ducked just in time. Dorcas's and Tabitha's laughter rang out through the superheated, sulfurous air as they swooped closer to him.

No fear . . . no fear.

He took a halfhearted swing at the pudgy ghosts, stumbled, and dropped to one knee as red-hot lava lapped at his feet.

Dorcas grabbed one of the chains. Tabitha grabbed another. They swung them around as if they were rodeo cowboys twirling lariats. The shimmering circles of metal dropped over Luke's head and settled around his neck.

No fear . . . no fear . . . no fear . . . concentrate on your surroundings . . . don't let yourself be distracted . . .

Bile rose into my mouth as Luke made a choking sound and grabbed for his throat. Those girls played rough. For all his years as a cop, I wasn't sure he was prepared to go one-on-one with a pair of old ladies. Even if they had been dead for a few hundred years.

Crap . . . don't think . . . empty your brain . . . no fear . . . no fear . . . don't give them anything to use against him.

The spirits swooped over him, laughing, mocking. He was gasping for air, frantically clawing at the lights around his neck. If he was aware of Tabitha and Dorcas, he gave no indication until the moment when, with a howl, he broke free of the stranglehold and launched himself into the two spirits like a cannonball.

The moment they collided an explosion slammed me back against the rock wall, knocking the breath from my parched lungs.

I slid down the wall until my butt hit the narrow ledge and I clung to it, blinded by the chaotic fireworks display before my eyes. Each successive concussion sent shock waves through my body. When the light show ended, I wasn't surprised to see that Luke had disappeared, along with Tabitha and Dorcas.

It's okay . . . everything's fine . . . he's a cop . . . he knows what he's doing . . . it's probably some kind of plan he and Sam —

I forced myself to stop thinking, stop feeling, stop doing anything that could put him in danger. He had plowed the road for me. Now I had to do the rest.

If only I knew exactly what that was.

The volcano, which had been shooting plumes of lava one hundred feet into the air every few seconds, fell quiet. The temperature began to drop noticeably and I realized I was shivering. The velvety darkness that had greeted us returned but this time it was punctuated by a starry "sky" that took my breath away. One star, brighter than the rest, flickered on and off with metronomic precision.

A couple of ghosts, some lava, a few fireworks, and it was all over? I didn't think so. Luke's actions had probably derailed the plan, whatever it was, and they were regrouping.

Fine with me. I had been taken by surprise in the antique shop when the spinning wheels had rallied against me and —

I tried to push the images away but it was too late. They were literally dancing in front of my eyes. Six Scottish wheels hovered in front of me like enormous hummingbirds. A traveling wheel nudged my right hip.

Spinning wheels.

Seriously?

If this was old magick, I wasn't impressed. At this rate the talisman would leap into my arms and pledge its undying devotion.

I grabbed the traveling wheel and flung it into the Scottish wheels. It caromed off the first, the second, all the way through to the last, shattering each in turn. The silky wood splintered into thousands of toothpicks that scattered through the starry darkness like pollen in spring.

Before I could congratulate myself on a job well done, seven glittering orbs of light rose up in front of me in the place where the wheels had been. They spun counterclockwise, giving off sprays of butter yellow, lime green, tangerine orange, chestnut brown, aquamarine, orchid, and lemon yellow glitter. Under different circumstances this would have been a real Kodak moment.

"So here we are," intoned the lime green orb. I recognized the voice from the Salem antique shop. "We've been waiting for this."

"But there's one problem," the lemon yellow orb said, also in a voice I'd heard before.

"We think you'd feel more at home somewhere else," the glittery tangerine orb chimed in. The four others bobbed as they spun and murmured agreement.

I wasn't crazy about where I was but better the devil you know. Not that I had a choice in the matter. The interior of volcanic hell was instantly replaced with a scene I knew all too well: the abandoned highway rest stop where I had gotten my ass kicked and only Samuel's timely intervention had saved me.

Okay. I could deal with it. This was like green screen effects on a movie set: it was only as real as you allowed it to be. And I refused to let it be anything more than a minor distraction.

Funny thing, though: even though the sparkling night sky had gone dark, that same lone star still sparkled from the highest point.

Whatever.

I told myself it was all a façade, that nothing I was seeing or feeling had any basis in my reality, but my bone-deep fear of loneliness was stronger than logic. The scene looked like something from a Stephen King novel after the apocalypse. A weird hybrid of normal and bizarre that played into every dark night I ever spent wishing for a family, a home, some place where I belonged.

I was standing in front of an abandoned rest stop in the middle of a desert that stretched to infinity in every direction. No birdsong. No distant rumble of highway noise. Not even the faint whoosh of the wind moving across all of that emptiness. Just . . . nothing.

"She doesn't like it," one of the orbs observed.

"Look at the way she's breathing," another offered. "Any second and she'll need a paper bag to keep from passing out!"

The rest of them bounced with laughter, bumping into each other in what seemed to be the glitter orb equivalent of high-fiving.

"I don't care how powerful her magick is," said a third, "she's still half human and where was it written that a human could lead a clan?"

Let them talk, I told myself. They wanted me to lose my temper and forget why I was there but it wasn't going to happen.

It would take a lot more than some misguided high school taunts to make me forget that the future of Sugar Maple and everyone in it was hanging in the balance.

This time I was ready for whatever they threw my way.

Insults? Bring 'em on.

Bad-tempered wheels? No problem.

A tiny windowless room with no ventilation, no way out, and wall-to-wall spiders?

I might be in trouble.

31

CHLOE

Clearly they had been saving the good stuff.

I was inside the front lobby of the abandoned rest stop, feeling like the scientists in *Jurassic Park* just before T. Rex showed up on the scene. A banner reading ALL YOU CAN EAT AND MORE hung lopsided over the locked door of the once-popular buffet. The doors to the restrooms had been boarded over. Crumpled coffee cups and bent straws littered the scuffed tile floor. I could still smell the memory of french fries and sweat in the underoxygenated air.

I wanted out.

I wanted out *now.*

Deep breaths, I warned myself. Nothing was the way it seemed. For all I knew I was still on the snowy field between the woods and Sugar Maple's old footprint and these were nothing but a string of Fae mind games meant to bring me to my knees.

Another deep breath. Square my shoulders. Have a backup plan in mind. March my butt to the exit as fast as I could.

Too bad the exit was gone. And the buffet. And the trashed-up hallway. I was in a tiny windowless room with no ventilation and no way out. Once again the only constant was the twinkling star that seemed to hang high above it all, even though the ceiling was so low it grazed the top of my head. The walls were pressing inward and I was starting to feel like a panini when something soft brushed against the back of my neck. I managed to turn around in this hideous little vertical coffin and saw the most magnificent handknitted shawl imaginable clinging to the wall. It shimmered like diamonds scattered across a field of moon-washed snow.

I instantly realized there were no purl-back resting rows involved in this design. It was pure lace technique, long row after long row of yarn overs and beadwork mixed with intricate, perfectly balanced decreases.

Maybe you had to be a knitter to understand but my whole life was about manipulating whisper-fine yarn into something beautiful. I dreamed in stitches. The love of fiber was woven through my DNA as far back as you could trace.

340

All of my attempts to keep my mind a total blank went up in smoke when I touched that mind-blowing shawl. It was like holding a cloud of dreams in my hands. Diamondlike crystals had been handknitted into the shawl at precisely calculated intervals. The level of workmanship was far beyond anything I had ever dreamed possible. I was good but, as far as I knew, nobody was *this* good.

That should have been my first clue but I was too in love to think straight.

Oh, the spiderweb fineness of the silk yarn! Oh, the dazzling sparkle of the crystals!

Oh, the thousands of hairy silver spiders leaping from that intricate web of beauty and onto my head, my shoulders, my arms.

I opened my mouth to scream and two of the fuzzy monsters perched on my lower lip, leaking acrid juices that dripped into my mouth and launched me into the dry heaves. The room was the size of an old-fashioned phone booth. The walls were covered with arachnids. The shawl was completely obliterated by the sheer number of them. They smelled musty and hot and the more I slapped them off my body and picked them from my hair, the faster they swarmed back to take me out.

My legs were covered from my ankles to my thighs with fat hot crawling hairy spiders. I felt the sting of their bristles as they slid under my jeans and crawled up up up. I swatted, smacked, screamed, smooshed myself against the spider-covered wall in a crazed attempt to kill as many of them as I possibly could before they did a *Star Trek* move and crawled into my ear and burrowed through my cerebral cortex.

The magick side of my brain knew these spiders were illusions courtesy of the Fae but the human side was in control. For the most part my brain entirely shut down and I was reduced to a state of shrieking mindless primitive terror. If I'd been behind the wheel of my Buick, I would have driven off a bridge to escape these hideous creatures. Anything to escape them.

They were inside my T-shirt, crawling into my bra, slithering around the curve of my left ear, moving across my cheek toward my nose, gliding over my knees and up my thighs until I was reduced to nothing but one long scream.

They were on the button of my jeans, the zipper pull, along the stitching on the pockets. One dived into my ear and a wave of fury rose up inside me and I knew I had my answer.

I battled to push fear aside and let rage take its place. And the angrier I got, the more my fingertips began to tingle, and the more they tingled —

Here's some unsolicited advice. If you're ever trapped in a room with seven million spiders, embrace your inner rage. Sometimes a bad temper is the only thing separating a girl from a total meltdown.

The flames shot from my fingertips, crisscrossing in midair, turning spiders into charcoal briquettes at an amazing rate. Sizzle! Sputter! The stink of burning arachnid in that small airless room was stomach turning but I could live with it. The more I killed, the more disappeared of their own volition. For every one I blasted with firepower, another twenty fell from my body and disappeared.

I let out a whoop of triumph when the walls pulled and the room expanded, growing wider and deeper as more spiders met their maker.

I zapped the last one and watched it shrivel into a dried-up spider patty. A moment later the ceiling lifted up and away but the solitary star remained in position and I laughed out loud in a combination of exhaustion, glee, and amusement.

Old magick? Old technology was more like it.

The Fae had a surveillance camera watching me!

They could watch me all they wanted. It wasn't like I was about to stage a strip show for the camera unless dead spiders had a thing for lap dances. Now there was an embarrassing way to make a buck. In fact, anything that even remotely included dancing was way out of my comfort zone. The thought of lap dancing anytime, anyplace, for anyone, brought on a wicked case of the giggles.

Great. Now the Fae could observe the rightful leader of Sugar Maple dissolve into helpless laughter like a five-year-old in church.

"Stop it!" I ordered myself. Nerves, that was all it was. A bad case of post-traumatic spider syndrome. Relief was pouring out of me in gales of laughter. Nothing wrong with that as long as I managed to keep my focus on Sugar Maple while I rode it out.

A door opened up where the beautiful shawl had been and I dashed through it before it could have second thoughts.

Instead of the desolate main lobby with the crumpled paper cups and bent straws, I found myself in a narrow whitewashed hallway punctuated every ten feet by doors right and left. The ceiling had been replaced with a dome of glass. Brilliant sunlight flooded the space, bouncing off the highly polished hospital-white tiled floor and back up to the sky.

I waved at the twinkling surveillance camera, hoping I looked casual and not at all concerned about this latest turn of events.

The camera didn't wave back but then I didn't really think it would.

I don't know how you feel about closed doors but they were giving me the creeps. In fact, I would put closed doors right up there with circus clowns and hockey masks. My heartbeat accelerated painfully as I passed a pair of doors then by the time it even considered returning to a normal rate, it leaped up again in anticipation of more doors. My chest actually started to hurt and I was thinking 911 and who the heck would give me CPR.

The only thing that kept me putting one foot in front of the other was the hope that each step brought me closer to bringing Sugar Maple and the friends I loved back home where they belonged.

I kept a sharp eye out for runaway spiders but so far, so good. Every now and again a shiver ran down my spine that felt uncomfortably like phantom legs dancing across my skin. Every inch of my body screamed for a week or two under a hot shower where I could wash away the traces of sticky spider residue. A lobotomy wouldn't be bad either if they could just remove the part of my brain that held memories of being trapped in that upright casket with wall-to-wall spiders.

Thinking about the spiders almost took the edge off all those closed doors.

Almost but not quite.

Gunnar hated horror movies, too.

I refused to think about my best friend, who had died saving Luke.

Luke was so vulnerable that night, so terribly mortal —

I wasn't going to think about Luke either. That would be like opening my heart, my dreams, my hopes to them.

No.

Absolutely not.

The hallway ended at a T intersection where I could turn right or left. A faint buzz of apprehension moved along my skin like the hum of bees. The decision took on epic proportions. Beads of sweat trickled down the back of my neck as I stood there, unable to choose. I wished I had a coin to flip, some way to avoid making the decision my-self.

My inclination was to go right so I went left. At the time it made a kind of loopy sense to me.

This hallway was identical to the last. Stark white. Blindingly brilliant sunshine reflected everywhere. The surveillance camera twinkling from on high.

And those doors. I hated those doors. Blank faces staring out at me, shielding secrets I didn't want revealed.

Terrible things hid behind closed doors. Stolen goods. Dead bodies. Murderers with cleavers the size of legs of lamb.

Stop it! Don't give them any more ammunition.

Think of bluebirds in spring. Think of crackling hearths on cold winter nights. Think of a truckful of Malabrigo wound into center-pull balls and ready to knit.

I made it past the first two pairs of doors without incident. This was old magick so it figured they would trot out the haunted house scenario. Why mess with success? Haunted houses had been scaring the Halloween costumes off kids for as long as anyone could remember. When it came to thrills and chills, it was a golden oldie.

And I hate to admit it but it worked. The

unknown scared the crap out of me. The doors were probably props that led to nowhere but they still managed to give off a malicious vibe.

I forced my shoulders down from my ears and kept walking. If I was going to convince the talisman, wherever it might be, that I was the right one to lead Sugar Maple, I had to exhibit both courage and resolve. Not to mention the ability to kick a little ass when necessary.

This was one of those times when a girl just had to act *as if.*

I strode down the hallway, head held high, a confident spring in my step. First the spinning wheels, then the spiders, and now these ominous closed doors. If they wanted to play childish parlor games, that was fine with me. I could handle whatever they chose to dish out and keep coming back for more.

At least that was what I thought until I reached the next-to-last door on the right. It swung open and a black-robed giant leaped out, grabbed me, and pressed the sharp edge of a dangerously curved sword against the soft part of my throat.

The steel was cold and I stopped breathing. The slightest movement and I'd be sliced like a Christmas ham.

I couldn't tell if the creature was male or

female. The only thing I knew for sure was that it wanted me dead.

Up until that moment I had labored under the belief that everything I saw, everything I was experiencing, was the result of an elaborate series of illusions created by my very inventive Fae opponents. But this time I knew that wasn't the case.

Magick knows magick. We recognize each other in a crowd without saying a word. There was definitely magick in the air but the sword that nicked the tender skin of my neck was of this world and meant to kill a half-mortal sorceress.

32

CHLOE

I gasped as the blade pierced the skin of my throat. The warm trickle of blood made me shiver as it moved slowly down my neck and inside my shirt. Except for that, I felt nothing. No pain. No discomfort. Just amazement that I'd been cut, maybe seriously, and felt nothing at all.

The black-robed figure repositioned the sword until the tip of the blade rested against the soft vulnerable spot below my earlobe, next to my jaw. I saw a flutter of lime green glitter spin slowly across my line of vision.

Sugar Maple is already gone. Build your life out there with your human and leave this world to us.

I heard the voice from somewhere inside myself. Light, melodic, undeniably female, but laced with the kind of determination that never ended well for anyone.

"This is my destiny," I whispered. "This is where I belong."

You belong with your human. That is your destiny. The world of humans will welcome you.

The blade angled down, pressing harder against the vein throbbing beneath the skin.

"I belong here."

Sugar Maple is gone. Its day is done. We will rebuild stronger than before on the land our ancestors claimed.

I wasn't about to get into an argument about the relative merits of Salem versus Sugar Maple with someone who was itching to run me through with a sword the size of a two-by-four.

"There is room in this dimension for all of us. Rebuild your community in Salem and we'll restore our community here in Sugar Maple. We'll coexist in peace."

Wrong thing to say.

I heard the pop as the blade broke the skin and dipped into the rich vein below, felt the quick rush of blood, the sense of release that was almost sexual. Was this it? Was this the way my time was supposed to end, the way the Hobbs legacy was supposed to end?

I felt like I was trapped in a dreamworld, drifting away from all that was familiar. Was this how my father felt when his life was ebbing away on an icy road one dark winter's night? This fuzzy, distant feeling as if everything that had happened before was nothing more than a dream, as if nothing mattered but giving in, giving up, giving over to the inevitable that faced all humans sooner or later.

I loved my human side. I loved that my blood ran warm inside my veins and that I was a link in the long chain of human history, but I wasn't that girl any longer. I couldn't go back to the time before magick. My powers were part of me now. They informed every move, every choice I made. The mortal world — Luke's world — had so much to offer but Sugar Maple had my heart and soul and I wasn't ready to leave it all behind.

My shirt was soaked with my blood. The narrow hallway spun crazily as I struggled to remain conscious. I tried to cauterize the wound with flames from my fingertips but I had waited too long. The flame was nothing more than a sputter.

I let out a cry of frustration or at least I tried to. The creature in the dark robe suddenly released its hold on me and I slipped to the blood-wet ground. The saber glittered in the reflected sunlight and for a moment I thought I saw Penny the cat watching me with sad golden eyes.

The twinkling surveillance camera silently watched it all.

I was dying. I knew that. I waited for the past life parade but except for Penny and the dark-robed creature, I was alone.

Or was I? I felt strong arms around me, holding me close. A whisper of softness in my ear. A practiced touch at my throat. The faintest smoky haze of purple that was there and gone.

Janice, I whispered in my mind. *Are you here? Was that you?*

But the only sound was the beat of my heart growing stronger, steadier inside my chest. The pool of blood beneath me vanished. No bloodstains on my T-shirt.

And maybe a handful of seconds before the saber-wielding creature tried again.

I'm not exactly an athlete but when your life is on the line even a couch potato like me could qualify for the Olympics. I didn't know where I was running and I didn't care. Anyplace without a crazed lunatic with a sharpened sword was good enough for me.

The ground shook beneath my feet as the creature lumbered after me. I reached another intersection and veered right this time. A door on the left swung open and what seemed like a thousand knitting needles — size 15s, 35s, and greater, in lengths I'd never seen before — flew out like a convoy of fighter planes and buzzed my head.

I swung at them and took out at least three pairs of wooden 17s with points sharp enough to puncture a paint can. I didn't want to think about what they could do to my carotid artery.

The knitting needles split up into two separate flights, diving at me from different directions. One pierced my right forearm. Another scraped the left side of my face. The faster I knocked them down, the faster they came back like crazed mosquitoes looking for blood.

The creature in the robe was having trouble keeping up with me. If I could manage a little more speed I might be able to put serious distance between us.

The hallway curved sharply to the right then to the left. I skidded against the wall, regained my balance, and kept running. Doors swung open and closed, deflecting the flying knitting needles that seemed locked on me like lasers. Another intersection loomed and a crazy thought leaped into my head.

Why turn right *or* left?

Why not break through the wall.

I'm not sure if it was magick or adrenaline or a crazy combination of the two but I went through that wall like it was made of paper and exploded into a winter wonderland.

Walls of snow everywhere. Mountains of it. All sparkling beneath a pale winter sky. Ribbons of ice cut through the accumulation, carving pathways to nowhere.

Keep moving. You have to keep moving.

I dove for the nearest pathway, slipping and sliding on the ice, pushing relentlessly forward.

Heavy footsteps sounded behind me.

I heard a whoosh as the creature's sword slashed the air.

Maybe the Olympic track team wasn't an impossible dream after all. For a gawky, clumsy girl who couldn't walk through a room without knocking something over, I was really hauling ass.

Still I couldn't seem to gain traction. At one point I was pretty sure I was hydroplaning but I was moving too fast to worry about it. Normally navigating ice makes me sick to my stomach. I hate that out-of-control feeling, that one-step-away-from-disaster sensation that filled my stomach with something close to panic.

But I'd rather be skidding on the ice than going mano a mano again with a giant saber-wielding maniac.

The pathway narrowed. I turned a little bit sideways, balanced myself with my hands, then kept going and I was going to keep going until there was a reason to stop.

Which happened about thirty yards later when I burst into a clearing that looked strangely familiar.

The world had fallen silent again. No more footsteps pounding behind me. Just the cushioned white noise of a snow-covered world.

I was standing along the curve of a half-plowed two-lane country road at dusk. Here and there a deer poked an inquisitive nose into the clearing then retreated back into the shadows.

The temperature was dropping. My skin felt like it was freezing from the inside out. I considered magicking myself a down-filled jacket and some handknitted mittens but five seconds from now I could be standing on a beach in the blazing sun. No point in depleting my stores of magick until I knew what was around the next corner.

I started down the icy roadway, arms held wide for balance. There was barely enough plowed road for me, much less two cars going in opposite directions.

Crap. I had to stop putting thoughts in

their mind. Old magick was like a boomerang. Put something out there and you could be sure it would come winging back at you with a bomb attached.

Right on queue I heard the rumble of a car approaching. I turned and started to run back toward safety. I slipped and fell to one knee. Pain shot through to my hip. I scrambled to my feet and pushed myself back into the clearing seconds before a black pickup truck roared past then disappeared.

Dusk was giving way to night. I wasn't sure whether or not this was part of the illusion. Exhaustion, the cold, everything was conspiring to make me punchy. I was tired of dodging bullets, tired of trying to figure out what was real, what was trying to kill me, what was just trying to screw with my head.

I wanted it to be over. I wanted to be with Luke. I wanted Sugar Maple to reappear. I wanted to see my friends again, walk the streets I played on as a kid, claim my heritage, and get on with my life.

Was that asking so much?

And that was when it all came crashing down.

33

CHLOE

I heard the crash before I saw it. The sound of brakes screeching. A scream rising up into the darkness. The slam of metal against wood.

And then silence.

I started to shake and this time it had nothing to do with the falling temperature.

I knew those sounds. Those sounds had been with me almost every day of my life.

I was frozen in place, once again helpless to stop the inevitable as the seven glittering orbs returned to enjoy the show.

"Don't do this," I shouted, even though I knew better. "Please don't do it."

They hovered, rays of glitter pulsating to some internal rhythm, and took turns moving slowly past my face. They smelled vaguely like thyme and grass clippings and something I couldn't identify. Elation flowed from them like snowmelt. They were waiting for me to lay my broken heart on the snow for them to see.

But they ceased to matter when I saw the car.

Oh, how I had loved the big green late 1970s Thunderbird with a backseat made for napping. As a little girl I had thought it was the most beautiful car in the world. It had been my family's magic carpet to exotic places like Burlington and Montpelier. Anyplace is exotic when you're not quite six years old.

The T-Bird didn't look so beautiful crumpled and broken and lying on its side, wheels spinning, windows smashed, steam punctuating the frigid night air from the crushed front end. I heard the sound of a little girl crying from somewhere close by but I didn't turn to look. I couldn't turn away from the horror in front of me.

"Ted!" My mother's voice, slightly husky. Utterly unforgettable. "Oh, please, Ted, talk to me! Say something!"

Her anguish was like another presence. Even though one of Isadora's sons had thrown down the black ice that caused the crash, my mother's guilt knew no bounds. If she hadn't cast a spell over my father that bound him to her forever, the accident never would have happened.

359

"Why are you showing me this?" I cried out.

Because we can, came the answer.

I cried out as the crumpled side of the car lifted up and away and I saw my father lying in my mother's arms.

They were both twenty-five years old and doomed.

I had no photos of my parents. No scrapbooks or old letters or birthday cards to remember them by. Over the years I had blocked all memories of my father, letting my anger at my mother overshadow everything else. In time I was so successful at it that he was nothing more than a whisper on the winds of time.

But now a thousand long-buried memories came at me in a tidal wave of sweet pain.

Riding through town on his shoulders as he showed off his little daughter to Lilith and Archie and Midge and the Griggs family and anyone else in town who stopped to talk to the strapping young mortal and his half-sorceress child.

How hard it must have been for him to give up all that he knew, all that he was, to be with my mother and me in Sugar Maple. Was he resentful? I would never know.

The memories I saw spinning before me showed nothing but joy.

I drank in the sight of him: tall, lanky, dirty blond hair and melted choco brown eyes that crinkled when he laugh His hands were big and callused from carpentry work. Strong hands that made child feel safe in all the ways that mattere

I loved you so much. The realization fe like coming home. He wasn't a shadow. H wasn't just a name on some long-forgotte birth certificate. Some shared DNA.

That was my *father.* The all-too-mortal man I had called Daddy. And as I watched my mother cradle him as he bled out in her arms, I felt like I was losing him all over again. Losing them. Losing my childhood and my future in one terrible moment.

"Such a shame," the tangerine-glittered orb said with a note of mirth in her voice. "So young!"

"A waste of fine human flesh," said the lime green orb.

"Oh, he was a pretty one," said the chestnut-tinted orb. "Guinevere always did have an eye for fine young men. I've always wondered who would have been next if she hadn't left the way she did."

Rage exploded inside my head. Powerful, destructive, ugly rage that sent me spinning up into the air in a crazed attempt to tear

those glittering balls apart with my bare hands.

Every ounce of magick at my command, everything I had ever learned through the Book of Spells, all that Sorcha had taught me came pouring out in an eruption of vengeance that made the volcano from hell seem like a child's chemistry experiment.

Conscious thought vanished. I didn't want the cruel and vicious Fae to claim my beloved hometown but the only clear motive at work inside me at that moment was to make them stop. To make them pay for the fact that one of theirs caused the accident that took my father's life.

With every sob ripped from my mother's broken heart, I hit them harder. I tore the lime green ball into two and laughed as it disappeared from sight. I sank my teeth into the lime green and spat the glitter at the other. I laughed out loud when I dug my thumbs into the tangerine-glittered orb and its lifeblood spilled over my fingers.

Familiar flames shot from my fingertips and incinerated the aquamarine orb. My heart filled with powerful elation. My need to destroy knew no limits.

I could have ripped apart the entire Fae world, all of Isadora's old followers, the descendants of Da'Elle, the clan members

who'd stayed behind in Salem, destroyed every single one of them with one mighty blow. Orchid, chestnut, both lemon and butter yellow — one by one I fought and obliterated the glittering orbs.

"I know you can hear me!" I roared into the night. "You'll never be able to harm the ones I love again!"

Bold words, heedlessly spoken.

I should have known better.

Your daughter, a new voice said. *How long will you be able to protect the daughter?*

"I don't have a daughter," I shouted. "Are mind games all you've got left?"

Another orb appeared before me, but this one was huge and the color of onyx. It obliterated the wrecked T-Bird and the terrible scene playing out in front of me. The orb glittered darkly like ice on a moonless night. A faint hum emanated from it, steady, toneless, unsettling enough to raise the hairs on the back of my neck.

The orb suddenly split apart and Luke spilled out on a sea of bloodred foam. He was alive and in one piece and a surge of love, violent and fiercely protective, almost knocked me to my knees.

Luke rose to his feet as the orb healed itself and ascended to a point a few feet above our heads, where it hovered. If you had asked me yesterday if giant glittering disco balls from hell were high up on my list of fears, I would have laughed in your face.

But if you asked me now, I'd pencil it in at number one.

The orb began to trace slow circles over Luke's head.

"Stop," I said in a deadly calm tone of voice. "Don't do that."

The circles slowed to a lazy crawl as the orb dropped down closer to him.

"I told you once," I said, still sounding calm, "but I'm not going to tell you a second time. This isn't his battle. It's mine."

I saw Luke's expression flatten into his cop face, a sure sign he was about to do something we might both regret.

A sick feeling washed over me as I realized his temporary powers were quickly disappearing. His reflexes had slowed to human speed, which made him vulnerable to attack. Twenty-four hours, Samuel had said, but I could see the estimate had fallen dangerously short.

Here's a present for you, mortal, a deep, rich voice intoned as a shimmering screen unrolled from the top of the orb and a little girl on a bicycle trundled into view. The daughter reference now made horrifying sense.

It was Luke's daughter, Steffie. Any second she would ride that bicycle into the street and her tiny body would be crushed beneath the wheels of a neighbor's car.

The need to destroy filled my heart and soul. A dark red mist clouded my vision. I would do anything to spare the man I loved the sight of his daughter taking her last breath on this earth.

Sugar Maple didn't matter any longer. I didn't give a damn about talismans or clans or leaders or any of the thousands of things that get in the way of what was truly important.

This was important. Love was important. Husbands, wives, lovers, partners, parents, children in any combination. I hated my world of magick for taking my parents. I hated Luke's world of mortals for letting his daughter die. It didn't have to be this way and the fact that it was had me spinning out of control.

Luke tried to stop me as I threw myself at the orb but my powers, as well as my rage, were beyond his reach.

I started shredding the black orb inch by inch, using everything at my command. My nails, my teeth, my magick, my fury. I aimed bolts of fire at its heart. I pierced it with daggers conjured from years of loneliness.

I raged against the senseless death of a little girl and the unending pain her parents endured. I raged against the fact that the town I loved, the creatures I called family, had been taken from me because I had been found wanting. I raged against the fact that I hadn't understood how far I would have to go to win.

I was grotesquely alive. Fully aware of everything I was doing in a way I had never been before. The adrenaline rush of blood madness was the kind of high not even hand-dyed pure cashmere or a bucket of Ben & Jerry's had ever delivered. Was this how Dane felt when my parents' car skidded across the carpet of black ice he had prepared just for them? Was this the way Isadora felt when she watched Suzanne Marsden sink below the surface of icy Snow Lake?

Was this how you became a monster?

34

CHLOE

"Chloe!" Luke's voice came to me from a distance. "Chloe, stop! It's over . . . stop . . . you did it . . . you won . . . it's all over!"

The red mist parted just enough for me to realize Luke was next to me. I was still flying on pure sensation and had trouble taking in my surroundings.

His shirt was ripped. A jagged gash bisected his left cheek. I had a fuzzy memory of him fighting by my side but my fury had all but blotted it out.

I was standing in the middle of an empty field with Luke. It had the scruffy, hopeful look of early spring in northern Vermont. A few snowdrops dotted the expanse. Here and there a yellow daff poked out its head to test the surroundings. Winter was gone but spring hadn't quite made up her mind.

The snow was gone. So was the totaled Thunderbird. And the wreckage of my parents' lives. The screen with Steffie's image. The ashes of the orbs I had destroyed. The last vestiges of the rage that had carried me through battle to this place.

Was this what you wanted me to become, Samuel? I asked silently. I had crossed the divide between civilized being and monster to save the town I loved.

But where was the talisman? Why wasn't I basking in its golden glow right now? Maybe I had won the battle but lost the war.

Seven beings watched us from a point some twenty feet away. They were the height of human children but unmistakably adult and undeniably beautiful in the way only the Fae could be. Each was garbed in a simple robe matching the color of one of the glittering orbs I had vanquished just moments before.

They looked fragile in defeat, as if a gust of wind would tear them apart like dandelions on a hot summer day.

I had to remind myself that they were ruthless warriors who, if the tables had been turned, would be rejoicing at my death and Luke's with no reservations.

They spoke in one voice. "We have been defeated. We are prepared to be banished into the eternal darkness."

So that was the next step. I wasn't sure

even the Book of Spells had instructions for a situation like this.

I recognized their collective future was in my beginner's hands. I had banished Isadora gladly and with no regrets. She had preyed upon the weak and taken lives for sport. Banishing her had been the right thing to do.

These warriors had waited centuries to claim a birthright promised them by their ancestors and when the moment came, they had fought fiercely and without remorse to achieve it.

Hadn't I done the same thing?

"Chloe," Luke whispered in my ear, "they're waiting."

I knew what he expected me to do. It was what Samuel had coached me to do in order to win over the talisman. A total commitment to Sugar Maple that allowed no room for doubt of any kind. It was exactly the same thing I had expected of myself up until a half second ago.

I knew that my decision might cost me Sugar Maple but if I was ever going to be a true leader, now was the time to start.

I stepped forward and looked toward the Fae. "I'm not going to banish you."

My voice was strong. My resolve was unshakable.

If they sensed weakness they would strike but I wasn't weak. I had never felt stronger or more powerful in my life.

"You have two choices," I continued as the Fae watched and listened. "You can choose to leave this dimension and go beyond the mist or you can choose to stay here in Sugar Maple, build a place for yourselves in the community, and finally live in peace."

I felt Luke's eyes on me and I knew what he was thinking. I wasn't totally crazy. I would build safeguards that would protect all of our citizens, Fae and magick and human, from mischief or harm. One transgression and the entire clan would be banished. I finally understood my enemy. I understood how deep the bitterness ran but I believed there was no other way to achieve the goal Aerynn had set all those years ago.

Once again the seven Fae spoke as one. "There is no Sugar Maple. The talisman didn't return it to you."

My answer surprised even me. "Then we'll rebuild Sugar Maple together and we'll make it better than it was before."

I didn't expect them to jump up and down with excitement but I had expected more than the silence that greeted my words.

"I need a decision." Okay, so maybe working together had been a crazy idea but it was worth a shot. Beyond the mist was looking more and more likely.

"Chloe." Luke stepped forward. "Look!"

He pointed toward a twinkling dot in the northwestern sky.

"The surveillance camera?" I said. "That's not possible."

Luke shot me a quizzical look. "What surveillance camera?"

"The one that watched everything that went on inside the dome."

"I don't think that's a surveillance camera, Chloe."

Whatever it was, it was burning brighter and hotter with every second that passed. A murmur of excitement rose up from the gathered Fae as it began a rapid descent then headed straight for me.

LUKE

The disk stopped inches away from Chloe. A flat gleaming circle of intricately detailed gold that could be only one thing: the talisman.

Samuel's voice rang out across the open field.

You are all she was and more, daughter. You will achieve everything Aerynn dreamed of before you are done.

371

Tears flowed down Chloe's cheeks as she held out her hands and the talisman dropped into them.

The seven Fae representatives swirled closer.

"We will join with you here," they said in unison, "and help you rebuild Sugar Maple. It is the right thing to do."

Chloe beamed with happiness and welcomed them with more genuine warmth than I would have believed possible. Call me a suspicious, cynical cop but I would be keeping a sharp eye on them from this point on.

She turned to me and gave me a smile that was equal parts elation and embarrassment. "It looks like an Olympic gold medal," she said. "Maybe I should wear it around my neck."

"That's some serious bling," I said as she moved into my arms.

"Too bad a town didn't come with it." Her voice caught on the last word. "Damn," she whispered. "I came so close."

"We're still here," I said. "We got through the worst they could throw at us." We both had stories to tell and now we'd have the time to tell them.

She looked up at me as the Fae swirled around us doing their equivalent of the happy dance. "I hope that was the worst."

"Gutsy choice, Hobbs. I'm not sure I'd have been so generous."

I felt her shoulders lift and fall in a shrug. "I thought —" She stiffened in my arms. "The forest," she said, pulling away slightly so she could get a better look. "It's gone!"

Something was happening. The air buzzed with energy. The Fae were swooping and diving with what I hoped was excitement and not some kind of doomsday plan.

The forest was gone but stands of sugar maples took its place, studded with evergreens and trees I knew by sight if not by name.

"It's coming back!" Chloe cried. "Sugar Maple's coming back!"

We ran toward the perimeter of town. I steeled myself for the thwack I would get when I ran face-first into that weird memory foam barrier that had thwarted us in the beginning but it wasn't there. We were inside the township limits for the first time since the incident at the waterfall.

"The roads!" I sounded every bit as excited as Chloe did. "The grids are appearing."

First faint gray lines in the grassy dirt, then paths worn smooth by horses and wagons, followed by the asphalt of our day.

And where there were roads, there were people. Houses small and large popped up like mushrooms everywhere we looked. Quaint cottages. Sturdy brick two-stories. Uncompromising capes and saltboxes.

And if you had people, you had businesses. Thriving mom-and-pop shops that were the lifeblood of every small town in this country. Appliance repair shops and beauty salons, delis and grocery stores, dress shops and tailors and dry cleaners and banks and one very special shop right in the middle of town that had put Sugar Maple on the map.

Standing in front of Sticks & Strings, Chloe began to cry. She buried her face in her hands and she sobbed as the people we'd thought we'd lost suddenly walked out of the shadows and gathered around us.

Paul and Verna Griggs and their sons. Archie the troll and his wife, the beautiful Lilith from the library. Chloe's good friend Lynette and Lynette's husband, Cyrus, from the playhouse. The girls from Fully Caffeinated. Frank, Manny, Rose, and the rest of the crowd from Sugar Maple Assisted Living. Chloe's old friends Renate and Colm Weaver, from the Sugar Maple Inn, had been hovering nearby. *Hovering* being the operative term since they were Fae who did a lot of hummingbird maneuvers. They finally expanded to more human dimensions and approached Chloe.

The Weavers had been deeply angered by Isadora's banishment last December and they had been responsible for much of the chaos that led to the talisman pulling Sugar Maple off the grid. The friendship had been strained to the breaking point and I wasn't sure what was about to go down.

"Renate," Chloe said in a calm tone of voice. Then, "Colm."

Renate opened her mouth to say something but burst into tears instead and the next instant she and Chloe were hugging and crying and saying all those things women say to each other after a fight. The other Fae joined them and I imagined glitter was flying everywhere like confetti.

Colm and I shifted position a few times, cleared our throats, checked our cell phones for messages.

"Good to see you," Colm said, extending his right hand.

"Good to see you, too," I said, accepting it.

And just like that we were back where we had started, in the town Chloe had fought to save, surrounded by the people who had been her family since the day she was born.

With one exception.

Lorcan Meany was leaning against the doorway of Janice's Cut & Curl. He was a big, broad-shouldered guy with a mop of curly black hair and an easygoing disposition. I don't think I had ever seen him when he wasn't smiling.

Until today.

His head was down. His kids stood a few feet away from him, hands jammed in pockets, heads down as well.

I nudged Chloe. She looked over at Lorcan and took my hand.

He lifted his head as we crossed the street and approached him. The disappointment in his eyes when he realized Janice wasn't with us felt like a sharp kick in the gut.

"She'll be here," Chloe consoled him. "She's in Salem. She's fine. I know she'll be here."

I pulled Chloe aside. "Maybe she isn't fine. I was the one who asked for Janice's help when you were in danger." What if something had gone wrong when Janice summoned up her healing powers to save her friend.

"What do you mean you asked Janice for help?"

I gave her the abbreviated version. "When I tackled those spirits in the dome, the explosion flung us into another realm. You couldn't see or hear me but I saw everything that was happening to you. I tried to break free and get to you but time was running out so I pulled together all the powers I had left and reached out to Janice."

"I don't imagine Dorcas and Tabitha were too thrilled with that turn of events."

"How do you think I ended up in that onyx orb?" I stole a quick glance at an increasingly more distraught Lorcan. "You'd better contact Samuel. He'll know where Janice is."

But, as it turned out, she didn't have to.

Suddenly there was Penny galloping toward us like a shiny black Hummer. You could hear her purr from twenty feet away. She leaped onto Chloe's shoulder but before Chloe could say a word, the cat coughed once, twice, then spat out a fat yellow canary.

The canary flapped frantically, sneezed, flapped again and then in a burst of purplish smoke morphed into Janice right before our eyes.

Talk about making an entrance.

The naked look of joy on Lorcan's face as his wife flew into his arms — well, let's just say even tough cops can get a little misty-eyed.

All around us Sugar Maple was settling back into its familiar patterns. There would be time for questions later. Right now it was all about getting back to normal. Kids were hustled off to school. The girls at Fully Caffeinated got ready for the midday rush. Paul and his sons went off to repair Midge Stallworth's powder room sink. Lilith flipped the sign on the library door to OPEN. Lynette and Cyrus hurried back to the playhouse to finish painting scenery for their next production.

Chloe and I stood there on the sidewalk across from Sticks & Strings, arms around each other, Penny securely perched on her shoulder, and watched as another day in the life of Sugar Maple unfolded.

Lucky? That didn't begin to cover it.

"I wish Aerynn could see this," Chloe whispered against my neck. "I think she'd like it."

"Maybe she can."

"Starting to believe in magick, are you?" she said with a soft laugh.

Vanishing towns. Volcanoes from hell. Bathtub ghosts. A four-hundred-year-old knitting sorcerer. Glittering disco balls with attitude. Attack cats. And despite it all, a happy ending.

"Magic and love," I said as I ducked my

head to kiss her. Maybe love was the best magic trick of all.

"Luke?" She peered up at me. "Are you okay?"

I wasn't okay. I was about to explode with all of the emotions I'd kept trapped inside for days. Fear. Rage. Relief. Joy. Bottled up and ready to explode all over the place. I wanted to tell her that what she'd done was off-the-chart magnificent, that she was a warrior goddess, that when they wrote the history of Aerynn and her descendants, it would be Chloe's name in big bold letters.

Luckily a big brown UPS truck rolled to a stop in front of us and I didn't have to say any of it.

Joe, the regular driver, beeped his horn and waved. "Hey, Chloe! That was a helluva bad storm, wasn't it? I got at least twelve giant boxes of wool for you and more at the depot."

"Bring 'em around the side," she said with an enormous smile. "We'll help you unload."

"We?" I asked with a grin. "I'm chief of police around here, not a yarn jockey."

But she kissed me on the mouth, a kiss of such promise, that I would have taken up crochet if she'd asked me to.

"I'll make it up to you," she said.

"Damn right," I said, then I kissed her until it was either breathe or die.

Her golden eyes glowed with happiness. Her skin was translucent. Her blond hair shimmered in the sun. The last few days fell away from her like a bad dream. She was back where she belonged, in the town she loved and fought for, surrounded by the people she called family.

Tonight we would go back to her cottage, feed the cats, nuke some frozen pizza, sprawl together on the sofa while she knitted and I watched *Dirty Jobs*. Later in the darkened bedroom maybe I could find a way to tell her all the things I couldn't say in the bright light of day.

I took her hand and we ran back across the street toward Sticks & Strings.

It was good to be home.

EPILOGUE

CHLOE

Samuel pierced the veil a few moments before midnight.

There was no flash of lightning. No earth-shaking clap of thunder to announce his leave-taking. No astral visitors bearing messages of farewell. I was lying next to Luke, listening to the even sound of his breathing, when suddenly I knew that Aerynn's mate was gone.

Samuel had been part of my life for less than a human day but for that brief span of time I had been reminded of how it felt to be connected to someone by blood. The thought of what might have been pierced my heart. The stories, the wisdom, even the chance to make up for the years he had chosen to remain hidden away at Bramford Light — all gone in the blink of an eye.

My angry words to him at the lighthouse reverberated inside my skull. Who knew our time would be so painfully limited?

But he was with Aerynn now. Or at least that was what I wanted to believe. I tried to picture the two of them, beautiful and in their prime, building their life together in another dimension. The life that should have been theirs back in Salem all those years ago.

Maybe Hobbs women did have happy endings after all — they just had to wait longer than other women to get them.

My brief time with Samuel had been spent mostly in anger and confrontation. My heart had been too filled with resentment over the lost years to grab hold of the hours I had been given.

Tears slid down my cheeks and onto the pillow. "Damn," I whispered, wiping my eyes with the back of my hand.

Next to me Luke mumbled something in his sleep and sank back into his dreams. I maneuvered my legs around Lucy and Pye, who were dozing at the foot of the bed, and made my way into the kitchen to start a pot of tea, my all-purpose cure for just about anything.

The pot of tea led to a bag of Chips Ahoy, which led to the need to work off some of those calories at the wheel. I'm not sure spinning does much for the cardiovascular system but it definitely does wonders for the soul.

In seconds I was under its spell. The only sound in the cottage was the faint click of my wheel. Moonlight spilled through the windows. Tree branches cast eerie shadows across the floor. The heady scent of merino and blue-faced Leicester filled my head.

This was my legacy, I thought as the fiber slipped through my fingers. Every time I sat down at a wheel, every time I picked up my needles, I was tapping into my history, keeping alive the traditions that Aerynn and Samuel had both held close.

And magick. Not that I was about to forget about that, but the truth was I'd been knitting and spinning a whole lot longer than I had been casting spells and battling Fae enemies.

"Chloe."

I turned at the sound of Luke's voice in the entranceway. In the splash of moonlight washing over him I could see the toll our battle with the Fae had taken. The left side of his jaw was bruised and swollen. His left cheek bore a jagged cut. A shiner was blossoming beneath his right eye.

He had been overmatched from the start. He could have played the human card and backed away and nobody would have faulted him for it. But he fought by my side every step of the way and I loved him so much I thought my heart would split open like a piñata.

"What are you doing up?" I asked, hiding my emotions behind my spinning.

"I woke up and you weren't there." He struggled to stifle a yawn. "I like it better when you are."

I love spinning but not even the pleasures of the wheel were any match for straight-up love.

"I like it better when I am, too," I said, and moved into the warmth of his arms, chuckling softly at the hazy spray of sparks our touch ignited.

"Do you think we'll still be striking sparks a year from now?" he asked as they faded into the moonlit room.

"I think we'll still be striking sparks a hundred years from now." I told him about my certainty that Samuel had pierced the veil and he held me tight as he listened to my regrets.

"Come on," he said once my emotional storm had passed. "We both have a busy day ahead. Let's get some sleep."

I had almost forgotten that a group of gay knitters from Cincinnati was coming up for a design workshop in the morning. They would be joined in the afternoon by a ladies church group from Nashua for an advanced finishing class that promised to turn good knitters into great ones. Both groups were repeat attendees I had grown to know and love but it would still be a very long and very busy day.

Arms wrapped around each other, we headed slowly down the hallway to the bedroom.

"Are you still planning to go back to Salem tomorrow?" I asked.

"Paul's taking me up to Montpelier around lunchtime. I'll drive a one-way rental down there, pack up the Buick, settle the motel bill, then drive back."

A big fat lump formed in my throat. "You hate my Buick but you'd drive it all the way home for me?"

"Guess I'm just a fool for love."

Who needs chocolates and roses anyway? Sometimes true love shows up behind the wheel of a dented gray clunker with Vermont plates. My overheated emotions threatened to get the better of me so I quickly shifted gears.

"I'll make you a lumberjack breakfast before you leave. You won't need to stop for food until you're on your way back."

"Didn't you say something about pancakes

and bacon the other morning before things got crazy?"

It seemed like a lifetime ago. "Blueberry pancakes, a river of maple syrup, eggs over —" I stopped as a loud noise rattled through the cottage. "Did you hear that?"

"They could hear it in Montpelier." He snapped instantly into cop mode. "Since when do they pick up the trash at two in the morning?"

"Maybe they're playing catch-up," I said. "Things haven't exactly been normal around here lately."

The rumble grew louder.

And a whole lot closer.

Luke tilted his head. "If I didn't know better I'd say that sounded like the Buick."

"That's crazy," I said.

Still, this was Sugar Maple where *crazy* was a relative term. It wouldn't hurt to check.

We swung open the front door in time to catch a major display from Mother Nature. The sky erupted in flashes of lightning that slashed the firmament and lit up the landscape like the Fourth of July times ten.

"Damn," Luke said as we stepped out onto the porch where the roar of an invisible engine almost drowned out conversation. "That really does sound like your car."

"My car's in Salem. Remember?"

He shot me a look. "Are you sure?"

Beads of sweat broke out on the back of my neck. "I was five minutes ago."

Twin beams of light appeared near the curve in the road, heading straight for us at warp speed.

I froze in place but Luke quickly threw me to the ground, then threw himself on top of me.

The front porch shook as something huge and heavy crashed into the saplings at the edge of my driveway, then hit the ground with a monster thud.

"Guess you don't have to rent a car in Montpelier," I said to Luke as we stood up and brushed ourselves off.

"Guess not," he said.

My Buick was back. Okay, so it was half in the rhododendron bushes and smoke was spewing from under the hood, but it was definitely back and so was Aerynn's wheel and mountains of yarn trying to escape through the open windows.

It would have been an almost-perfect ending to the craziest few days of my life when an all-too-familiar voice rang out from the depths of my battered car.

"Don't just stand there, missy. Help me out of here."

Luke and I locked eyes. He looked as horrified as I felt.

"Elspeth?" we said in unison.

"And who else would it be?"

I could think of any one of a thousand people, living or dead, but I managed to hold my tongue as Luke and I pulled old Buttercup from the backseat of the car.

Her mob cap was askew. A skein of sequined cashmere was draped around her neck. Her plain white apron and voluminous black skirts were wrinkled and definitely worse for the wear.

Luke tried to check for injuries but she batted him away like he was a pesky fly.

"Hands to yourself," she said, visibly recoiling from his touch. It isn't easy to show disdain when you barely reach a human's navel, but somehow the yellow-haired troll managed just fine.

"He was trying to help you," I snapped, annoyed by her old-school prejudices. "What are you doing here anyway?"

Which probably wasn't the most hospitable thing I could have said but Samuel's friend didn't exactly bring out the best in me.

"Samuel sent me," she said, puffing up like a blowfish. "It was his last wish."

I aimed an eye roll at Luke that made him

grin. Even my cats could come up with a better story than that. "You're telling me that Samuel's last wish was for you to deliver my car."

"No, missy," she tossed over her well-padded shoulder as she stomped up the steps to our front door. "I'm telling you his last wish is for me to deliver your baby."

BARBARA BRETTON'S ROAD TRIP PROJECTS ROUNDUP

Like Chloe and Janice, I'm a big fan of road trip knitting. Give me a long stretch of open highway, a circular needle, and a fat ball of yarn and I'm a happy knitter.

I'm also not alone. I surveyed some of my knitter friends and came up with the following unscientific findings.

#1 Favorite Road Trip Project: Socks

We love socks! If you're a sock knitter, you're probably a road trip sock knitter as well.

Rho loves making socks on a magic loop (Lifestyle pattern and fleegle's no-holes heel pattern with Judy's Magic Cast-On and Jeny's Surprisingly Stretchy Cast-Off):

- Magic Loop
  http://www.knittingdaily.com/blogs/
  daily/archive/2009/09/16/the-magical-
  magic-loop.aspx

- Lifestyle pattern: http://www.k1p1design1.com/lifestylesocks
- Fleegle's heel: http://fleeglesblog.blogspot.com/2007/09/no-sock-holes-for-you.html
- Judy's Magic Cast-On: http://knitty.com/ISSUEspring06/FEATmagiccaston.html
- Jeny's Surprisingly Stretchy Cast-Off: http://www.knitty.com/ISSUEfall09/FEATjssbo.php

Marietta takes two pairs of socks-in-progress when she travels and knits them with sock-weight yarn on size 1s or 2s.

Cathy R believes that "the selection of a new sock pattern and appropriate yarn is very crucial for the retention of sanity over the long miles." Jellidonut knits them two at a time on circular needles and loves it when people think she's a magician! But Katminder says it all: "Socks socks socks!"

#2 Favorite Road Trip Project: Dishcloths
Surprisingly popular. I'm not a dishcloth knitter myself. I can't imagine putting in all that effort only to use the end result to scrub out a pot. But that's just me. (If someone else does the knitting, it's a differ-

392

ent story. Handknit dishcloths are environ-
mentally friendly and beautiful.)

Sue3331 keeps a set of short needles and
several balls of kitchen cotton in the car so
she's never without something to knit. Ni-
cole Simmons and Jeanne Hickling do the
same thing. Kathy Minder likes to whip up
a dishcloth or two en route to a weekend
visit with friends and relatives. She presents
the finished knits as thank-you gifts.

#3 Favorite Road Trip Project: Hats

There is a vocal contingent of knitters on
our blog, Romancing the Yarn, who swear
by hats as favorite road trip knitting
projects.

Megan Boesen once made three Jayne hats
while driving through South Dakota with
her significant other's family but then
wondered why she couldn't find any buffalo
yarn! (The Jayne hat: http://www.craftste
.org/forum/index.php?topic=19076.20)

Julie S votes for hats — "just plain ol'
stockinette, knit in the round, hats."

Lynne Welch likes to "knit uncomplicated
things when I travel. I do a lot of hats (using
doubled wool worsted and size 10 needles,
cast on 72, k2p2 for 11 inches or so, k2tog
around for several rows till I get down to 1
stitches, then cut yarn and draw through)."

#4 Favorite Road Trip Project: Scarves

I'm only surprised it didn't rank higher in my unscientific survey. Scarves are long and repetitive. Once you master the stitch pattern you can keep on knitting for miles. A long and intricate scarf could take you from New York to Florida and back again. (And what's more beautiful than yards of seed stitch? Perfect guy scarf!)

Ellen H loves to knit scarves on road trips but admits she loves reading even more. Kozmic says, "After a couple of semi-nasty accidents with dpns on road trips, I've gone back to knitting scarves using a circular needle." Estella loves scarflets and small shawls while on the road. Jeanne Hickling travels with her Sunday Morning Shawl (which can be found on Ravelry at http://www.ravelry.com/patterns/library/Sunday-morning-shawl).

And Sara Brockunier (a knitter after my own heart who can be found at http://fabricnfiberfanatic.com) loves seed stitch scarves.

#5 Favorite Road Trip Project: Baby Items

This one surprised me. I think of baby knits as fiddly and intricate but my knit pals have me reconsidering my options.

Grandma Moo says, "Hats and small toys

are my favorites except that I can't do toys if I have to help with directions. We once missed an exit by 45 miles because of a bear's nose." Holly Abery-Wetstone is making all of her road projects baby sweaters and will stock them away until she needs a baby gift. Her current favorite is from Ravelry: http://www.ravelry.com/patterns/library/seamless-baby-kimono.

Susan Lantz loves Elizabeth Zimmerman's famous (all garter stitch) Baby Surprise Jacket in Noro Silk Garden or Dream in Color Classy.

#6 Favorite Road Trip Project: Bags

Sally at Rivendale Farms and Page Pennington agree that bags make for great road trip knitting. Page says, "Once the bottom is started, you just knit in the round until it is as big as you, then stop."

Don't forget to felt!

And My Favorite Road Trip Project: Pet Shelter Blankets

I love to make blankets for rescue animals awaiting adoption in shelters. That little bit of softness and warmth can make a big difference. (I also like to think that a colorful blanket might lure in a loving adoptive family for a deserving pet.) A few years ago I bought up a ton of Red Heart's Light & Lofty from Smiley's http://www.smileysyarns.com.

Light & Lofty is a machine-wash-and-dry acrylic that's perfect for busy shelters, which need easy-care items that can withstand rough treatment. I use it double and crochet (yes, crochet!) it up with a monster size N plastic hook. Shelters can use anything from 12-by-12-inch squares to 36-by-36-inch squares. Rectangles are okay, too. Make a chain to your approximate width, *single crochet (sc) in the second chain from the hook (or do a half double crochet [hdc] in the third), chain 1, repeat from * across the row. Turn. If you're working single crochet, chain 1, sc in second sc, *chain 1, sc in next sc, repeat from * until end of row. Continue in pattern. (If working half double crochet, chain 2, hdc in second hdc, *chain 2, hdc in next hdc, repeat from * until end of row.)

Keep going until you reach desired size or run out of yarn. Don't worry if it's midrow. Weave in all ends carefully. You want a fairly tight fabric so little paws and claws don't get stuck. If your local shelter can't use them, check Hugs for Homeless Animals (http://www.h4ha.org/) for shelters that would welcome your handiwork.

DAWN BROCCO'S
MINI STOCKING CAP

This little cap is a quick-to-knit, yet not boring-to-knit, tree ornament or egg cozy for the holidays. Techniques include cabling without a needle and wrapping a stitch.

Materials
Shibui Knits Merino Kid (55% kid mohair, 45% merino wool): 1 hank (218yd/100g) Chinese Red (color #1797) size 6 (4 mm) double-pointed needles; cable needle; tapestry needle

Dimensions
7 1/2 inches from edge of cap (with cuff folded up) to tip of poof; 6 1/2-inch circumference

Gauge
5 1/2 stitches and 7 1/2 rows per inch in stockinette stitch with size 6 (4 mm) needles or size to give gauge; gauge is not crucial

with this cap

Abbreviations

2/2RC = slip 2 sts to cn and hold in back, k2, k2 from cn

BO = bind off

cn = cable needle

CO = cast on

dpns = double-pointed needles

k = knit

k2tog = knit 2 sts together

ndl = needle

p = purl

rem = remaining

rep = repeat

rnd(s) = round(s)

RS = right side

ssk = slip 2 sts, separately, knitwise, then knit them together from this position

st(s) = stitch(es)

WS = wrong side

Technique: Wrapping a Stitch

Slip next st purlwise to the right-hand ndl, bring yarn to front, slip st back to the left-hand ndl, turn work around (so the WS is now facing you). The wrap is completed.

Technique: Crossing a Cable without a Cable Needle

For a 4-st cable: Slip all 4 sts to the right-hand ndl. Pinch the last 2 off between your fingers, then either hold them in back or hold them in front (depending on the pattern) while you slip the rem 2 sts from the right-hand ndl back to the left-hand ndl. Then put the 2 pinched sts back onto the left-hand ndl and knit them in this new position.

This method ensures the sts are never dropped while you're repositioning them.

Knitting Tip

Feel free to use ssk, instead of k2tog, in the shaping — just be consistent.

Cabled Fold-Up Cuff

CO 42 sts onto dpns.
Rnd 1: (p1, k4, p1, k1) around.
Rnd 2: (p1, 2/2RC, p1, k1) around.
Rnds 3–5: (p1, k4, p1, k1) around.
Rnd 6: (p1, 2/2RC, p1, k1) around.
Rnds 7–9: (p1, k4, p1, k1) around.
Rnd 10: (p1, 2/2RC, p1, k1) around.

Turning Ridge

Rnd 11: (p5, p2tog) around — 36 sts rem.

Cap Base

Knit 7 rnds.

Wrap first st of next rnd, turn, knit around, knitting wrap together with the last st of rnd. WS of work is now facing you. This will be the RS from here on, so pop the work, and the beginning yarn tail, up through the center, to make knitting easier.

Knit 13 rnds.

Cap Shaping

Dec Rnd 1: (k4, k2tog) around — 30 sts rem. Knit 6 rnds.

Dec Rnd 2: (k3, k2tog) around — 24 sts. Knit 6 rnds.

Dec Rnd 3: (k2, k2tog) around — 18 sts. Knit 6 rnds.

Dec Rnd 4: (k1, k2tog) around — 12 sts. Knit 6 rnds.

Dec Rnd 5: (k2tog) around — 6 sts.

Dec Rnd 6: (k2tog) around — 3 sts. Break yarn, leaving a 3-inch tail; end off by pulling tail through rem 3 sts.

Make Poof

With tail threaded into tapestry ndl, place finger at peak of cap. Wrap yarn around finger (to make a loop) and sew through top of cap; rep until 5–6 inches of yarn tail rem — approximately 14 loops made.

Thread tapestry ndl through center of loops, near the base, then bring around and through loops again. Rep on other side of loops, then weave tail in on WS to secure.

Soak briefly in cool water with your favorite detergent or wool wash. Rinse in same temperature water. Squeeze out gently. Lay flat to dry.

DAWN BROCCO began her designing career working freelance for most of the major knitting publications. She has been self-publishing for the past fifteen years, and now has over one hundred patterns available. Her style embraces classic design with modern twists and whimsical design based on a love of nature. You can find Dawn Brocco Knitwear Designs at http:// www.dawnbrocco.com and you can reach Dawn at dawn@dawnbrocco.com.

GEORG HAWKS'S
MINIATURE SOCKS — TOE UP

These socks will fit the miniature sock blockers found on the Internet, or you can add a loop to make it a decorative ornament.

Cast-On and Toe

Use the Turkish cast-on or Judy's Magic Cast-On, for 12 stitches total. Begin by holding the yarn between the two needles with the tail hanging down in front of the lower needle. Wrap the working yarn up and over from back to front, down and under from front to back, six times. At the end of the required number of wraps, your working yarn is at the back, coming up from behind the lower needle. Slide the lower needle farther to the right and the upper to the left, and just start knitting across. Turn and do the second needle the same. I find it easier to split the sock across four dpns or two circulars at this point. Then we do the increases. Knit 1. Make 1 — by lifting the bar between the two stitches or by knitting into the stitch below the next stitch. Knit across the top of the row until one stitch shy of the end. Make 1 — by lifting the bar between the two stitches or by knitting into the stitch below the previous stitch (so it mirrors the other side). Knit 1. Turn work and repeat on bottom half. Then knit a full round. Repeat until you get the desired number of 24 stitches over all needles on the round.

Body

Knit until when you insert your thumb into the toe the edge of the knitting reaches your knuckle. It should be about 5 rows after you finish your toe.

Gusset

Because your ankle is wider than your foot, one usually needs a gusset. On the bottom half, do an increase row: Knit 1. Make 1 — by lifting the bar between the two stitches or by knitting into the stitch below the next stitch. Knit across the top of the row until one stitch shy of the end. Make 1 — by lifting the bar between the two stitches or by knitting into the stitch below the previous stitch (so it mirrors the other side). Knit 1.

For the miniature sock, you only need one stitch on each side of the sole. Then knit across the top of the sock, and begin the heel.

Short-Row Heel

All heel directions look weird and confusing until you actually try them. Work *only* on the bottom half of the sock.

Row 1: Knit 13 stitches (all but one of the bottom). Move the working yarn as if to purl. Slip the last, unworked stitch from the left needle to the right needle. Turn your work. This is called wrap and turn, because you are wrapping a stitch and turning the work.

Row 2: Slip the first, unworked, stitch from the left needle to the right needle, finishing the wrap and turn. Purl the next stitch and purl across to the last stitch. Move the working yarn as if to knit and slip last stitch. Turn.

Row 3: Slip the first stitch and knit across to the last stitch before the unworked stitch. Wrap and turn.

Row 4: Slip the first stitch and purl across to the stitch before the unworked stitch. Wrap and turn.

Repeat Rows 3 and 4 until 3 of the heel

405

stitches are wrapped and on left side, 8 stitches are "live" in the middle, and 3 are wrapped and on the right. At this stage, you should be ready to work a right-side row. Your heel is half done.

Now you'll work the second half of the heel:

Row 1: Knit across the 8 live stitches across to the first unworked, wrapped stitch. To work this stitch, pick up the wrap and knit it together with the stitch. Always pick up the wrap from the outside of the sock. Wrap the next stitch (so that it now has two wraps) and turn.

Row 2: Slip the first (double-wrapped) stitch and purl across to the first un-worked, wrapped stitch. Pick up the wrap and purl it together with the stitch. Wrap the next stitch and turn.

On subsequent rows you will pick up both wraps and knit or purl them together with the stitch. Continue until you run out of wrapped stitches on a knit row. You will go back to knitting across the top of the foot. When you reach the bottom of the foot and the wrapped stitches there, pick up the wraps and continue around.

Gusset Removal

Now we have to get rid of the extra stitches we put in for the gusset. At the start of the next bottom half of the sock, slip 2 stitches and then knit them together. At the end of the bottom of the sock, knit 2 together. For the miniature sock, you only added 1, so do it once.

Ankle

Just knit. Again, you can use your thumb and knuckle as a guide, or fold the sock at the heel, and when you reach the start of the narrowing of the toe, you've got enough.

Ribbing

A little ribbing on the top looks nice and helps your sock stay up. Three rows of k1, p1 suffice. You can do the whole ankle in ribbing if you like ribbing.

Cast-Off

I have a nasty habit at this point of getting out the crochet hook. But a simple repeat of k2tog, move loop off right needle and back onto the left needle, also works well.

GEORG HAWKS is a professional Tserf and office monkey for the Tsarina of Tsocks and Holiday Yarns. She lives in

upstate New York with her husband, two dogs, and three cats. She freely admits her sock addiction, but refuses to seek help.

Work: http://holidayyarns.com

Play: http://thegeorg.blogspot.com

Contact: thegeorg@stny.rr.com

LAURA PHILLIPS'S
THE MARA SCARF

I've long suspected I was born in the wrong century, for I've always delighted in arcane crafts and skills. Few things are more exciting or satisfying to me than watching a lamb's first steps and shepherding its care through adolescence and beyond. The first year's harvest of fleece is spun into a fine, soft yarn to knit into lace patterned scarves or a cabled sweater. Subsequent years bring more fiber for sweaters and, if I'm fortunate, daughter lambs to increase the flock.

The more intricate the knitting pattern, the more interesting, I think. Simply knitting the patterns isn't enough. It's such fun to adapt them to handspun, to mix, match, and experiment. What's the worst that can happen? The results are ugly? So what? What's knit is easily unraveled into yarn again for a fresh start on something else that might turn out better. Imagine if life were so manageable.

Despite this taste for adventure in fiber land, I've realized I spend the majority of my knitting time with the simplest of stitches. I like to blame a hand injury that left me with three numb fingers for months, but the truth is, I simply love the mindlessness of knitting something so simple I could continue in the dark without dropping a stitch if I'm careful — very, very careful. Instead of straining my already tired eyes, I can relax with friends, watch television with the family, or keep my fingers busy through a tense meeting and project an air of calm attention that is so unlike the real me that's hiding inside, fidgeting and tapping away in irritation as I await my turn to speak.

My MARA scarf features probably my favorite of these simple stitches — so called because for some ten years now, I've carried my knitting bag along to meetings of my writing group, the Mid-America Romance Writers, MARA for short. When one scarf reaches an appropriate length, I bind off, add fringe, gift it to someone deserving, then cast on for the next one. The pattern is a loose seed stitch, usually on U.S. size 9 or 10 needles, knit with an angora or mohair blend. The halo of the yarn creates a soft, luxurious scarf that hides the occasional minor stitch error.

Knit into the fabric of each scarf are a hundred memories — smiles, giggles, outright belly laughs, a few grumbles and frustrations, and maybe even some tears. Each scarf has lived with me through at least one or two crises and has known the touch of many friends, for who can resist the sensual allure of a well-spun baby-soft yarn?

The pattern is a simple seed stitch, repeated throughout the entire scarf. Cast on an uneven number of stitches — 25 for a 7-inch width, 35 if you prefer something closer to 10 inches wide. In every row: k1, p1, repeating across and ending with k1. In each subsequent row, you'll be knitting in the previous row's purl stitches and purling in the previous row's knit stitches. That makes it easy to tell when you've goofed and easy to know how far to frog (unravel your work) to correct a mistake. The only thing easier would be a simple stockinette or garter stitch, but the seed stitch creates a prettier fabric that's reversible. When the scarf is as long as you want it to be, bind off loosely and add fringe. Or not. Gift it or keep it, or if the results aren't to your liking, unravel the whole thing and make something else.

There's only one unbreakable rule for making the MARA scarf. You must use yarn that you love. The sensation of soft yarn as it slides over tender flesh should be a quiet pleasure. No matter what's happening in the world around you as you knit, your yarn should be a pleasant companion for the many hours you'll spend with it.

LAURA PHILLIPS can be found at laura@lauraphillips.net and www.laura phillips.net and also at www.thelandof moo.com.

KIM HELMICK'S BASIC RIBBED SOCKS — CUFF DOWN

Socks are a wonderful knitting project. They are small and portable, so I can work on them anywhere. They also provide the opportunity to learn every knitting skill imaginable without a huge commitment of resources or time. Different forms of short rows, color work, lace, or cables — socks allow the knitter to experiment with new techniques. This is my basic, no-frills beginner sock pattern, written so that even fairly new knitters can succeed with their first sock project.

Materials
6-ply sock yarn of choice
U.S. size 3 double-pointed needles — set of five
Tapestry needle for grafting toe and weaving in ends

Gauge

5 1/2 to 6 stitches per inch

Abbreviations

k = knit

k2tog = knit 2 sts together

ktbl = knit through the back of the loop

p = purl

p2tog = purl 2 sts together

RS = right side

ssk = slip 2 sts, separately, knitwise, then
  knit them together from this position

WS = wrong side

Cuff

Cast on 48 stitches loosely. (Cast on over two needles if necessary.) Being careful not to twist stitches, join in the round.

Work in k2, p2 rib pattern until sock leg is desired length (4 to 7 inches).

Heel Flap

Leave half the total stitches (24 sts) aside for the time being. Place the remaining 24 stitches on one needle, and work back and forth as follows:

Row 1 (RS): sl 1, *k1, sl 1, repeat pattern from * to last stitch, k1

Row 2 (WS): sl 1, k across row

Repeat these two rows 11 or 12 more times (ending with Row 2) until heel flap measures approximately 2 inches.

Turn Heel

Continuing on the 24 stitches of the heel flap and beginning with a right-side row:

Row 1: sl 1, k12, k2tog, k1, turn (8 sts remain unworked on end)
Row 2: sl 1, p3, p2tog, p1, turn (8 sts)
Row 3: sl 1, k4, k2tog, k1, turn (6 sts)
Row 4: sl 1, p5, p2tog, p1, turn (6 sts)
Row 5: sl 1, k6, k2tog, k1, turn (4 sts)
Row 6: sl 1, p7, p2tog, p1, turn (4 sts)
Row 7: sl 1, k8, k2tog, k1, turn (2 sts)
Row 8: sl 1, p9, p2tog, p1, turn (2 sts)
Row 9: sl 1, k10, k2tog, k1, turn (0 sts)
Row 10: sl 1, p11, p2tog, p1, turn (0 sts) — 14 sts total remain on needle

Pick Up Gusset Stitches

Knit across the 14 stitches on your heel. Using an empty needle (now designated as Needle 1), continue on and pick up and knit the 12 or 13 slipped stitches along the side of the heel flap. Pick up an extra stitch at the end (close to your instep stitches) to help avoid a hole at the top of your gusset.

Needles 2 and 3 hold the instep stitches.

Work in k2, p2 pattern across these two needles.

Grab the last empty needle (now designated Needle 4) and pick up and knit an extra stitch at the beginning plus the 12 or 13 slipped stitches from along the side of the heel flap. Continue to knit 7 stitches (half of the 14) off the original needle holding your heel stitches. Slip the other 7 sts onto the beginning of Needle 1. You now have an empty needle to continue knitting in the round.

Gusset Decreases

Round 1: Needle 1 — k7, k remaining sts *through the back of the loop* (ktbl). (This twists the stitches and prevents a line of small holes.) Needles 2 and 3 — work in k2, p2 pattern across. Needle 4 — ktbl until 7 sts remain, k7.

Round 2: Needle 1 — k to last 3 sts, k2tog, k1. Needles 2 and 3 — work in k2, p2 pattern across. Needle 4 — k1, ssk, k to end.

Round 3: Needle 1 — k across. Needles 2 and 3 — work in k2, p2 pattern across. Needle 4 — k across.

Repeat Rounds 2 and 3 until 12 stitches remain on Needles 1 and 4.

Foot

Continue to knit the stitches on Needles 1 and 4 (sole stitches) and follow the rib pattern on Needles 2 and 3 (instep stitches) until sock measures 1 3/4 inches less than total length of foot. (You can gently try the sock on. You want to knit the foot up to the point of the bottom of your big toe.)

Toe Decreases

Round 1 (decrease round): Needle 1 — k to last 3 sts, k2tog, k1. Needle 2 — k1, ssk, k across. Needle 3 — k to last 3 sts, k2tog, k1. Needle 4 — k1, ssk, k across.

Round 2: Knit all stitches around.

Round 3: Knit all stitches around.

Round 4: Repeat Round 1 (the decrease round).

Repeat Rounds 3 and 4 (knit all round and a decrease round) until 8 stitches remain on each needle. Then do decrease rounds only until 4 stitches remain on each needle.

Graft toe using kitchener stitch.

Sew in ends.

KIM HELMICK is a freelance writer and photographer from Iowa who also edits the monthly magazine *Fort Dodge Today*.

Her knitting and photography blog can be found at http://kshotz.blogspot.com.

RACHAEL HERRON:
HOW TO KNIT IN THE DARK

Touch is as important as sight. A purl bump is as evocative as a smile, and a ribbed ridge can suggest where to turn next.

A double-point needle, left in the wrong place underneath a pillow, can be a fine murder weapon, if one knows just how one's enemy might fall heavily asleep. It would be hard to prove, of course. And that's just the point.

In the dark, soft is always soft.

The soothing sound of knitting needles clicking in the dark becomes even more relaxing — a nighttime chant, a prayer, the rhythmic rosary of craft.

Doing something when you can only trust the tips of your fingers to guide you is a good test of skill. Close your eyes right now. Do what you're doing. See how far you get.

Night knitting, folded correctly, is the best kind of pillow.

The working yarn has to trail across

something. And if it happens to trail across the person next to you, make it count. Make it work.

Glow-in-the-dark needles are like the Captain EO ride at Disneyland — it was a good idea for a limited time, but was the headache really worth it?

When you wake from a good dream, knit a few stitches. This way, you catch the dream and keep it forever.

Keep just one candle lit when you're working on something important. He'll tell you he's happy his sweater is almost done, but you'll know what he really means — you look more beautiful than ever in the soft glow, and you feel it when he kisses you over the needles.

RACHAEL HERRON is the author of *How to Knit a Love Song* (AVON), the first of the Cypress Hollow Yarns series. She writes a blog (http://www.yarnagogo .com) and lives in Oakland with her family, many spinning wheels, and a collection of animals that defies enumeration.

TERRI DULONG:
DON'T LOOK BACK!

My mother taught me how to knit as a child and although I learned all the basics, after I reached my late teens it would be a forty-year hiatus until I had needles in my hands again. It was my high school girlfriend Alice who coerced me to return to knitting five years ago and since then . . . I've never looked back. Seldom does a day pass that I don't knit at least a few rows.

Between all the wonderful yarns now available and a multitude of patterns, I'm fully and completely addicted to this extremely relaxing activity. Knitting soothes my soul, allows my mind to wander, and produces lovely handmade items both for myself and to give as gifts.

Courtesy of my friend Alice Jordan, I'm sharing a very simple pattern to make dishcloths or facecloths and they're a nice gift for friends and family. Great for the seasoned knitter or the new beginner. So

421

grab that yarn and those needles and get started!

Yarn: 100% cotton (such as Sugar and
  Cream by Lily)
Needles: U.S. size 8

Cast on 35 stitches.
Row 1: k3, *k1, p1, repeat from * to last 3
  sts, k3
Row 2: k3, *k1, p1, repeat from * to last
  3sts, k3
Repeat Rows 1 and 2 until the piece measures 7 1/2 inches or desired length.
Bind off. Weave tails in.

TERRI DULONG is the author of *Spinning Forward* and *Casting About* (Kensington), the first two books in her Cedar Key series. You can visit Terri at www.terridulong.com and contact her at terridulong@bellsouth.net.

CAROLINE LEAVITT:
THE SWEATER

I've been knitting since I was a Girl Scout, but I'm not an expert knitter. I'm often impatient and what I really love is simply the peace and pleasure of easy knitting while I'm watching a movie (I can never do just one thing at a time). There was a time, though, when I made very intricately designed sweaters. My first husband wanted a sweater. "Make it with a brontosaurus feeding on vegetation on it," he said, and because I loved him, I said I'd try. I had no idea how to do it, but I first made countless drawings of what I thought the sweater should look like. Then I used graph paper and colored pencils to block it out, and finally I was ready to fling myself into the project. Surrounded by balls of brown, green, red, beige, and sky blue, I made a scene on a sweater! The sweater took me four months but it was exquisitely gorgeous. Worth every stitch! My husband loved it

423

and wore it. Right up until the moment I found out that he had been cheating on me. I took the sweater from his drawer and scissored it up and threw it in the trash. He took it out and tried to sew it back together. I scissored it up more. Now, happily remarried and still knitting, I know I shouldn't have destroyed that sweater. The marriage was over, but there was no reason for that gorgeous sweater to be!

CAROLINE LEAVITT's ninth novel is *Pictures of You* (Algonquin Books). A book critic for *People Weekly* and a book columnist for the *Boston Globe*, she can be reached at http://www.carolineleavitt.com.

JEAN BRASHEAR: THE FOURTH TIME'S THE CHARM . . .

You could view me as a walking knitting disaster (which I have been) or perhaps a moderate success story, I guess. My first attempt at knitting, I was eight or nine and a Camp Fire Girl with a leader who wanted us to learn — quickly. Picture little kid, skinny needles, wicked splitty yarn. Add too-tight stitches, short deadline, no one at home who knows how to knit, and you have a recipe for tears and a sick stomach. It was years before I could make myself tackle knitting again.

Fast-forward to the young woman who decides to create her own dress from a yarn halter top attached to cascading rows of scrap fabrics (don't ask — I have no idea what I was thinking). I was still too traumatized to knit, so I quickly switched to crochet, and because I was poor, I found a great deal on rug yarn and jumped on it. (Yes, ouch.) The dress actually drew a great deal of admiration (probably because of the lack of undergarment, but let's not go there) but *scratchy* does not begin to describe the experience. Add in summer heat, well . . . Disaster Number Two.

I live in the South, and there's not much call for warm knits (thank heavens nowadays there are summer yarns) so I cannot begin to tell you what was going on in my head with Disaster Number Three, the floor-length knitted skirt (in bold red, white, and blue stripes, no less) I decided I needed to make. Straight skirt? Oh, nooooo — could I be that rational? That circumspect? (Impulsiveness remains, to this day, a challenge I haven't conquered — with a sizable dose of stubborn thrown in, an occasionally lethal combination.) This was a full skirt, row upon row upon row that I got so sick of (not to mention so hot working on) but wouldn't quit, that my grandmother took pity on me and spelled me. (Though I'm pretty sure she was shaking her head the whole time — love is a wondrous thing, isn't it? Not only did she swelter along with me, but she never told me I was an idiot.) I have no idea what happened to that skirt, but a whole village could stay warm inside what amounted to a knitted teepee, I swear.

Later on, when I had children, I tackled

knitting again and actually turned out some sweaters — with patterns, even! A gray vest sweater for my beloved and a memorable (never let four-year-old boys pick out their own yarn) green and orange striped one for my son (don't know what happened to that one either . . . a mercy, IMO). So . . . fourth time's the charm. Sort of.

Except that I still have Fear of Socks (one sock on the needles as we speak . . . been there for six months, and I've finished at least a dozen other projects in the meantime — but I'm not giving up, I swear, just . . . steeling myself). And I still have a lamentable tendency to charge off on my own, sans pattern . . . only I'm no knitting genius and there's no budding pattern maker in me. I still don't know what all the abbreviations mean and I don't want to have to think too hard while I'm knitting because I mostly do it while I'm visiting with people or watching whatever, um, interesting TV choices (because there can't be just one, right?) my beloved is making (so I can stay near him without lunging for the remote) and so . . . I guess the moral is that you don't have to be a gifted knitter like Barbara Bretton or any of the other knitting goddesses who allow me to hang around when I'm clearly the B Team . . . knitting can still be fun. And therefore.

Award-winning romance author JEAN BRASHEAR brings a wistful, funny voice to women's fiction in *The Goddess of Fried Okra* (Bell Bridge Books). "Wholly original, funny and poignant," says *New York Times* bestselling author Susan Wiggs. Details at www.jeanbrashear.com.

MAURA ANDERSON:
THE WEDDING SHAWL

I'm a firm believer that gifts you make for another person are some of the most precious gifts you can give. Every part of the process of creation and crafting is focused on the person you are making the gift for, from the choice of pattern and material to the actual crafting. You can't help but think of the person as you work, and those thoughts, memories, and wishes seem to permeate the item you're making, becoming one with the gift forever. This gift becomes one of the magical gifts whose meaning far surpasses the physical item.

This is the tale of one of those special gifts.

When I moved to the Pacific Northwest in 1995, I was introduced to a woman, Sue, who shared a lot of interests and we became good friends. She and her husband helped encourage me in my career and my private life. They were guests at my wedding and were goddess-parents of my youngest son.

We were often in touch and shared a lot. Sue's husband was having some serious health issues and Sue had her own physical problems but when I needed to touch base or just vent, Sue was only a phone call or instant message away.

I tried hard to be as good a friend in return, though I admit I often felt helpless to do much more than provide a friendly hug and a soft shoulder. It wasn't a pleasant feeling to not be able to do more, but I did my best. Then the unthinkable happened — Sue's husband died, most likely from a medication interaction in his prescribed medications. The police called my husband and me in the middle of the night and we raced to Sue's house. My husband took care of Sue while I helped with her husband's body. I know it sounds gruesome but I am still grateful for the chance to say good-bye to her husband and preserve as much of his dignity as I could while shielding Sue as best I could as well.

Sue's loss was traumatic. I can't even begin to understand or say I know what she felt because I did not. I still do not. I tried to show her that I loved her and cared about her but eventually she moved out of the local area to try to figure out how she was going to continue on as a widow and what she wanted to do. We fell out of touch for the last three or four years with only the occasional update or e-mail but I still thought about her and wished her well.

About six months ago, I got a call from Sue with some fantastic news. She had met a wonderful man and was living with him but wanted to know if I would be her maid of honor at her upcoming wedding. She sounded great — probably the most upbeat and positive I'd heard her in years and really happy. Everything I wanted for her — happiness and security — was on the horizon. I told her I was thrilled to be her maid of honor and we shared a lot of updates before I had to get off the phone.

I immediately knew I wanted to make her something for her wedding. Something special. Something that spoke to her and myself and the journey we'd traveled together and apart. Something that could capture the memories and the dreams we'd shared with each other. I'd taken up knitting after she moved away; I loved lace knitting and I remembered how much Sue loved lace and also how much she hated being cold and that she hated clothes with sleeves. Not the best combination, especially in the Pacific Northwest. Suddenly, I knew what to knit — a shawl. The very first lace shawl

431

I ever knit would be for Sue.

From there I went on a hunt for a pattern. There are a lot of patterns out there and I'm a fan of a site called Ravelry (www.ravelry.com), where knitters and crocheters gather and you can see patterns, yarns, and people's projects and even buy patterns. I must have looked at hundreds of lace shawl patterns — I must have saved two-thirds of them because I knew someday I wanted to knit them — but when I saw a pattern called Oriental Impressions Triangle by Sylvie Beez, I knew that was the right shawl for Sue. If you want to see the shawl pattern I chose, you can go to http://www.ravelry.com/patterns/library/oriental-impressions-triangle.

Oriental Impressions is a symmetrical triangle where a center line separates two identical sides that are a pattern of squares, triangles, and eyelets. When I looked at the sample shawl on the pattern page, it looked like the winding path my friendship with Sue has taken, complete with walking together, then away, then reconverging. A large area of eyelets seemed to indicate the time of only spotty contact and then a lovely border that looked like the eye of a peacock's feather — something I've always associated with happiness and beauty.

Pattern decided, I needed to make a deci-sion on color and fiber. By this time Sue had sent me a link to the picture of her dress so I knew she was wearing a sea green sleeveless dress for this second wedding. I knew I wanted something that would coor-dinate but I didn't want to take the chance of clashing or being "close enough but not quite." I also wanted something warm and luscious and not too heavy. Something that would enfold and embrace my friend but not weigh her down or seem too oppressive. A friend at work had done a large lace piece in Jagger Spun's Zephyr yarn — a lace-weight wool-silk blend — and I loved the feel of it, so I chose a lovely vanilla color of the same yarn for Sue's shawl.

By the time I got my supplies, the wed-ding had been moved up to Beltane (May 1) to accommodate other obligations. I cast on with size 2 needles (little!) and started knitting. I'm relatively new to lace and this is finer yarn than I've used before so I can't multitask while knitting Sue's shawl. I have to keep my attention on the work or I either miscount or drop a stitch. Because I have cats who love yarn and want to be on me all the time, I can't work on it downstairs where the TV is. Instead this shawl is being knit in my bedroom with my full attention.

Every stitch is accompanied by thoughts of our friendship, memories of times we've shared, and wishes and dreams I have for Sue's future. There are moments of intense concentration when I have a tricky series of stitches mixed with coasting along on the return row of only purl stitches. It reminds me of the give-and-take of a friendship — times of complexity and working to feed the friendship alternating with being fed by it. Through it all, the yarn is unbroken. There are no knots or joins; it's all one long, long thread that ties us together.

Right now I'm about halfway through the pattern and am working at it every night to get it done on time. There are a few flaws — I miscounted once or twice — but none of these are horrible or ugly. I thought about ripping back and fixing them but I decided not to. This wedding shawl is not about perfection or illusions of infallibility. I'm flawed, Sue is flawed, our relationship has had flaws and bumps; so it's right that her wedding shawl should keep the flaws it has, despite my care and attention.

Even tears have touched this shawl. Several times I've had memories move me to tears and a few have fallen on the yarn. I left them there to soak in and dry. What friendship has no tears?

I want Sue to be able to wrap this shawl around her and think of the love that went into making it. It can warm her when she's cold, touch her softly when she's fragile, hug her when she needs a hug, and be a visible symbol of the beauty that emerges from years of friendship, even though the whole was never without flaws, wounds, and scars.

I already have a card made to go with it that says:

Sue,

My arms to hold you,
My heart to love you,
My friendship to sustain you,
My energy to fuel your dreams,
May beauty surround you, always.
           Blessed be on your wedding day,
                   Maura.

MAURA ANDERSON is a published technical writer by day and an e-published fiction writer by night, at least when her time isn't spent reading, knitting, making jewelry, or being a wife and mother. She's lived on the beautiful Puget Sound for the last fifteen years along with her husband, youngest son, and a

herd of various rescued animals. She recently translated her lifelong love of storytelling into writing and works in a variety of romance subgenres; currently she is working on an urban fantasy/steampunk novel based in an alternative Egypt. Every day is filled with new ideas and new challenges. You can read more about Maura and her current projects on her website at http://www.realmsoftheraven.com.

ABOUT THE AUTHOR

Barbara Bretton is the *USA Today* bestselling, award-winning author of more than forty books. She currently has more than ten million copies in print around the world. Her works have been translated into twelve languages in more than twenty countries.

Barbara lives in New Jersey but loves to spend as much time as possible in Maine with her husband, walking the rocky beaches and dreaming up plots for upcoming books.

You can write to Barbara at
barbara@barbarabretton.com
or visit her website,
www.barbarabretton.com